About the Autor

David Wiggins the author was born in Burslem, Stoke-on-Trent, Staffordshire, UK. Parents, Aubrey William (Bill) Wiggins and Elsie Wiggins (nee Woodhart).

Educated in Stoke -on- Trent at Cauldon Road, Secondary Modern Boy's School. A school of hard knocks, if ever there was one. Then after this school was burnt down, by two of the pupils. I was transferred to, Queens Street, Boy's School, Fenton. A very disciplined headteacher kept order and confiscated any matches or lighters!
Much later as a mature student the author gained a degree from The Manchester Metropolitan University. David was then employed as a High School Science-Teacher in the UK. David is now retired and with his wife, Diane, and their teenage son, Zachariah. Recently, relocated to Bendigo, Victoria, Australia. David has three grown up stepchildren and two daughters from his previous marriage, he has thirteen grandchildren.

During the Covid lock-down period. I was unable to go to work as a Science Teacher. Therefore, I began to write, and now in retirement I am continuing with this endeavour, to write good honest tales of Adventure, Mystery, Fantasy, Comedy, and Romance.

DEBUT NOVEL DEBUT NOVEL DEBUT NOVEL

Welcome to POUTIA Secret Hidden Place. This is my Debut Adult Novel. Written with the British zeal for Intrigue, and an Adventure. Holding true to our obsession with regard to solving a Mystery. The narrative twists and turns, and is interwoven with a heartfelt Romance or two. Hoping my debut novel will entertain you, using wit, intuition, and imagination. A keen reader of everything, who enjoys the countryside. Especially, the beauty of the Peak District of Derbyshire. It was inevitable that my first novel, would endeavour to capture the spirt, charm, ambience, of this majestic land.

POUTIA Secret Hidden Place

David Wiggins

POUTIA

Secret Hidden Place

Dedication:

This book is dedicated to all those who enjoy walking, either in the park, or out in the wider countryside. There is peace and beauty to be found in the plants, wildlife, and also in the landscape. The author spent many a carefree day, walking in and around North Staffordshire. Such as The Roaches near Leek, and Manifold Valley. Then there is the Peak District of Derbyshire. The rolling hills and wooded vales, the babbling rivers, are all breathtakingly beautiful places to meander, on a summers day. This unique and idyllic landscape never fails to make the visitor smile. Especially, with acknowledgement, of a grand walk enjoyed with family or friends. In places that spring to mind such as, Dovedale, Matlock Bath, Cromford Mill, Bakewell, Buxton, Castleton, with a visit to nearby Blue John mine. Every place mentioned above are magnificent, and inspirational in their own right. All must be visited, by the enthusiastic walker, if they have not already done so.

CONTENTS

ISBN 978-0-6459858-1-8 (Paperback)

Published (First Edition 2025) .

Any references to historical events, people, or real places, are used fictitiously. Names, characters, and places, are purely products of the author's imagination.

Front cover image of Bruce Knight by Artist Diane Wiggins.

Acknowledgement

With love to my dearly departed Mother Elsie Wiggins.
Taken to soon, leaving far too many heartbroken.
Fond memories of my childhood with you are always in my
heart. You were kind and thoughtful, you motivated me to
work hard at what I wanted, and to be honest with myself
always. God Bless you, till we meet again.

Quotes from the formidable and prolific author:

Arnold Bennett.

The walk up the hill is sometimes difficult. There are many setbacks, and it is so easy to give up and not to try. Some are just contented to walk around the hill. However, to be truly honest, the view is far better from the top.

Arnold Bennett.

The biggest wall you have to climb is the one you build in your mind. Never let your mind talk you out of your dream, trick you into giving up. Never let your mind become the greatest obstacle to success. To get your mind on the right track, the res t will follow.

Another aspirational Quote:

We shall never have more time. We have, and have always had, all the time there is. No object is served in waiting until next week or even tomorrow. Keep going day in and out. Concentrate on something useful. Having decided to achieve a task, achieve it at all costs.

By Arnold Bennett.

The purpose of life is not the pursuit of happiness; the purpose of life is to gain happiness from the pursuit.

By Arnold Bennett.

POUTIA

Secret Hidden Place

by David Wiggins

Prologue:

My name is Bruce Knight; I am twenty-four coming on twenty-five. I live in a city mainly because it is great here. What I mean is, it has everything I need. A place to work, a place to eat out with mates. Plus, there are several cinemas, a sports and leisure centre, with a good gym and a ten-pin bowling centre.

At the weekend, I chill-out usually down at the local park, with a couple of my mates. We meet up on Saturday morning and play footie, five a side if enough turn up, or it's just a knock-about, till about lunch time. Then we go to the Marquis of Granby, for a sarnie and a few pints. Maybe after lunch a few games of pool, before going home for a snooze. At about 8ish it is time to shower before I go downtown for a good night out. Doing a few pubs first and then finally, in a club till about 5 in the morning.

Sunday is so cool; I get up at about 2 o'clock in the afternoon. Then after a quick shower I go to my local Wetherspoons for lunch. Meet my mates and watch the footie on the big-screen TV. Then finally, go to a mate's flat for a take-away meal. I like, pizza, or Chinese, with sweet and sour pork balls, this is my favourite. But, if not, a chicken tikka masala curry, will do just as well. I heard this great joke the other day.

A Dung Beetle walked into a café and the person serving behind the counter spoke.

"Take a seat bud, I'll be with you in a minute to take your order." "Thank you," said the Dung Beetle. "I'll have that stool over there."

I get back to my place, at about eleven and totally crash out, like a zombie. Then Monday morning, the dreaded alarm goes off at 6:45 and it's back to work! I work in the City University, in the canteen. I am the Assistant Catering Manager. This means I am responsible for food ordering and storage. It is a decent job and easy enough to do, even though it can be hectic when we have a delivery.

I had a regular girlfriend at school, Sarah-Louise. She was drop dead gorgeous, a real looker even from the age of twelve. We went out together for 5 years right from year 8 onwards, up till she was seventeen and in the sixth form.

Then, just after her 17th birthday, she went to Australia with her brother and her mum and dad. I will see her again one day, they said I could. But that was almost 7 years ago, and I am terribly busy these days, with my work, my mates, and other stuff. I would like to get a job as a football coach, maybe with the university or at a sports college. Something like that anyway, one day maybe I will be a football coach for Arsenal!

My mum and dad moved to the Midlands about a year ago. They said, they wanted to escape the rat race. I have been to their new place, and it is all right. I mean the house is cool with a conservatory and a walk-in shower room. But the village where they live is dead boring, with just a few dozen houses, a church, a pub. Mum and dad have kept a bedroom for me and another for my sister, if we want to go and stay with them for a holiday. But believe me, any more than 2 days staying there in the middle of nowhere, would drive you stir crazy.

I like the city life too much; it has things to do in abundance. Plus, there are loads of things to see and do. My mates all think the same. My best mate is Josh, he once said to me.

I went to the countryside for a visit once. I looked at it for an hour or so, then got bored and came back home.

That's just how I feel too. My Mum and Dad are cool with me living here. My big sis is in Madrid teaching English, so, we don't get to see her much these days. I have been working at the Uni for 2 years now. My mates say it is time I moved on to better and bigger things. But I don't know really. I do like my job, and my manager is a cool guy, and very easy to get on with. Josh said that I should apply to UCAS to see which Sports Coaching courses are available. It was then early July. Josh also said.

"If you want to find a place to study, then this is the best time to do it."

I spoke. "Josh, I agree with you, I will call UCAS."

Over the next few weeks. I thought about nothing else but enlisting on a university course. There was a few that really interested me. One was at Leicester University, another at Swansea, another at Loughborough. But they are all too far away from London. Then in late July UCAS called me, saying that clearing had commenced and that I should apply quickly to my first and second choice, as all the places would soon be gone for this academic year. I phoned my mum, and she said that I should take a week's holiday and come up and see them. Whilst there, I could discuss my plans with mum and dad. Also, I could take long walks around Monyash, the village where they now live. Exercise should focus my thoughts on what was the best course for me to do, suggested mum.

However, this kind and thoughtful suggestion was at an awkward time, especially to be away and visiting the countryside. Because in mid-August. The Premier football league season would have begun, and my mates were eagerly waiting for that first game. Plus, the night clubs around here in London would be buzzing with people back from their summer holidays - where the ladies are always eager to flash their tans!

However, there I was in my parent's lounge! Mum had collected me from the coach stop in Bakewell. Dad was busy in the kitchen cooking a pasta bake; and making ready for dinner. *Was this really a clever idea?* I thought. My dad is 66 years old and is losing his hair on the top of his head. He is not overweight but not muscular either. He reminds me of the Comedian Eric Morcombe. Mum once remarked.

"That sons usually turn out like their fathers."

"I sincerely hope not." was my reply.

My dad had not been to university. He had worked for most of his life on the milk marketing board. After that he sold life insurance. Mum, on the other hand, had been to college to study hair and beauty. She worked as a full-time hairdresser, but she took a break for about 5 years because of having us two kids. My mum is so sweet! She is a real gem of a mother. I do miss her - especially when I get home from work! Mum always kept the house clean and tidy, and she is a brilliant cook. Every evening, without exception, she had prepared and cooked a delicious dinner. My mum is sixty-one, but she always looks amazing. She wears lovely clothes, and her makeup is beautifully done – and so is her hair, always tidy, always curly, and shiny. Anyway, I thought, *what would they know about university places for Sports Coaching and Management?* I watched the two of them doing their best to set a table and bring out of the kitchen dad's pasta special. I wondered if possibly, a long walk might clear my head after dinner, and especially if I should go back to London tomorrow morning, on the next available coach.

Chapter 1

After dinner, I offered to wash the dishes. Mum asked,

"Do you all fancy a walk to burn off those calories?"

We all thought we should, so off we went walking into the heart of the village - where I noticed a finger sign that was marked. Public footpath to Lathkill Dale. I stopped at the finger post which was placed against a drystone wall. There was two protruding flat stones built into the wall to be used as steps to help the walker to get over the wall.

"How about a walk down there?" Dad walked up to the finger post.

"No not this one, it is a bit of a way, possibly 3 miles each way."

Mum walked up behind dad, and she slapped him on his back.

"What! 6 miles that is just a mere stretch of the legs. Come on. Let's go," she insisted with a cheeky smile.

The footpath led over several pasture fields, and it was easy walking along a well-trodden footpath. Dad commented on the song of a skylark and mum pointed to a curlew that was calling nearby. The footpath then split to the left - with the same marked finger sign as before, Lathkill Dale. I asked.

"Where does that other path go to on the right."

Mum replied. "We have not explored that way yet."

I suggested. "Well maybe next time, we could go that way."

After walking for about an hour and a half on the same public footpath that crossed several country lanes. The landscape gradually lost the open fields, and it became more of hills and dales. Then finally, we arrived in Lathkill Dale via a narrow path that descended into a small valley. Lathkill Dale is an abandoned mining settlement, which went back originally to Roman times. However, the settlement was now in total ruins and was last occupied in the late 18th century. This valley was once rich in Galena, a Lead baring ore. When the Galena was finally all removed, the settlement gradually emptied. The people moved elsewhere possibly to find work in the new factories of the industrial revolution.

"There are a number of these ghost settlements in and around the Peak District."

Exclaimed Dad, as he stopped in what was once the centre of the village. He pointed and continued to say.

"Look, at those buildings, they are now gradually blending back into the natural landscape."

We had enjoyed the walk. It was interesting, and it was nice to be back with Mum and Dad. I do miss seeing them regularly. However, I was also already missing my friends back home! I wondered what they might think of this forgotten place. Josh would have probably said.

"Was there a Greggs or a Costa? No! Then get the hell out of there and be quick about it."

After about 3 hours of continuous walking, we were back at Mum and Dad's house. We had talked about my idea to go to university to study, sports coaching, and management. They both thought it was a particularly promising idea, and a way of establishing a new career path. They explained to me how in their opinion, I could stay in my flat and study locally and possibly, still do my regular job. But work part-time in the evenings and at the weekend.

I quicky replied.

"Hang on a minute, dad. What about me and my social life, like going out with my mates in an evening and at the weekend?"

Dad then mentioned something like. That sacrifices will be needed, and weekend binges, might need to stop; or at least be curtailed for a few years.

"What!" I replied in a raised voice. "You must be joking! My social life is sacrosanct."

Anyway, they said that I should sleep on it, and I would see things more clearly in the morning. But I really doubt that!

In the morning dad was already up, in the garden pruning his roses. This was not unusual for him. He was always an early bird. I got up at around 10:30. That walk had tired me out. Mum had driven down to Bakewell to collect some groceries from a supermarket. Dad said, "morning Bruce. What are you going to do today?"

I replied with a smile. "It is such a nice sunny day, so I might take another walk." Dad agreed that was a good idea. He said, "if I got back by 5ish they would take me out for a meal at a local pub." I thought that was an exceptionally innovative idea. I looked at dad as he stood in the back garden. "I will be back well before 5 o'clock, no worries".

I had a piece of toast and a cup of coffee, then put on my walking shoes. I took the same footpath as before; the one marked to Lathkill Dale. At the point where the footpath split, I went along the right-hand path.

After a mile or so of walking across open moorland the path narrowed and came upon a wooden style. Built into a barbed-wire fence. I climbed over it and stood at the side of a country lane. I walked a hundred metres up the lane towards a big old house that was set in a very unkempt and overgrown garden. On the garden gate was a small plaque which was rusty, but I could just manage to read. "Yew tree Cottage." There was a very large old oak tree with many branches, standing almost proudly in the corner of the garden. There is a dirt road next to this big old house. At the corner of this dirt track and the country road. There is a wooden finger post with "Public Footpath" etched into it. This part of the public footpath was just a dirt track - which twists and turns for about half a mile. The track then split in two. To the right was a sign on a big, old, solid wooden gate - which read, "Dead of Winter Farm." I remember thinking, that sounds like a nice cosy place!

To my left, the dirt track descended a shallow slope with a rusty metal finger post. On it was marked in green paint, "No Place."

I decided to see what this "No Place," looked like. So, I continued walking. First, down the slight incline, the path then crossed a small babbling brook. A little concrete bridge wide enough to be driven over in a car, but nothing much bigger. When over the little bridge the way forward was cut through a delightful shady narrow wooded vale, but not much more than fifty metres in total length.

Suddenly, on the left was a dry-stone wall, close by there was an old-style iron gas streetlight. The dirt track turned sharply to the left. A cobble stone road was now the way ahead. There was on the left-hand side of this cobbled road. A row of red brick terraced houses. Set back from the dry stone wall, by a small garden. Opposite the firs house I noticed a wishing well, that had been overgrown by weeds, mainly nettles and ivy. It was clearly no longer in use, almost derelict. The well had a little roof with some letters obscured by the ivy and cobwebs. Clearing the cobwebs away with a stick that I found close by. I could now make out the letters which spelled, "POUTIA Wishing Well."

I continued to walk along the narrow lane, passing four more terraced houses. Then two detached houses that were made of stone with slate roofs. I kept following the lane and, in a few metres, there was another small bridge, that went over another little brook. Immediately to my right was a large timber building with "Blacksmith," ceremonially written over its large double doors in yellowing paint. That was probably once white paint. By now I was looking for signs of life but there was no one to be found, everything seemed to be closed. Was No Place a deserted village, much like Lathkill Dale. However, this village had not yet fallen into dereliction. I continued to walk eagerly on as my curiosity got the better of me. I came across two Tudor-style semi-detached cottages with thatched roofs, and pink roses climbing up the wattle and daub. These were on the left-hand side of the lane. Opposite them was a small Chapel. Written above the Chapels double doors was an inscription set in stone. "Inclicte Paradisi Praepositi." I tried to Google what the inscription meant but found I had no internet signal.

The small chapel building looked rather charming. It was made from red bricks with a slate roof (which appeared intact) - apart from the odd slipped tile here and there. There was the customary wooden Chapel notice board perched on the edge of the lane. The notice board had an A4 lined paper fixed to it with drawing pins. The notice gave details of a Bring and Swop afternoon, on the coming Bank-Holiday Monday at 3pm. It read "Please bring items you no longer need, but others might find useful." Also, on the notice board was a small white card. 'Exchange wanted.' A dependable person to help with the repair of a tiled roof, ladders are available, as are the 30 new tiles. House owner now too old to climb up on the roof but is a keen gardener and will gladly reciprocate by doing work in your garden."

I sensed somebody was watching me, so I turned around quickly and noticed an elderly woman, hurrying away. There was a small Village Shop. Located nearly opposite to the chapel. I tried to catch the elderly woman's attention by coughing into my hand. But sadly, she had disappeared into a nearby house, before I had a chance to say anything. I walked over to the village shop and it seemed to be open. I noticed that it was called "Peace and Goodwill." A small note had been stuck on the Shop door which stated. "We exchange what you have for what you need; all others pay cash, sorry no cards taken." I pushed the door handle down to enter in, not knowing what to expect. The door swung inwards, and a little doorbell tinkled.

Inside the shop it was dark and dated, with a slightly musty smell. A tall thin lady came in from a back room situated behind the shop counter. She was wearing a yellow apron over a blue knitted cardigan and black leggings. She was about 60ish, she had a pale complexion, and light brown eyes that matched her light brown hair. Her long hair was piled up onto her head in a tight top knot. She spoke in a local Derbyshire accent.

"Hello, can I help you love?"

I really needed something sweet to eat and a cold drink.

I looked at the lady and replied.

"Hello. Can I have a chocolate bar." I helped myself to one from the counter display. "I also need something to quench my thirst. Do you have any cold drinks?"

"Yes, my dear, we do."

She pointed over towards the cold drink's chiller in the corner of the room. So, I walked over to look and collected a can of Elderflower and Grape juice; one of my favourite soft drinks.

"Is that everything. That will be £3.80 please luv."

I gave her a fiver, and she offered me the change.

"Thank you. This is a very out of the way place."

The lady answered with a smile.

"Yes, my dear, we are as far away from anywhere else, as we can be."

I left the shop, closing the door behind me. It was then that I noticed the amazing contrast in this village. Manly between old and new. There were some new bungalows further on down the lane, on the right-hand side. There were three in total, with beautiful gardens. Each garden was full of brightly coloured flowers, surrounding an immaculately cut lawn. Yet, compared to the village shop, which was a rickety old wooden building roughly two hundred years old. However, if you thought that was old. Next to the village shop was a garage forecourt, with two very antique looking petrol pumps. One pumps with a petrol label and the other with a diesel label. Both were rectangular, standing upright and each with a round globe on the top, with 'Avery Fuels,' written across. The garage did not look very modern to say the least; it was rather a dump really. Filled with out-of-date fittings and signs. One of the signs was an upside-down triangle, red in colour. Alvis Motor Cars. What a mixture of old and new this "No Place" is. Half of the village is full of old junk, and very old-style buildings. Yet, some of the houses look very modern – (almost new builds) - and their gardens are beautifully kept, with weed free, manicured lawns!

I walked on for about another fifty metres. Then directly in front of me was an ancient oak tree, with the village green behind. Standing next to the Oak tree was an old man wearing blue jeans, a green shirt, a flat cap, and walking boots. He seemed to be out walking his little dog. As I walked towards him, he called to me.

"Are you lost my young friend?"

I walked up to him, and I bent down to pat his little terrier dog.

"No, I am not lost, but I have no idea where I am."

"Well, my friend you are in "No Place.""

"That is an unusual name. I noticed the name on the old wishing well was POUTIA."

"Now that is an incredibly old name for here abouts, going back centuries. We only use that name now during early May. When we have a traditional Well Dressing."

The old man then asked.

"Are you here to see someone, in the village?"

"No, my parents live in Monyash This was just meant to be a walk for an hour or two. But I think I may have gone further than I had intended."

"Well, in that case, you had better start to head back. The hills around here soon go dark, especially if a mist comes down. Many a walker had got lost on those misty hills."

"Yes, I suppose, I should head back. Is there an alternative way back to Monyash?"

The old man retorted.

"No! Young man. You must return the way you came in, or you might not return at all."

I was a bit puzzled by that statement; it was a bit odd.

"OK. Thanks, goodbye."

I turned around to walk back the way I came in. The thought that I might not be able to return home, unnerved me a little. But then I thought, strange people do sometimes, say strange things!

Walking back along the narrow-cobbled lane, I noticed the lady from the shop. She was watching me from the shop window. I didn't give her any eye contact I just kept on walking. However, at the point where the terraced houses ended, and the stone wall turned right. A man was standing in the garden of the very last house. He looked at me and spoke.

"Goodbye stranger, till we meet again."

I thought what a strange thing to say to me.

"Yeh, cool mate, see you later."

I felt very unnerved talking to this stranger - a man who looked remarkably like my father and about the same age.

Well on the walk back to Snipe Cottage. My thoughts were that No Place, was indeed a very strange village. All four people, I had seen there were as old and odd as some of the buildings, and yet some of the houses looked brand spanking new. An anomaly in a modern world, was my thought.

On entering the back door, mum spoke to me.

"Have you had a nice walk, dear?"

"Yes, it was all right, I went to the next village over the moor called No Place. I went into the village shop there, for a cold drink and a bounty bar."

Dad then walked into the kitchen.

"Glad you enjoyed your walk. Can we get ready now. I have planned for us to share a lovely meal in a charming old inn."

"Change your shirt Bruce," suggested mum. "I have ironed several and they are in your wardrobe."

"Ok thanks mum. I will have a quick shower and change my shirt and be back downstairs in twenty minutes."

After my shower and change into clean clothes, we went outside and got into dad's car. Dad asked mum.

"Debs if Bruce and I have a pint or two tonight, will you drive the car back my dearest."

"Oh! go on then, you two men can have a drink or two with the meal."

The pub that dad drove us to was, The Star, Taddington. An old country inn with real oak beams holding up the ceiling. On the walls there were brass horse fittings, from years ago, when horses pulled the plough. On the walls there were several old paintings of farming practices. Scenes of workers cutting the wheat with a scythe, and loading wheat sheafs on to a cart. On arrival we met up with two of my parent's new friends. Trevor and Brenda Williams. Trevor is a tall thin man, aged about mid-fifties, he had a closely trimmed beard, and he was wearing round spectacles.

"Hello, I am Bruce, how are you?"

Trevor smiled and offered to shake Bruce's hand.

"Hi Bruce, I'm Trevor, and this beautiful lady is my wife, Brenda. I'm a local estate agent; I helped your parents to find Snipe Cottage. So, if you ever need to rent or buy a property around here, I could help you."

Brenda had a pale complexion, and she had a wonderful head of Curley blonde hair. Brenda was a semi-invalid. She walked with the aid of a stick. Mum had mentioned to Bruce that her new friend Brenda, had suffered with Polio when she was a young girl. Polio had left Brenda with a slightly curved spine and one leg shorter than the other. Brenda smiled at Bruce and offered her hand.

"Hello Bruce, your mother has told me all about you, that you work in a university in London."

"Yes, I do, I am the assistant catering manager."

"That sounds very interesting. How long are you up here?"

Mum quickly answered.

"Bruce is here for the week, giving him time to think about going to university to study for a diploma or a degree."

"Brilliant, good idea. Which university are you thinking of going to?"

"I don't know at the moment. But, if I can get into a university in London, then I can probably keep my job."

"What do you do again, Bruce." asked Trevor.

Bruce was about to give him his job title all over again. When a waitress arrived at their table holding a notepad and pen.

"Are we ready to order now."

Everyone quickly picked up the menu and Bruce spoke first.

"Dad, can I have the mixed grill with extra onion rings, and a side order of garlic bread. I am starving after that long walk earlier."

"Bruce went on a good walk today, exploring for miles over the moors," replied Robert. "He was gone for about 5 hours, a real stretch of the legs."

Brenda looked up at the waitress. "Can I have the Lasagna with chips, please." Then looking at Bruce.

"Do you enjoy walking Bruce, the moors are unbelievably beautiful in the summer, and hiking is now a very popular pastime."

Bruce smiled and nodded in agreement.

"Yes, I do like walking, and it was very peaceful and quiet over the moors, I can definitely say that."

"I suspect it is so different here, especially with you coming from London, with all that noisy traffic and air pollution," quipped Trevor.

"Yes, London is quite different from here. But there are some beautiful parks, and there are several interesting walks such as Hampstead Heath. Plus, there are many quiet places in London, where you can sit and read. It is not all noisy and bustling with traffic."

All the others were now giving their meal requests to the waitress. Bruce continued to say.

"Speaking of a contrast. I went to a little village today, it was so quiet, no traffic, no people hardly, no anything really. Not even any mobile connection to the internet. I did not expect to see such a place as that ever. Especially, this side of the Ural Mountains. It looked as if time had stood still there for about two hundred years or more."

The waitress had now taken everyone's order. She suggested that because the pub was terribly busy, that the meals could take up to half an hour or more.

"Thank you. That is not a problem." replied Robert.

"Speak for yourself, Dad!"

"Where did you go to on your walk," asked Trevor.

"I went to a village called, No Place."

"What." remarked dad. "You must have gone somewhere."

Hearing Roberts raised voice. Debbie quickly responded. "Yes Bruce, the village with the little shop you told us about, what was it called?"

"No! You don't understand the village was called "No Place."

"Parden me. I have been an estate agent around these parts for over 36 years. Believe me, there is nowhere called, "No Place." What utter nonsense."

"Oh yes there is," replied Bruce defensively. "I was there today. It was a small village, with a shop, a chapel, an old garage, and a blacksmith. Oh, and that garage was a real antique, the sort of place a salvage hunter would love to get their hands on. It must be one hundred years old and hardly changed since the day it opened, possibly by Queen Victoria herself."

Trevor again responded, with some authority.

"Well, sorry, but I have never heard of it!"

Debbie was feeling uncomfortable with this apparent situation. She looked at Brenda for some clarity.

"Brenda, have you heard of that village, No Place?"

"No, Debbie not around here, and I'm a local Taddington girl, born and bred."

"Well, it was there alright today, definitely this afternoon. It was real enough to me," insisted Bruce.

Robert wanted to change the subject.

"Never mind all that mystery village talk. What would everyone like to drink?"

"Can I have my usual, a pint of dry cider please?"

Debbie spoke to Brenda.

"Should we ask the waitress for a jug of iced water for now, then we could have a coffee later, after the meal."

Trevor was feeling a bit uneasy about Bruce's mystery village, so he stood up.

"I will come to the bar with you Bob, to get the drinks."

At the bar, Trevor wanted to ask the Landlord a question.

"Hey, Jack, have you ever heard of a village called "No Place?" Jack swiftly replied.

"What around here? No, never. I would like to call this pub. "No Place Like Home." But the bloody brewery will not allow it."

Robert and Trevor chuckled to themselves. As they carried the drinks over to their table. No place like home? They liked Jack's suggestion.

"Trevor just asked the Landlord if there is a village called, No Place, around here and he had never heard of it."

"Well, I am telling you it is there alright."

Mum snapped.

"We will go with you tomorrow, alright Bruce. We will put an end to this mystery village once and for all."

"Thanks, mum, I remember it had an old wishing well, with writing on it, POUTIA Wishing Well."

Trevor gasped as he took a swig of his pint.

"POUTIA Wishing Well; I think you drink too much of that strong cider my friend."

"Don't be so rude, Trevor." Replied Brenda in a raised voice. "Now that is enough joking for one night. I thought we came out to enjoy a meal together."

"Hear, Hear," replied Robert.

"Sorry Bruce, no hard feelings. Let us raise our glasses to Bruce and good luck at university."

They lifted their glasses to a cheer.

"Good luck Bruce."

Bruce smiled and felt more at ease.

"I heard this great joke the other day. A man walked into a bar with a car steering wheel between his legs. The bar person said. Blimey that must hurt. The man replied. Yes, its driving me nuts."

"Now that is funny," answered Trevor.

After the meal Mum drove the car back to Snipe cottage. They went straight to bed, saying they were tired after such a long day. It was only 10 o'clock. Getting into bed, Bruce thought I have enjoyed the mixed grill it was mega. After the meal I had a banoffee pie with ice cream for dessert, that was also mega. However, nice the food was Bruce was bored here. He needed to go back to his flat, his job, and most of all, his mates. Honestly, he couldn't wait to leave. He was up early the next morning, just before 7 o'clock. He asked mum over breakfast, if she could take him to Bakewell. She was a bit upset about him leaving.

"But you have only just got here, please stay awhile longer."

"Please understand mum I need to get back home. I am going to get the 11 o'clock London coach this morning."

"Are you sure love, you should consider staying for a few days more, we do miss you, dear."

I considered her kind words for a brief second, but only one brief second. No on refection, I decided. Not to stay. It was time to go home. Honestly, I couldn't stand the empty feeling of being here anymore, even though it is great to be with mum and dad. I was bored rigid, and I wanted to get back to some normality, and to be with my friends again. Therefore, as mothers so often do, she relented and after I said goodbye to dad. Who admittedly would have been glad to have me out from under his feet. He gave me a man hug and said goodbye and good luck with the university course.

Mum drove me to Bakewell. We were standing by the coach stop.

"I still have half a week of holiday left. I will use it to find a place at uni. I am sure there will be a suitable place somewhere in London."

Mum waited with me at the coach stop. When the coach arrived. I showed the driver my e-ticket on my phone. Mum gave me a kiss on the cheek and a big hug.

"Love you, Bruce. Don't forget to call me to let me know you got back safely."

I got onto the coach, and found an empty window seat. I watched mum waving goodbye to me, she seemed a little tearful and was dabbing her eyes with a paper tissue, as the coach pulled away. I thought freedom at last. I considered myself to be the master of my own destiny, I am just a city boy at heart, so let's get a game on.

After the long journey to Victoria coach station. I picked up my shoulder bag and headed home. I arranged on my mobile to meet up with my mates later that evening. Then after a quick snooze at my flat, it was time to shower and get ready to party. Oh, the joy of being at home I thought, this was better than perfect. Firstly, I won all the best of five games against Josh. He had to admit, that I was the grand master pool player, that evening. Secondly, we went afterwards to a Greek restaurant. The food was mega, and the live music had Josh and me and others there dancing through the restaurant.

However, my feel-good factor was short lived. Beause when I arrived at my flat, it had been broken into. The door was smashed open, and the lock broken. I called the landlord, and he said he would fix the door tomorrow. I then called the police. But, because I had said, that it looked as if nothing was taken. The police said, they would give me an incident number. However, no one from the police would be coming over, as nothing seemed to have been taken. I phoned and told Josh, and he said, it happens all the time mate, the robbers are looking for forms of identity these days. Such as passports and driving licence's, there is good money to be made in supplying fake identities.

The following morning, I called mum about the incident and Mum was terribly upset. She said I told you to stay here a while longer.

I then tried to explain to mum that there was no harm done, only to the door which had been smashed in. However, all my stuff was still there, even my tv and my laptop. Which did seem very strange to me at the time, as nothing had been taken. Mum mentioned that maybe the robbers were disturbed and ran off empty handed. I told her not to worry and I would be waiting in now, for the landlord to come and fix the door. Mum also said she would speak to dad later, about them going on a walk to solve this "No Place" mystery village. Alright mum I replied, have a nice day and take some photos of the village. A few hours later the Landlord turned up with a new door and a new lock and keys.

In Monyash, mum, Deborah (Debbie) and dad, Robert (Bob). Had decided to take a stroll across the moors to find, "No Place." They followed the same path as before. Turning right at the fork in the footpath, just like Bruce had done. Then after climbing over the style, they stood on the narrow lane. They turned to the right and walked up to the big old house.

"Just look at this magnificent old oak tree Debbie, it must be 500 years old."

Debbie admired the majestic tree and noticed the nearby dirt track.

"Bruce mentioned a finger post pointing down a dirt track by the house with the old oak tree."

Robert considered the absence of a finger post.

"Well maybe the finger post fell over, anyway onward my love, onward to the unknown."

Debbie just gave him one of those looks, that say everything about how you feel about that person at that moment. They walked along the dirt track about half a mile. Debbie and Robert then stopped at the old farmgate. The gate was chained up and pad locked. The sign on the gate read, Dead of Winter Farm.

"Well love this is a dead end. Maybe Bruce climbed over this gate and the track then continues over there somewhere," suggested Robert.

"Yes, I suppose so, but this track only seems to go to that old farm. Anyway, I cannot climb over that old gate, it is far too high."

The couple turned around and walked back down the track. Reaching the tarmac lane, they took a left turn. But, after at least another mile of walking they found no other footpath, and no other dirt track.

Arriving back at Snipe cottage about an hour later.

"Bob put the kettle on for a brew, and I will phone Bruce."

"Hi love. How are you, did the Landlord fix your door?"

"Yes mum, he has and it is a much more sold door than before, and the lock is also a stronger make."

"Good news, about the door. We went on that walk of yours today. But it took us to an old farm gate and nothing more. Did you climb over that gate?"

Bruce was now confused.

"Yes, I know the Dead of Winter Farm. But, just before that farm gate there was a small lane, not much more than a dirt track, going off to the left."

"No love there wasn't a lane on the left, just a tall hedgerow."

"Mum, I am telling you there was a lane there, it went down a slight slope to a little bridge over a brook."

"Well, I don't know what has happened to it, because there was no lane there today pet."

Bruce was exacerbated by this response. He thought they must be in the wrong place.

"Look mum, you must have missed it, did you two look properly, were you in the right place?"

Then Bruce ended the call abruptly as he had another incoming call.

"Ok mum I need to go now, but I will call you later, bye."

Debbie went into the kitchen to talk to Bob.

"Bruce is adamant that there was a little lane on the left, just before that farm gate."

"Here Debbie, have a nice cup of tea. Bruce must be mistaken. We saw nothing there; he must have the wrong dirt track, or something like that. He possibly forgot that he had climbed over that farm gate and the lane he mentioned is somewhere beyond that gate."

Bruce was busy on his laptop trying to find a university place, and he found one. However, it was at Greenwich University which is miles away from Tottenham. Bruce text Josh about it. Should I go to Greenwich? Better at UCL mate, came the reply. Red Lion 9 b there. That evening Bruce met with Josh, and they had a few ciders. Bruce decided that he needed to balance his study life, with his work life and most of all keep his social life. Bruce asked Josh for his opinion.

"If I stay at my job at the city university and if I could study part-time, Then, we can still chill at weekends and sometimes in the week."

"You have it my man, fancy another Strongbow."

"Sure do, I'm getting a taste for this stuff."

Bruce was happy with this idea, so he texts his mum. Hi, mum will keep hold of my j at ucl study pt at ucl keep my s life lol x.

Mum text back. Not sure what you mean, but sure it will be fine xx

Bruce arrived back at his flat, at a little after midnight. He opened his new door and in the dark, he noticed something on the floor. Bruce turned on the light and there on the floor was an envelope. He thought it must have been pushed under the door, maybe by the landlord. Picking up the envelope and turning it over. He read, **"Warning"** thinking it was just a joke from one of his mates. Bruce left the envelope on the coffee table, as he walked into his bedroom desperately wanting a good night's sleep.

In the morning Bruce was awakened by the bright sunlight shining through a gap in the curtains onto his face. Bruce sat up and made his way to the kitchen area. There he put some tap water into the kettle and switched it on. Bruce walked back into the lounge and there he opened the curtains. Bruce then noticed the brown envelope. **"Warning"** had been stamped on to the front of the envelope. Bruce opened the envelope with his right index finger. Inside was a small piece of blank paper and written on it was. "Please do not go back there again, you are being watched." Bruce thought who is watching me? Bruce picked up his phone and he called his mum.

"Hi mum, did I tell you I had my door fixed and now there is a more secure lock on it. Anyway, mum. I have had an envelope pushed under my door."

"Who is it from."

"I don't know, the writing on the envelope just says, Warning, and even that was rubber stamped on. Inside the envelope is a note, that says. "Please do not go back there again, you are being watched."

"Call the police dear and tell them that you are being bullied or even stalked."

"Hang on a bit mum. I don't know what this is all about, and I don't want to get the police involved."

"I am not happy about this Bruce, first you are broken into and now you are receiving threatening letters, you need to tell someone."

Bruce reassured his mum that all was okay.

"You know best love, just be careful. By the way, dad and I are going to look for that little village again today."

"Good idea and remember to take the track, by the old house with a big oak tree in the garden. Then when you get to the Dead of Winter Farm gate, take the little lane to the left."

"Will do love, have a nice day, love you, I will call you back later xx."

Bruce sat down with his mug of coffee, and he looked for any distinguishing marks or a postage stamp, on the brown envelope. Funny, he thought, *who would send this to me*? What is the warning. Maybe, it is Josh, he likes a laugh at times. I will see him later, and with that thought in mind, Bruce put the envelope into his trouser pocket.

Meanwhile, in Monyash, Debbie and Robert, were full of determination to find the strange little village, No Place. Debbie had prepared somethings for their outing. She put into a small rucksack, a flask of tea, four corned beef sandwiches with mustard pickle, two each. Two pink lady apples, and two bananas. Oh, and a scotch egg for Robert, and a camera. They set off from Snipe cottage at about 10:30 on a clear and sunny morning. The weather forecast was to be Hot 27c with a calm to moderate breeze. Not really too bad at all for a walk on a late August day.

Back, in London, Bruce had also been out walking around, with no general purpose in mind. It was still his holiday, so he was making the most of it. At lunchtime he went into a Costa Café. Whilst waiting in the queue, someone behind him tapped him on his shoulder.

"Hi Bruce, do you remember me?"

Bruce turned around and there was Gemma, a friend of Sarah-Louise, from their high school days together.

"Hi! Gemma, how are you."

"Fine thanks, what are you doing these days. I have not seen you in ages, are you still in contact with Sarah-Louise."

"No, I have not heard from Sarah-Louise in yonks. I am too busy working these days, then I meet up with my mates, going out clubbing, then sleeping, that sort of thing."

"Are you not at work today, Bruce?"

"No, I have had a week's holiday. I went up north to see my mum and dad. However, I came back after 2 days, it is so boring up there in Derbyshire. What about you Gemma. What are you doing these days?"

"I am going to uni. in September, to study Physiotherapy."

"Brilliant Gemma, which uni. are you going to?"

"UCL" Happily smiled Gemma.

"What! No way. That is where I was thinking of going on a full-time, Sports Coach and Management course. But now I have decided to just study there, part-time and keep my full-time job there as the assistant catering manager."

Bruce was now at the front of the queue and ready to order.

"Must get my steak bake and a cappuccino. Well, good luck Gemma, hope to see you in September."

"Yes, nice to see you again Bruce."

On Friday night Bruce was eager to go out and socialise. He arrived at the Red Lion pub at 7pm, and within minutes he had a pint in his hand. He stood by the bar waiting for Josh to turn up. The Red Lion is a typical old London pub, set in one of the busy side streets in Tottenham. There is not much space inside the pub, basically consisting of two medium sized rooms. One a bar and the other a lounge. However, outside on the pavement there are at least five large tables, with umbrellas, that seat six around each table. Josh sent a text saying he will be late, about eight, OK.

Bruce thought he would talk to his mum, while he had nothing else to do. The phone rang and rang and then went onto answer phone. "Mum, call me back can you, thanks love you." Then Bruce phoned his dad, but his phone was turned off, so went straight to answer mode. Bruce left a similar message there too. "Hi dad, give me a call back, when you can, or get mum to call me, thanks dad."

Bruce was bored stiff and almost comatose by 8 pm.

"Thank heaven you are here, Josh. I have been playing kick the buddy, on my phone for almost an hour now."

"Sorry mate my sister needed me to pick her up from work, as her car is in for repairs. Do you want the same again?"

"Yes, please mate."

Bruce tried his mum's phone number again. But as before it went straight onto answer phone mode. "Hi mum, give me a call back, please." Bruce and Josh then went from the Red Lion pub, to another, The Vine Tree. This pub stands on a busy street corner and there are two interior rooms. The public bar and a very comfy lounge where sweethearts meet for a chat. There is also a large beer garden, and this is immensely popular on summer evenings. Bruce and Josh were meeting Toni, Ben, and Rikki, at 9:30 in the beer garden for another drink or two before going clubbing at Fabric night club.

Toni is the only women in this group of friends. She is hoping to persuade the others to go with her to the Notting Hill Carnaval, on the following Bank holiday weekend.

"Now, admittedly it was a bit hectic the last time we went to the carnival, and we lost Ben and Rikki within the first half an hour. However, this time we know better, don't we? We need to stay together as a group, and to follow each other. No drifting off to buy a drink, of homemade rum, eh Ben!"

Toni is a nice young woman, extremely easy to get on with. Originally from Camden Town. But, now lives in Deptford and compared to the men, she is a truly local London girl. Toni is 24 years old with short chestnut brown hair, hazel eyes, and a fair complexion. She is of medium build and about 5'5'' tall. Toni almost always wears jeans, trainers, and a top. Her hair is usually untidy, and she rarely wears any make-up. Toni is usually a happy go lucky type, but she is also sensitive about certain subjects such as the homeless. She often talks about how some people make her so angry, because they don't care enough about the plight of the homeless. Such as people who think that homelessness should be made illegal. She would say do you really think that people planned to be homeless. That one day at school when they were asked by a careers teacher, what do you want to be when you leave school? The student replied. I would like to sleep in shop doorway and have drunks urinate on me!

Toni works at the Home Office as an administration clerk. Toni previously had a boyfriend named Alex, who played the saxophone in a local band Blues band, so she is well known in the local pubs. However, she is single now and was another one of Sarah-Louise's original friends from high school.

Ben is a degree student at Goldsmiths; he is studying Humanities. Ben is 25 years old and about 6' 4" and stocky build with it. He was born in Bristol and of Afro-Caribbean descent. Ben is a gentle giant of a man, with a typical Bristol accent. He can often be heard saying "alright my lover." He also says that Toni, Rikki, Josh, and Bruce are his London family. Ben lives in student accommodation in New Cross, whilst attending university. However, he goes home to his parents in Bristol whenever he can, especially during end of term holidays. Ben has two older brothers and three younger sisters; he says that his family means everything to him and the only reason for returning to London early is when the football season begins.

Rikki is the youngest at just twenty-two and originally from Brighton. He lives with his mum, and two younger brothers and they were neighbours of Sarah-Louise when she lived in Camden Town. Rikki works as an administrator with the NHS Health Trust at St. Thomas's Hospital. He is very tall about 6' 2" and very thin in appearance, with pale skin, blondish hair, and light blue eyes. Rikki often wears stylish clothes and today he was wearing new jeans and an orange tee-shirt that stated, (Same old Twat New tee-shirt). Rikki is aware of his good looks. He is very photogenic with a strong jaw line that most other guys would kill for. He is also noticeably confident and can hold down a conversation on most subjects. I think the term is he is well read. Rikki's mum is a single parent. She would leave Rikki alone when he was younger, with a book to read to his two younger twin brothers. Usually, in the local library for several hours, whilst she went shopping on a Saturday morning.

Josh is the oldest of this group of friends being nearly 27 years old. He originally came from Hatfield and unlike the others. He, like Bruce, is not university educated. He is employed by Carphone Warehouse, in New Cross. Josh looks older than his 26 years. He has shoulder length hair that was obviously dyed blonde at some point, but now the original light brown hair is starting to grow back through. Josh is roughly 5'9'' tall, and he usually wears a black leather jacket with metal studs on the back spelling. "Arsenal." Josh and Bruce hit it off from their very first meeting in the bar of the Marquis of Granby. They both have a wicked sense of humour, and they tell jokes to each other constantly. Josh has a flat in Tottenham, which is just a few blocks away from Bruce, and all the group of friends met originally, either from personally knowing Sarah-Louise or by meeting in the bar of The Marquis of Granby. The

Marquis of Granby pub is usually their focal point; it has two large rooms a bar and a lounge. Plus, a further room next to the bar with two pool tables.

"Are we all agreed then. We will be going to the carnival next weekend." Ben said, "I am up for it." Rikki "Me too." Josh said, "I will come along if Toni holds my hand."

Ben replied. "We should all hold hands."

Bruce then spoke. "I sometimes wonder about you lot. So, we have five yes's." Toni was ecstatic, "Yes, it looks as though we are all going." Bruce then concluded, "But I am not holding anyone's hand, OK."

Bruce spent the following week back at work and he had an acknowledgement card from UCL. Stating that he was now enlisted on their, Part-time, Sports Coaching and Leadership; HND Course. Bruce instinctively phoned his mum to tell her his good news, but he could not get through to her phone again. Bruce had also tried his dad's number. However, still nothing there either. Bruce had arranged to meet up with Josh, at the Royal Albert pub on Wednesday evening. So, they could watch a European cup match on a big wide screen tv. Bruce mentioned to Josh that he couldn't get through to either his mum or dad.

"I have phoned them both several times, but their phones must be turned off or something."

"Where do they live?"

"Derbyshire, in the Peak District."

"Well maybe they don't get a good signal up that way, mate. It must be very remote around there, is it also hilly?"

"No, the signal is usually alright. I have called them before and not had any problems."

"Do you know what phone system they are on?"

It is either, EE or Vodafone."

"Well then phone EE and Vodafone tomorrow, and ask them, if they are having any problems with their transmitters in Derbyshire."

"Good idea, will do, thanks mate,"

"That kind of technical information cost's a pint thanks." Josh offered Bruce his empty glass.

"I heard this great joke the other day. A man handed a glue stick instead of a chap stick to his wife by mistake, and she still isn't talking to him."

"Nice one," replied Josh.

On the next day, Bruce tried to phone his parents, but again with no luck whatsoever. Then he called EE service help line, to ask if there were any problems with calls in and out of Derbyshire. He was told that no engineers had reported any problems with their signals. He then called Vodafone and asked if they had any problems with their mobile signals in the Peak District. He was assured that the signal strength was satisfactory. Then whilst Bruce was at work. Bruce asked Andrew Dolby, his manager, what he would do.

"What would you do if your parents didn't answer their phones?"

"If I were you. I would go after work, and call in to see the police. Ask them if they will contact the Derbyshire police, and if they could contact your parents for you."

"Thank you, Andrew. That's a great idea; I will try that later."

Bruce went to the local Tottenham police station after work that evening.

"Can I help, Sir?" Asked the police Sargent at the reception.

"Hello, I have been trying to phone my mum and dad. They live in Monyash in Derbyshire. I have been calling them regularly over the past 5 days, and still there is no answer."

"I see you are concerned Sir. If I could take a few details. Your name is?" "Bruce Knight." "Your address." "Flat 18, Deptford House, Tottenham." "Their address." "Snipe Cottage, ST. Leonards Road, Monyash." "When did you last have contact with your parents?" "I went to Derbyshire 3 weeks ago, just for 2 days. My mum then drove me to Bakewell when I was leaving, and I spoke to her later that day; and on the following day also."

"Alright Sir, we shall contact an officer up there in Bakewell, and they will most likely send a patrol car around to your parents' home. Basically, to see if all is fine, etc. You will receive a call from the police, in a day or two. Stating that a police officer had been around to their house, to let them know, that you are trying to contact them."

"Thank you very much Sargent, I will look forward to that call."

Bruce felt much more contented now that the police were going to call in and see his parents.

Two days later, whilst Bruce was at work, the police in Bakewell called him on his mobile.

"Hello, can I speak to Mr Bruce Knight."

"Yes, this is me speaking."

"This is a return curtesy call from Derbyshire constabulary regarding an enquiry about a Mr & Mrs Knight of Snipe cottage, Monyash. I am afraid to say, that after two visits, on two consecutive days; we have been unable to make any contact with Mr or Mrs Knight. However, the house is securely locked, and it seems unoccupied, at this present time."

"My mum and dad are retired, and they don't really go anywhere much these days only on local walks."

"Sorry, Sir, that we have not been able to contact your parents. Maybe, you should try other relative or friends to see if they know anything more about their whereabouts. Again, sorry we couldn't be of more help to you, goodbye."

Bruce was now in a puzzle. Where could they have gone? After work Bruce phoned his parent's numbers again and again. He then remembered, Josh saying that maybe the transmitters are down. Bruce called EE service help line. After negotiating the mental anguish of press this number for this service, now press this number for that service. He finally, after 20 minutes of listening to Beethoven's 5th on a perpetual loop. He eventually got through to a service engineer based in the Midlands.

"Hello, I have been trying to call my parents for at least a week now. They live in Monyash, Derbyshire. But all the calls go straight to their answer phone service, can you see if their numbers are available or not."

"Please give me a moment and I will check those numbers for you.

Hello, I am sorry, but both those numbers are unavailable at the moment. Their phones must be switched off."

"Is there a signal problem up there in Derbyshire, could that be the problem?"

"No, the signal status is fine, it is presently somewhere between 2.5 and 3.5 Gig. Their phones definitely must be turned off. Thank you, for calling EE help line service, is there anything else I can assist you with."

"No thank you, that is all."

Bruce then decided to call the Vodafone help line, and after selecting 1 to be connected to an operative, then 2 to be connected to an engineer, 3 to be connected to a local service engineer. Bruce was then left to listened to Elbow, singing; one day like this a year. Then after what seemed like a substantial proportion of that year had passed by and Bruce was still waiting on the phone. A voice said.

"Hello this is Martin, North Midlands service engineer. How can I help you."

However, Bruce was now in the swing of things musically speaking, and was just about to get to the chorus.

"Throw those curtains wide. One day like this a year, will do me fine."

But then he remembered why he had phoned this number.

"Oh, hello Martin, could you see if there are any difficulties with the mobile phone signal in Monyash, Derbyshire."

"Are you advising me that there is a signal problem in Monyash, Derbyshire?"

"Yes, I mean no, I want to know if there is a problem there."

"No there isn't a problem that I am aware of Sir."

"Right, OK. Thank you." Bruce ended the call.

Bruce had never had this problem before, in his entire life. His parents were always available to talk to him day or night, they were always there for him. Whatever the circumstance was. He was now certain that something untoward had happened to them. Bruce then had an idea, and he called Bakewell hospital to see if his parents were in a car crash or something like that.

"Hello, can you help me please. I am trying to locate my parents, Mr & Mrs Knight. They live in Monyash, have they been admitted to the hospital."

"Hello, my name is Olga. I will check the register for you. Please hold the line for a moment. Hello, No, sorry we have no Knights on our system."

"Is there another hospital they could have gone too?"

"Where and when did they have the accident?"

"They are not in an accident; I just want to find them."

"No, sorry if you don't know where or when the accident happened, then I am unable to suggest which hospital they might have been taken to."

"There has been, no accident. I just want to know where my parents are." Bruce replied in a raised voice.

"We do take the safety of our staff seriously, and we have a zero tolerance of verbal abuse." replied Olga. "Therefore, our conversation is now being recorded." Bruce hung up.

Bruce kept trying his parent's phones over and over again, but it was the same response every time

, there was no answer. Bruce could not understand where they might be, this was so unlike them. Then he had another brainwave moment. I bet they have gone to Madrid to see Denise.

Bruce immediately rang Denise.

"Hello, sis are mum and dad with you?"

"Well, Bruce, it is so nice to hear from you too. Are you going to ask me if I am fine and keeping well. Enjoying life in Spain, etc."

"Ok, Yeh. Point taken, are you fine and well. Now, is mum and dad with you?"

"No, why should they be!"

"No sis. I have been trying to phone them for over a week. So, I guessed they might be with you. Their phones were turned off or they could possibly be abroad somewhere on holiday."

"Are you sure they are not on away holiday?"

"Well if they are they never mentioned it to me."

"Bruce, darling, they are now retired, and free agents, to do as they like. We are not children anymore. They can just go off somewhere, at the drop of a hat, if they want too, they have no ties anymore."

"I never thought of that."

"No, you were never a great thinker, were you sweetie? Anyway, it has been nice talking to you Bruce, and do call me when you hear from them, OK."

"Will do sis and thanks for the chat, bye."

Bruce was still not totally convinced that his mum and dad, had gone away on holiday. It was just so unlike them not to stay connected. Especially mum, thought Bruce.

The August bank holiday in London is famous for the Notting Hill Carnival. Toni loved the carnival atmosphere, with the music, the costumes, and the genuinely happy people that come here every year to take part in the carnival spirit. The streets all around that area of west London, are busy with people selling food and drinks. Some residents even make money by letting visitors use their bathroom. The whole place is buzzing with activities. There are lots of things to see and enjoy. Toni had asked the other guys to meet up with her, at 11 o'clock on the Monday morning. Toni would also be there on the Sunday if anyone wanted to enjoy both days. However, on the Monday morning, Bruce, Josh, and Ben, met at the Tottenham Court Road tube station at 10am. This was a mistake from the offset because the train was packed with likeminded people. Rikki had come down with his mother and his twin brothers, and they met up with Toni, in Notting hill high street outside the Santander bank. Where Toni and Rikki then waited and waited for the others to turn up. Finally, after being there for nearly an hour. Rikki recognised the tall figure of Ben.

The street carnival was by now festoon with bright colours, as participants were dressed in magnificent costumes and the live music was encouraging people to dance in the streets. There was as usual a mostly Caribbean feeling to the carnival, but there was also a Chinese dragon dance display and a Japanese drum group. The five friends tried their hardest to stay together and they succeeded for at least an hour. But, eventually, the sheer volume of people walking up and down, those connected streets. It was inevitable that someone would become lost or just swept away by the crowds going in the opposite direction, that they wanted to go. Bruce was with Rikki and Toni, but Josh and Ben had stopped to talk to friends and that separated them from the others.

The whole street was heaving with people, with plenty of pushing and shoving. Already some spectators, had succumbed to the heat and paramedics on motor bikes were in attendance. Bruce, Rikki, and Toni walked past a street corner and within the entrance to this side road, there was a group of Morris dancers. They stood in a circle; they began dancing forward and backwards. Going forward they would hit their sticks together. There were six Morris dancers, each wearing a black and white checkered tee shirt. With black knee length trousers, black boots, and a black rimed straw hat. Three others had black feathered costumes, and they were playing the music. One had a small kettle drum; one had a tambourine, and the other had a penny whistle. There was also one other, a tall man, in a similar black and white feathered costume. He was wearing a necklace made of small skeleton heads from birds, such as crows or pigeons.

He had a leather belt with a ceremonial dagger in a holder. However, where the Morris dancers and the musicians were white people. This other guy had his face, his bald head blackened. He made Bruce, Rikki and Toni feel uncomfortable because he was such an imposing figure.

They stopped to watch this unusual sight at a Notting Hill carnival. Then one female bystander who was standing next to Toni, she spoke.

"It is not right. They should not be allowed to blacken their face it is very disrespectful."

Then a man bystander replied. "We do not need this type of entertainer here. They are not your typical reggae band are they."

Prompted and inspired by these comments. Toni ran forward and put her hand on the tall man's blackened forehead. She tried to rub the makeup off. Several people in the gathering crowd cheered her on. Then the tall man with the blacked face, he grabbed Toni by the wrist, and he twisted it. Toni gave out a scream.

Rikki shouted. "Come on Bruce he is hurting her." Rikki grabbed hold of the man's arm, and the man let go of Toni. Bruce was now standing in the centre of the dancers. When one of the dancers shouted out.

"We have our intruder, the trespasser. Kill him now."

Bruce was motionless, just standing there transfixed, looking at these strange creatures in their black feathery costumes. Bruce became disorientated by the chain of events, when suddenly Bruce noticed the tall black faced man drew a knife on Toni and Rikki.

Toni screamed. "Look out he has got a knife!!!"

Toni and Rikki grabbed each other by the hand and they ran up the side road, away from the Morris dancers. Bruce noticed those two running away. So, he also ran up the road. Bruce's heart was pounding hard in his chest as he tried to take in what had just happened. The tall dark feathered cloak man, and the rest of the Morris dancers were now hot on their heels.

At the end of this short side road there was an alley way, where Rikki grabbed Toni's arm and pulled her into the alley. Bruce quickly followed. Then in the alley way Bruce, Toni and Rikki had stopped running. They turned around hoping that the chase had come to an end. However, after a second or two, the tall dark man, in his feathered cloak, and the other Morris dancers all entered the alley way. They too stopped running. They stood facing the three friends.

The tall dark man then shouted. "Stand still, you the trespasser. You must face me, your accuser."

Bruce, Toni, and Rikki could not believe their eyes, when the tall dark man, appeared to be getting even taller. He was growing upward before their eyes. He was already over 2 metres tall. The other Morris Dancers now spread themselves in a semi-circle behind the tall dark man.

The taller dark man then, pushed off his cloak of black and white feathers. He began to unfold black bat type wings from behind him. Within second's this tall dark man, became a different creature.

He was now at least 2.5 metres tall. He was completely black in colour. Not black as in someone with chestnut brown skin, from parts of Asia or Africa. No, not at all, this guy was totally black, charcoal or jet, whatever you consider is dark black, such as ebony. He was also naked, except for a pair of black shorts. He held a dagger before him. The dagger now changed shape, being transformed into a long two-edged sword.

Bruce and his friends stood still not believing their eyes. The Morris dancers who had remained standing behind the tall, now winged dark creature. They all began to laugh, then cheered, and shouted. "Ancient one! Ancient one! Ancient one! Kill the trespasser, kill your enemy, take your revenge now."

The tall black creature turned to glance behind him. He bowed to those Morris men that were cheering him. Then he turned and walked towards Bruce, holding the sword forward pointing it at Bruce. The dark creature then stopped about two metres away from Bruce, he smiled and bowed his head at Bruce. Then raising his sword arm up above his head. He momentarily glanced back at the Morris dancers. The Morris dancers cheered again. "Ancient one, ancient one, ancient one, kill your enemy now."

When suddenly in a flash of inspiration, Rikki ran forward in three large strides and kicked the tall dark creature in the crutch, as hard as he could.

Ricki then shouted. "What are you two waiting for an applause, run now."

Bruce and Toni quickly turned and ran up the alley way as quick as they could run, with Rikki just a stride, or two behind. Meanwhile, the tall dark creature was now growling in pain, doubled up and holding his not so happy sack. He then screamed out, full of intense anger.

"I shall kill you Trespasser, and your friends, mark my words I will have my revenge."

He then straightened himself up, took a deep breath, and accepted that the chase was back on again.

Bruce and his two friends were now running out of the alley way, and into the adjoining side road. Quickly heading for the main street, to re-join the carnival procession. The tall dark creature and the Morris dancers were still giving a hot pursuit, but by the time they reached halfway down the side street. Bruce, Rikki, and Toni were already in the main carnival procession surrounded by hundreds of carnival spectators.

Glancing back across to the side road. Bruce could clearly see the tall dark figure, standing in the side road with all the Morris dancers around him.

Toni then spoke. "We need to tell the police about those crazy people; I thought they were going to kill us."

The three friends pushed their way across the street to the other side, where they stood for a rest by a garden wall.

"Are you all right Rikki." asked Bruce. "You saved the day mate with your quick thinking."

"Yes, I am fine. I have always wanted to kick some jerk in the nuts, it was so, satisfying."

"How about you, Toni, are you alright." enquired Rikki. "Who were those jerks? That tall guy pulled a knife on us, we need to tell the police." retorted Toni.

"I don't know who they were, and as for that tall dark guy. He was totally freaky to start with. But then he turned into something else completely, and that knife became a bloody great sword. I really was panicking on what to do next, when Rikki kicked him in the balls."

Rikki smiled in recognition of his good deed.

"No worries, mate, it was my pleasure. You don't need to thank me."

Toni then spoke. "Come to think of it, it could have all been a scary costume game."

"No way," replied Bruce. "That was no scary costume game. They were for real; that tall creature, he even had a sword and threated to kill us."

"Well, Bruce I don't know who or what it was. But there is something not right about that whole group of Morris dancer freaks."

"I agree," remarked Bruce. "Talking about a tall guy, there's Ben over there, with Josh. Ben mate, over here," shouted Bruce.

With a lot of pushing and apologising. Ben and Josh made it across the street.

"Where have you guys been," asked Josh.

"We have had a very strange experience, with a group of Morris dancers," said Toni.

"Morris dancers at a Notting Hill carnival? I think you three have had some home-made rum at some point."

"No, rum mate, it was real enough, and a tall black guy pulled a knife on us." said Rikki.

"He was not actually, a black person as such. He was just blackened with costume makeup, and with wings, and he had a sword." explained Bruce.

"I think we all need a break and a drink." suggested Josh.

"Yes, indeed we do, let's get out of here. I suggest we go to the Marquis," exclaimed Bruce.

About an hour later, the five. Now very tired and thirst friends arrived at the Marquis of Granby. Ben and Toni were playing pool. Whilst Bruce spoke to Josh and Rikki, who were sitting down in the bar.

"The tall black creature, was, so strange. The guy was tall about 2 metres. Then in that alleyway he grew even taller."

"Yes, I know, especially after I kicked him in the tackle shop," remarked Rikki.

"He also had wings like a bat. Then the Morris dancers who had stopped behind him. Called him, the ancient one, and he came towards us with a bloody great sword," replied Bruce.

Josh had a cheeky smile, while he was listening to Bruce and Rikki.

"You guys have been smoking to much Ganj on carnival day, in my opinion. A tall black man, who turned into an even taller black man, with bats wings. Give me a break will you. He was black, yet not black, and he had a knife, that then turned into a sword."

"Yep, sounds crazy," replied Bruce. "But it is the truth mate, I swear on it."

Josh responded, "Sounds more like a normal carnival alcohol intoxication, exacerbated by marijuana abuse, causing hallucinations."

"You're, so wrong." Insisted Rikki, as he got up and walked over to join Ben and Toni at the pool table.

Bruce then tried to explain the facts to Josh.

"It might sound crazy to you mate, what happened to us today. But it was real enough. I am sure it was not a fake, or an illusion. The Morris dancers were behind this tall dark creature, and they called him, the ancient one, and they called on him to kill the trespasser. They all acted and looked like real people, in those costumes. Except for the tall guy, who became a tall creature, and I have no idea of who or what he was."

Josh thought for a moment. "OK mate, I believe you. What about your mum and dad, any news?"

"Well, I phoned Denise, in Madrid and she thinks, they had gone on a last-minute bargain, once in a lifetime holiday."

Then Josh replied. "But you thought they were missing, maybe lost in the moors, or they had been in a road accident somewhere. My point here being, that you thought the worst had happened to your parent's. Where now you see it for what it really is, they just went on a cheap last-minute bargain break holiday. No mystery, no harm, no problem. Now, what you saw at the carnival today, or what you think you saw. Is just as simple to explain. A group of ordinary men dressed up in costumes. Dancing around, playing music. Having a laugh on carnival day, at your expense. They were no different from hundreds of others on carnival day, just having a good time dressing up."

"Since you put it like that, you could be right."

Chapter 2

Two weeks later….

Bruce had just attended the first evening class of a 4-year Higher National Diploma in Sport Coaching and Management. Bruce is hoping that this qualification will lead him into employment with a sports college or university and eventually, he hopes to work for a high-profile football team. Bruce was extremely excited about his professional prospects. But, on the domestic front. Bruce had no contact with either of his parents, for at least 5 weeks. Even though he phoned them every day in the morning, then at lunch time and again in the evening.

Bruce also regularly phoned his sister, Denise.

"Hi sis, have you heard from mum and dad."

"No, they have not phoned me in months. Have you not been back up to see them?"

"No, I am terribly busy these days. I have started on a part-time uni. course, and I go to work full-time." said Bruce.

"Well, I can't call in to see them, I live in Madrid. You need to go up there this weekend and find out what has happened. They might have been in an accident or something like that, or someone like a neighbour of theirs might know something," remarked Denise.

"I can't go there this weekend, I have to meet my mentor at the university sports hall, it's my first tutorial."

"Well, you need to go up there sometime Bruce and the sooner the better. All this talk of our parents being missing, it is getting me worried too."

"OK, I will go up there the weekend after, I promise," said Bruce.

"Too right, you should, I don't like the mystery. Love you, bro, speak to you soon, bye xx."

Bruce phoned Josh. "Hi Josh, can we meet at the Marquis, later mate."

"Yes, can do, 8:30 is that alright," said Josh.

"Yes, thanks mate, sees you later."

Bruce now tried to phone his parents again, but there was still no answer, and the call was eventually transferred to the answer phone, where Bruce left the same message as previously.

"Hi this is Bruce can you please call me back asap. I am worried about you two, hope you are both well."

In the Marquis of Granby, Josh was waiting at the bar with 2 pints of cider.

When Bruce walked in, and seeing the drinks on the bar, he gestures as if he was firing arrows into the bar from an imaginary bow.

"Hi, Bruce or should I call you Robin Hood."

"You can call me what you like, after I have had a slurp of that pint. I have started my course at UCL and its looking, cool."

"In what way is the course cool," asked Josh.

"There is a student there named Bianca, and she is so fit, mate."

"I like your style." remarked Josh.

"Who cares about the practicality of the course work and all that academic stuff. When there is talent about."

"Drink up, mate. We will have another, and I shall tell you more about the vivacious, Bianca. Firstly, she is so beautiful. No, she is better than beautiful, she is gorgeous. Tall and slim, with a great figure. Secondly, she is olive skinned, with long black hair flowing halfway down her back, with a slight curl at the end. Thirdly, she has deep chocolate brown eyes, and a smile to die for, and she likes football."

Josh replied.

"She sounds heavenly, mate. Did you talk to her?"

"Early days," replied Bruce, "early days."

After another weekend of socialising and a week of work
and play, Bruce had booked a return ticket from London
Victoria coach station to Bakewell. Bruce had asked Josh, if
he could go with him, but Josh, Toni, Rikki, and Ben were
all going to the local match on Saturday, Arsenal are playing
Man city at home. Bruce settled down on the coach for a 4-
hour journey.

When he arrived at Bakewell, Bruce got a taxi to his parent's
house. Bruce rang the doorbell, hoping to be greeted by one
of his parent's. But, no reply, not a glimpse of anyone at
home. Bruce went through the side gate, and it was very
apparent that no one was there. His parent's left a back-door
key under an old dish cloth, which was draped over an
external patio light switch. Bruce retrieved the key and
entered the house via the backdoor. He shouted out, "mum,
dad, its me!" But no reply. The house was clean, but a bit
dusty here and there. Dads' car was parked in the carport,
and the car keys were hanging on a peg in the kitchen. Bruce
looked around the house, going from room to room. He was
hoping to find a note saying, gone to Timbuktu, see you
soon. However, Bruce was now beginning to realise the

seriousness of this situation, as he started to think that his parents' disappearance was much more than just going on holiday on a mere whim.

Bruce found the house phone in its holder, next to the TV in the lounge, and a telephone notebook. Looking through the book. Bruce noticed an entry for Trevor and Brenda. He used the house phone and called that number.

"Hello," came the reply.

"Hello, this is Bruce Knight, I am at my mum and dads house, and I was wondering if you know where they are?"

"Hello, Bruce," replied Brenda. "We have not seen Debbie or Bob in a month or more. In fact, it was when you came up here the last time, and we all went out for a meal."

Bruce enquired, "do you know if Trevor has seen or heard from them lately?"

"Trevor is at work right now, but I will ask him when he gets home."

"Thank you, Brenda, is there anyone else around here who might know where they are?"

"Well, they go to ST. Leonard's church on a Sunday morning. Maybe the vicar will know something."

"OK, thank you Brenda, bye."

Bruce, thought for a moment. I didn't know they went to church. Bruce walked along to St Leonard's. The church is surprisingly large for such a small village, thought Bruce.

On that Saturday afternoon the church was shut, and the doors locked. Bruce noticed a sign pointing to the vicarage and as he opened the gate. He heard a woman's voice from the garden.

"Can I help you dear?"

Bruce noticed a very pretty face on a slim, 30 something looking lady, who was hanging out the washing.

"Hello, I am looking for the vicar."

"Is he expecting you?"

"No, I want to ask him if he knows where my mum and dad are?"

The lady dried her hands on her apron, and she walked towards Bruce.

"Hello, my name is Lynette, and I am the vicar's wife. Who are your parents?"

Bruce answered, "Mr & Mrs Knight, from Snipe cottage, just over there in the village."

"I know your parent's Robert and Deborah. Why do you need to see my husband?"

"I live in London, and I have been trying to speak to my parents for over a month, but they are either not answering their phones, or their phones are turned off."

"Have you been to their house, said Lynette, as she gestured for Bruce to go to the front door."

"Yes, I have a door key, and I am staying there till tomorrow morning. Then I need to get the coach back from Bakewell to London."

Lynette opened the front door. "Please do come inside." Lynette then called to her husband.

"Michael, can you come here and meet Mr & Mrs Knight's son. What is your name again dearie?"

"Bruce, Bruce Knight."

The vicar walked into the entrance hall. He was a 30 something year old, slim-built man of average height, and nearly totally bald. Except for hair that grew from the side of his head just behind his ears and continuing around the back of his head to the other side. He had a very posh look about him, and with an accent to match.

"Michael, darling this is Bruce, who is Mr & Mrs Knight's son, from London."

Michael offered his right hand. Bruce shook his hand, and he asked.

"I am hoping you might know where my mum and dad have gone recently, they seem to have disappeared."

"Please do come on into my study, where we can talk." Michael led the way followed by Bruce and Lynette.

"I have not seen your parents in church since, well possibly, a month ago. You say they are missing what brings you to that conclusion, may I ask. Oh, Please do take a seat Bruce."

They all sat down, Bruce and Lynette on the sofa, and Michael sat at his desk.

"Let us start at the beginning," suggested Michael. "When did you last see your parents?"

"I came up here in mid-August for a couple of days."

"Did your parents mention that they were considering going away on a vacation or something similar?"

"No, they were not going anywhere, that I am aware. In fact, they came up here to Monyash, to get away from the rat race in London. They enjoyed the peace and quiet of the countryside," remarked Bruce.

"How strange that they have just gone off, like that, were they prone to going away suddenly."

Bruce replied. "No, not at all, it is very unlike them to go away, especially without telling me or my sister first."

Michael relied. "Had your parents ever talked about going away on an adventure holiday or something similar, possibly on a cruise or a walking holiday abroad."

Bruce smiled and commented. "No way, they are too boring to do anything adventurous like that. As I have already mentioned. They like peace and quiet, no noises, no glitter, no fun. That is why they moved up here to Derbyshire, to be in the middle of know where."

"So, you think it is boring here do you Bruce." Remarked Micheal.

"No, not that Monyash is boring. I meant that they are boring people, in the stuff they like to do, such as walking across the moors and looking at the wildlife. Etc."

Lynette interrupted. "Take no notice of him Bruce. We had a lovely parish church in Polegate in East Sussex, between Eastbourne and Lewes. Do you know that area, it is so heavenly." Bruce smiled and nodded in recognition.

"But Michael in his infinite wisdom decided we needed to get back to his common roots. He came from Glossop in Derbyshire originally, so we came here, didn't we my dear. Where if he would have listened to reason, we could have gone to Eastleigh in Hampshire, where I once lived with my parents, and a more beautiful area in England cannot be found."

Michael sat up straight in his chair. "Now, now, there are many qualities to be found here. We do not want to do our dirty washing in public; do we dearest?"

"If you say so, Michael! Lynette stood up. Anyway, I need to return to my household duties. Goodbye, Bruce. I hope you find your parents soon."

"Thank you, Lynette."

Michael also stood up. "Well Bruce, I do not think I can help you any further, have you contacted the police."

"Yes, when I was in London, they sent someone to look at the house. Then they phoned me back later to say, that no one was at home."

"You might need to contact them again Bruce, but this time contact the local police directly. The local constabulary might know if your parents have had an accident locally, or in nearby, Manchester, Derby, or Sheffield. They would be able to access, and check the national police data base, to see if they had been injured elsewhere in the UK. I would do that immediately if I were you. Please, let me know if you hear anything from the police regarding your parents. I will ask the congregation at the Sunday service for prayers for you and your parents."

"Thank you very much, that would be nice."

Michael led Bruce to the front door. "Goodbye Bruce and god bless."

Bruce returned to Snipe cottage, where he phoned the local Derbyshire police. A police constable, PC Degg, answered the call. He confirmed that Bruce's previous call was logged, and he would make further enquiries regarding the possible whereabouts of Mr & Mrs Knight though the national data base. Bruce thanked the police officer and mentioned that he was returning to London the following morning.

PC Degg then concluded the conversation by saying, that the police would contact Bruce immediately, if they had any new information. Also, that Bruce must not over-worry, because cases like this are all too common these days. Where the missing persons have just gone off on the spur of the moment. Maybe, for a romantic holiday to the Caribbean, or they were walking in the Himalayas with not a care in the world. Especially, if they had recently won a significant sum on the lottery, or through inheritance.

"Thank you, constable Degg, for your help."

PC Degg replied. "No problem, Mr Knight, you're very welcome, goodbye."

On the Sunday morning Bruce was awakened by the house phone ringing in the lounge. He hurriedly, got out of bed and ran downstairs. He picked up the phone, half expecting it to be the police. "Hello, this is Bruce Knight speaking."

"Hello, Bruce, this is Trevor. Brenda said you called yesterday. We have not seen or heard from your mum and dad in over a month. Don't you know where they are?"

"No, Trevor, it is a mystery to me, and my sister Denise."

"Well, my friend, I don't know what to tell you to do, have you contacted the police."

"I have, and the Police constable said, that it was quite common for people to just go away unexpectedly, and without telling others where they are going."

"Well, Bruce, maybe that is the answer, had they come into some money lately."

"The police constable asked me if they had won the lottery recently."

"Well, if they had good luck to them, I say."

"I must go back to London today the coach is at 11.30 from Bakewell. Could you let me know if you hear from them, please Trevor"?

"Sure, we will, have a safe journey home and I am sure they will turn up soon."

"Thank you, goodbye." He placed the phone back into the holder.

Bruce them remembered that he needed to book a taxi to take him to Bakewell. Bruce phoned and booked the cab for 10.30. Bruce then went back upstairs, had a shower, then he packed his small rucksack with his overnight things, and he went downstairs to the kitchen. Bruce put on the kettle to make a cup of coffee, and he suddenly had a eureka moment. If mum and dad had gone away for a holiday. Then surely, they would have taken the car and parked it at the airport?

Then after making the cup of coffee and having a sip or two. Bruce had another bright idea. Hang on a moment, their clothes, they would have taken most of their summer clothes, and their suitcases. Bruce quickly ran back up the stairs and went into his parents' bedroom. He opened the wardrobes; they were full of clothes. He looked in the dressing table draws. They were full of neatly folded clothes. Bruce noticed that there was a large suitcase, one on top of each wardrobe. Then Bruce, almost acting on instinct opened his mother's bed side top draw.

"Bingo" retorted Bruce, as he lifted up the 2 passports that were kept in a leather folder. Bruce took the passports with him back downstairs. He quickly drank his cup of coffee and went to the phone in the lounge. He pressed the return call for the local police. "Hello, this is Derbyshire police, how can I help you?"

"Hello, can I speak to PC Degg, please."

"I am sorry PC Degg is not on duty today, can I leave him a message, or can I help."

"No, I will call him later, will he be on duty tomorrow morning."

"I will look for you. No, but he should be available tomorrow afternoon after 2pm, is there anything else I can help you with?"

"No, thank you." He then put down the phone.

Bruce put the passports into his bag, and he left the backdoor key in its hiding place outside, after locking the backdoor. Bruce was standing outside the front of the house when the cab arrived.

"Cab for Knight," asked the driver.

"Yes please, and I am going to Bakewell to catch the London coach."

Bruce was in a daydream in the back of the cab. When the driver asked, "are you just visiting?"

"Sorry, Oh, yes. My parents have moved here."

"Do you live in London, Sir?" Inquired the driver.

"Yes, I do, in Tottenham." answered Bruce. The cab drew up into the taxi bay at the bus station. "That will be £21:75, please. Call it £20 for cash," remarked the driver.

Bruce took out his wallet and gave the driver a £20 note. The driver said," thank you kindly, Sir."

Bruce opened the cab door and suddenly the driver spoke. "Here is my card, just in case you need me again."

"Oh, thanks very much." Bruce took the card and put it in his jacket pocket. Then Bruce grabbed his rucksack from the back seat and closed the cab door. Bruce walked the few metres to the National Coach Stop. After about 15 minutes the London Coach arrived, then showing the driver the phone ticket. Bruce boarded the coach and settled down for a nice long snooze.

Arriving in London Victoria Coach Station. Bruce texted Josh to see if they could meet-up for a pint or two later.

Bruce dropped off his rucksack at his flat and he was soon in the Marquis of Granby, eating a steak pie and chips, whilst waiting for Josh to arrive. When Josh arrived, Bruce had just finished his evening meal, and they both went up to the bar.

"Any luck in you seeing your mum and dad?" asked Josh.

"No mate, the house was empty, and the strange thing is, that all their clothes were in their wardrobes. Plus, their passports were there too and their suitcases."

Josh replied. "It is very strange, I wonder where they can be?" "Anyway, Bruce, it is your shout, I think."

Bruce, put his hand into his jacket pocket to bring out his leather wallet, when something else came out and dropped to the floor. Josh bent down to pick it up, and he handed it to Bruce.

"Thanks mate, it is just the taxi drivers' card, he gave it to me in Bakewell."

"What is that written on the back," asked Josh.

Bruce turned the card over. "Your parents have gone away to No Place." Bruce read this out.

"What the heck does that mean, mate."

Bruce and Josh collected their pints and walked over to an empty table, where they sat down.

"I don't know what that means Josh. No place was the little village I walked to in the Peak District on one occasion."

"Does your mum and dad have friends there, who they might be staying with?"

"No, they don't and why didn't the cab driver speak to me personally when I was in his taxi. Especially, if he knew my parents, and where they are now."

"Why not try the number on that business card." suggested Josh.

"Yes, mate I will ring it now." An automated voice replied,

"The number you have called is no longer available."

Josh looked at Bruce and suggested. "Well, there is only one thing to do my friend, you will have to go back up their next weekend and go to that No Place yourself."

"Could you come up there with me," asked Bruce.

"No way man, it is the London derby next Saturday between Arsenal and Chelsea."

Bruce spent most of the following week wondering what he should do about his missing parents. They had obviously gone to No Place to see friends or something similar. He was obviously, not even on their radar. Bruce then remembered that he could not get a phone signal when he was in No Place.

That is, it, they hadn't turned their phones off. They had no signal up there and they were probably having such a brilliant time, they had completely forgotten about their son.

Also, that week Bruce began to get text messages from Rikki, Ben, and Toni. All asking if he was all right, and was he going to the big match on Saturday. Arsenal were playing Chelsea, texted Rikki. It doesn't get much bigger and better than that he told him. Bruce thought about his friends, good friends, great friends, magnificent friends, buddies, pals, mates for life. Then he compared them to his parents. Who are selfish, self-centred, uncaring, thoughtless, here today and gone tomorrow, with not a worry in the world. The type of people that turn their phones off when there is an emergency. Who in their right mind does that. Sod it, thought Bruce. I am going to the match on Saturday, with my mates.

Chapter 3

In early October Bruce and his friends enjoyed the spectacle of a classic premier league game between Arsenal and Chelsea. The final score of 0-1, did not bring anyone of the friends the satisfaction of their team winning. However, they gathered in the bar of the Marquis of Granby, after the match. Josh's analysis of the game. "That the 0-1 score, was all down to the manager." Ben quickly agreed. "Arsene Wenger had to go." Rikki replied. "It was only a blip that could soon be rectified."

"Yes, you wait, and see?" exclaimed Toni.

"The Gunners." replied Josh! They all raised their glasses.

"To the Gunners, Cheers."

Meanwhile Bruce, had been sitting down at a table in the bar. Deep in thought, whilst firmly holding his pint glass, seemingly daydreaming.

"Look Bruce is in a trance," exclaimed Rikki.

"He is probably dreaming about next week's game, where Alex Sanchez is dominating the game and scores twice against Asto Villa."

Heh, Bruce don't sulk, the match was not that bad, anybody would think we had lost 5 - 0" smiled Toni.

Bruce slowly raised his head.

"What, match? Who won 5 – 0? No, sorry, I am miles away, thinking about my parents."

Ben spoke. "Blimey, mate, are they still missing?"

"Bloody, hell Bruce, you need to call the cops," said Rikki.

"Ah, come here" said Toni sympathetically, as she sat down next to Bruce and gave him a friendly, reassuring hug.

Josh then gave his opinion. "It all sounds bloody strange to me mate. Two grown up people gone missing, people don't just disappear like that, do they?"

"I think it could be something really, serious!" replied Ben.

"What do you mean by serious," asked Bruce.

Toni, who was still hugging and comforting Bruce. "Hang on there, Ben. Don't make a mountain out of a mole hill."

Ben replied. "I am just facing facts. Mr & Mrs Knight were last seen by Bruce in August. Since then, about 8 weeks has passed, and nothing has happened. No contact, no phone calls. Bruce has travelled all the way up there to Derbyshire, on several occasions. Where he has been into their house, and it is just as they left it. Am I right, Bruce?"

All the friends were now silent, and those standing grabbed a chair and sat down at the same table with Bruce and Toni.

Toni finally broke the silence. "We need a plan. What have you done so far Bruce to find or contact your parents?"

Ben got out a small notebook from his jacket pocket. Toni, took it from him, opened it up to a clean page, and with a pen from within her jacket. Toni wrote. What, do we know so far?

"Right Bruce, has anyone you know spoken to or seen your parents?"

"No, replied Bruce. No one, not even my sister Denise in Madrid."

"Have you told the police?" Asked Rikki.

"Yes, I have told the police. Both here in London and in Bakewell. They think that my parents could have just flown off, unexpectedly on a special once in a lifetime holiday."

"Would your parents just go off like that?" Remarked Ben.

Bruce shook his head. "No, they are not like that?"

Josh then had an idea. "Have you called into or phoned the local hospitals nearby?"

Bruce quickly replied. "Yes, of course, I phoned the hospital, they had no one there of that name."

There was again another moment of silence, whilst Toni was writing down those facts.

Josh then exclaimed loudly. "I've got it mate. They are in a hospital, after they had been in an accident. Where they hit their heads on something, and they can't remember who they are?"

Rikki replied. "I once read about a couple who had lost their minds in a car crash, and it took months before their memories came back?"

"Now hang on a minute." Bruce insisted. "Their car was parked in the carport at their house, so it can't be that!"

"No, you don't get my reasoning Bruce. They were walking, and they were hit by a vehicle?" explained Josh.

Toni stopped writing. "Now that comment has gone right up my flagpole." she remarked. "Your mum and dad are in hospital somewhere up there, with concussion. It is a plausible cause for their unusual disappearance."

Josh replied confidently. "Bruce, you need to phone all the local hospitals in Derbyshire, everyone. To ask if they have a couple who can't remember their names or where they come from, due to concussion."

Toni then handed over the notebook to Ben. Ben tore out the page, that Toni had been writing on, and he gave it to Bruce.

Josh then concluded. "You need to go back to your flat Bruce, and make those calls. You really do need to know what has happened to your parents. You have waited long enough, about 2 months, am I right. That is plenty of time for them to have called you. However, now you must be more proactive, and find out where they are, OK mate?"

Bruce stood up and Toni again gave him another hug.

Ben offered to shake Bruce's hand. "Good luck mate, I am sure they are alright and as Toni says it is just a case of amnesia caused by concussion after a head injury."

Rikki patted Bruce on his back. "See you soon Bruce, and good luck on finding your parents."

As Bruce was leaving the bar. Josh gave him a pat on the back to reassure him. "I will catch up with you soon mate, possibly later in the week, keep in touch."

Bruce left his friends in the bar. He walked solely to his flat. In the flat he sat on the sofa, and he first called Derbyshire police.

"Hello, my name is Bruce Knight. I would like to speak to PC Degg."

"I'm sorry, PC Degg is not available, at the moment Sir. Can I be of assistance or you can leave him a message."

"Yes please, I am trying to contact my parents, and I was wondering if you had heard anything?"

"I will look on the computer for you, what are their names?"

"Robert and Deborah Knight and their address is, Snipe Cottage, Monyash."

Bruce could hear the tapping of the keyboard keys.

"Hello, PC Degg, has written that there has been no contact with Mr & Mrs Knight, and none of their close neighbours has any idea of their whereabouts. Sorry we cannot be of any more help at this time."

"Do you think I should phone the local hospitals and ask if they have a couple suffering from amnesia or concussion?"

"You could Mr Knight, but I think the hospitals would have contacted the police if they had such a couple."

"My friends think that something serious has happened to my parents?"

"I can understand your friends' concerns. However, I must reiterate what we have on file regarding Mr & Mrs Knight. That it is considered that your parents have most probably gone off on a spur of the moment holiday. Probably on a cruise or something similar. A last-minute bargain break and they will most likely return to their home shortly. Can I be of any further assistance, Mr Knight?"

"No, that is all, thank you."

"Thank you, Sir, goodbye" replied the police assistant.

Bruce sat there staring at the facts that Toni had written on the note paper.

1. Parents are missing, they are not in Spain.
2. Their friends have not seen or heard from them.
3. They had turned off their mobile phones.
4. They could have concussion after an accident.
5. They could have gone away on a wonderful dream holiday, in the Caribbean or they might be visiting No Place, wherever that is?

The latter part of number 5, resonated in Bruce's mind all that coming week. They must be in No Place, he thought. Then at work Bruce asked his manager if he could take a short holiday, possibly by taking a long weekend away. His manager agreed that he could take some of his annual leave on that following Friday, and the proceeding Monday. Great, thought Bruce. He could have a long weekend break in Derbyshire.

Bruce went to uni. on the Thursday evening, and he asked his tutor if he could be excused on the next Saturday mornings tutorial, as he was having a long weekend at his parent's house in Derbyshire. Bruce booked his coach ticket, and he had decided not to see his friends socially during that week, so he could keep a clear head.

Bruce was focusing his mind on finding his parents, he needed to know where they are, and that they are safe. He missed them dearly, even though they live over a hundred and fifty miles apart. But honestly, it was the unknown element that was getting to him. He was not feeling so secure or confident anymore in his abilities. He especially missed those ever so quick phone calls from his mother.

Such as. "Hi Bruce, are you feeling all right, is work OK. How are your friends, have you got a girlfriend yet? We miss you; we love you, hope to see you soon."

Then Bruce would reply. "Mum, everything is fine. I must go now; I am really busy. I will text you tomorrow or later in the week, love you, miss you mum xxx."

Bruce arrived in Bakewell just after 3 o'clock on Friday afternoon. His plan was to see and talk to as many people as he could, during this long weekend visit. He also thought the best person to start his conversations would be with the taxi driver who gave him the card, Clive Leach. A tall white man wearing glasses aged about 60ish, with a bald patch on top of his head. At the taxi rank, Bruce walked along the line of taxi's looking for that driver. But he was not there, so Bruce got into the first taxi and asked to be taken to Monyash. When the taxi arrived at Bruce's parents' house, he paid the fare and asked if the driver knew Clive Leach. The cab driver replied,

"Clive Leach, I have not seen him in years. He retired way back 6 or 7 years ago, or thereabout and moved away to Devon, I think?"

Bruce thanked the driver and then eagerly entered the house eagerly hoping to find his parents inside.

But, alas just as before, the rooms were empty and unoccupied. Bruce stared into the empty spaces and felt totally mystified by their absence. He sat down in the lounge, and he thought about what the cab driver had said about Clive Leach. How can he have retired and moved away, when I saw him just recently. Nothing in this dammed place ever makes sense thought Bruce. Then he picked up the house phone, and he called the local constabulary.

"Hello, my name is Bruce Knight, I would like to speak to PC Degg please."

"Hold the line please," said a female voice.

"I will see if he is free."

"Good afternoon, this is PC Degg, how can I help you Mr Knight."

"Hi, I still have had no contact with my parents, and I am at their house, and it is empty as usual. However, when I left here after my last visit. I had a cab driver take me to Bakewell, and the cab driver gave me his business card. I looked for that same cab driver when I got to Bakewell this afternoon. But he was not there at the taxi rank. Then taxi driver that brought me here said that the driver named on the card. A man named, Clive Leach and he retired and now lives in Devon. What is going on around here, everything is so confusing!"

"Do, you want to make a complaint about the cab driver, Clive Leach?"

"No, I just want to speak to him, he gave me his business card, and, on the back, he had written. Your parents are in No Place."

"Oh, I see, said PC Degg. Hang on a minute and I shall put that name in the computer. That's very strange," replied PC Degg. "It is noted here that, Clive Leach was reported missing and presumed dead, by his daughter after he disappeared from his home, some 5 years ago."

"That cannot be right," said Bruce. "Clive Leach drove me to Bakewell just recently."

PC Degg then replied, "I can assure you, Mr Knight he is recorded, as missing and presumed dead. The man who drove you to Bakewell, must have been an imposter. Probably someone driving the cab, to earn some extra cash. Totally, illegal I know, but it does happen occasionally. Anyway, thank you for the tip-off, Mr Knight. I shall investigate the matter further."

Now absolutely confused, Bruce said, "What about my parents, are you not looking for them?"

"We have their details on our system as a missing couple. However, until we have a lead to their present whereabouts, there is little more we can do. Sorry Mr Knight."

Bruce thought, what is the point in this conversation, and he said, "thanks for nothing," and he hung up.

Bruce then rang the number he had for Trevor and Brenda.

"Hello, can I speak to Trevor."

"Trevor speaking."

"Hello, this is Bruce Knight, and I was wondering if you had any news of my parents."

"No, sorry we have not heard a word. Have you contacted the police?"

"Yes, I have just spoken to them, and they have no idea where they are."

"Well, it is a mystery, Bruce. How long is it now since you last spoke to them?"

"About 10 weeks ago, Trevor have you ever heard of a cab driver named, Clive Leach?"

"No, not at all, should I have?"

"No, it was just a name that came up in a conversation with the police, I wondered if you might know him?"

"Sorry, Bruce, cannot help you there. How long are you up for?"

"I am here till Monday morning."

"Oh great! Bruce we might call round to see you on Sunday evening, around 6:30 if that is alright and take you out with us for a meal."

"Yeh OK, that would be nice, see you then, bye."

Bruce put the phone down and made himself comfortable on the sofa. Then after thinking what a bloody mess this whole episode is. He closed his eyes and fell asleep.

Bruce was woken up, in the morning by someone knocking on the front door. Hoping it was news about his parents

Bruce ran to answer the door. He opened it and an elderly man was standing a few feet back from the doorstep.

"Hello, my name is Chris Hughes, and I was wondering if Robert and Deborah Knight were here."

"No, they are not, I am their son Bruce, and I have not seen or heard from my parents in roughly 10 weeks."

"Sorry to hear that, I know your parents from St Leonards church, they go there some Sundays. We are having an open day today and we were wondering if they might like to come along."

"As I said, they are not here, do you know where they might be, asked Bruce?"

"No, sorry Bruce, as I said, I am here to see them. They have not been to church recently. However, would you like to come along later, maybe someone there might know something about where they have gone."

"OK, yes, that might be a good idea. What time does the open day start?"

"It begins at 10am and finishes at roughly 3pm. So, I shall hopefully, see you later today, Bruce, goodbye."

As the man walked away. Bruce thought this could be an opportunity to speak to the locals, and surely someone, could know something, anything.

However, first, things first. Bruce had decided to return to No Place. He got changed and put on his walking boots, that were kept by the back door. As he was putting on the boots, he noticed that his parents walking boots were missing. They must have gone for a walk, all this police speculation that they are in Las Vegas or on a Romantic Cruise is just utter rubbish.

Bruce opened the back door, and confidently walked towards the public footpath that he had followed previously. At the fork in the footpath, he took the right pathway. Then after roughly, 10 minutes of walking he came to the country lane. He stepped up and over the wooden style and onto the tarmac of the lane. In just a few seconds he came to the old house with the big oak tree in the corner of the garden. Bruce thought this must be it. But surely, I remember seeing a wooden finger post here pointing down this dirt track. However, he continued to walk, thinking that he might not have seen a finger post initially. Nevertheless, he was sure this was the dirt track he walked along before.

But surprisingly, at the point where the dirt track bends to the right. All that Bruce could see was the old farm gate, which had a sign on it. Dead of Winter Farm.

The gate was again closed with a hefty chain and padlock. Bruce thought, I know this was the place. I am dam well sure there was another lane here, opposite this gate. With a metal finger sign on a metal post. That pointed down a slope and had on it, No Place. What has happened here, I cannot have dreamt it, where is it, there is nothing here but a 3-metre-high hedge.

Bruce was feeling desperate to find the mysterious village called No Place. He thought I need to do something, anything to help me to solve this situation. He decided to climb over the farm gate and to ask at the farmhouse if they could possibly help him to solve this mystery of a missing lane.

After a walk of about half a mile. Bruce came to an old farmhouse. The two-storey house was made of stone with a slate roof. There were several brick-built out-buildings, with tiled roofs and a large timber frame barn next to the house. But, apparently, no farm animals. He would have expected to see chickens, ducks, or geese. However, Bruce, was on his guard in case there was a farm dog or two on the loose, that might not be over friendly towards strangers. However, as Bruce walked closer to the farmhouse there was not a sound.

The front door was within a porch with a boot scraper just outside. There was a brass bell hanging on a chain that dangled down from a big brass hook. Bruce could see the clanger within the bell, and he pushed the bell with his hand and the bell rang out several times. Bruce stood there motionless for a minute. Then heard a bolt being loosened behind the front door. The door swung open, and a very well-dressed man stood there looking at Bruce. The man was wearing a dark-blue suit, white shirt, red tie and polished black shoes. The man said, "can I help you."

"Hello, my name is Bruce Knight, and I was wondering if you could help me."

"If I can, Bruce, I shall be delighted. Please do come in."

"No, it is alright, I only want to know if you have ever heard of No Place."

"Oh, I see, please do come in, I insist. We can talk more openly inside."

Bruce walked through the door opening and the man closed the door.

"Please, follow me, Bruce."

The man walked down a wide stone stairway. That turned slightly to the right, it was like a spiral staircase, but much wider and higher and made of stone. At the bottom of the stairs there was a large room with no windows. There was a huge fireplace with a log fire burning. Two red leather Chesterfield sofas and a marble topped coffee table and a drinks trolly, were the only furniture in the room. The floor was covered with red quarry tiles.

The man was pouring a drink into a glass from a decanter; he raised an empty glass from the drinks trolly.

"Would you like a glass of red wine, Bruce."

"No thank you," said Bruce.

Bruce was noticing more about the man that stood before him. The man had a genuinely very nice dark tan complexion. Which Bruce decided must come from being a farmer and all that outside work. However, the man also had gold cufflinks and what looked like a diamond studded tie clip and a diamond studded watch, which twinkled brightly under the chandeliers light in the room. The man was immaculately well groomed with jet black hair that was slickly combed back away from his face. There seemed not a single hair out of place. He also wore a well-cut blue pin stripped three-piece suit. Bruce was momentarily mesmerised by this man appearance and his sophisticated attire. Bruce wondered whether he must be a very wealthy farmer, but he somehow did not look like your typical farming stock. He was slim and muscular but did not look as though he had done a day's hard work in his life.

The man had poured himself another glass of red wine after quickly drinking the other. He then spoke, "are you sure you will not join me, it is an excellent Burgandy."

"No thank you," replied Bruce, "it is a bit early for me."

"Not to worry. How can I help you, Bruce?"

"Well sir."

"Oh, do forgive me, I am so rude. I have not introduced myself. My name is Insidious Blake. I am pleased to make your acquaintance, Bruce Knight. What do you want from me, exactly?"

"I don't want anything Sir. But I had hoped that you might know where I can find the village No Place."

"No place, you say. Have you been there before Bruce?"

"Yes, I have Sir."

"So why do you not know where it is now?"

"I cannot find it Sir; I thought it was right opposite your farm's gate."

"Oh, I see, yes indeed. I might have heard of such a place once, but it is not the sort of place that I would care for or even visit myself. It is far to prim and proper for the likes of me."

The man poured himself another glass of wine.

Bruce nervously looked at the man and asked.

"If you could tell me how to get there, I would be incredibly grateful."

"Sorry, how to get where," said the man. "I could open a bottle of Claret if you prefer that?"

"No thank you I must leave now, sorry to have bothered you. But I really do need to find my parents urgently. Mr Blake, and I believe they are in No Place."

"How very interesting, you say, they are in No Place."

"Yes, they could be. I don't really know for sure. That is why I need to go there. Can you help me please."

Mr Blake stepped towards the fireplace, and he pulled on a cord that was hanging from the ceiling. On the other side of the room, double doors swung open and two beautiful young ladies walked forward into the room.

"Bruce, let me introduce you to Tanya and Jade. They usually look after my guests."

Jade looked like Perrie from Little Mix, and Tanya looked like top model Miranda Kerr. They stood on either side of Bruce, and they gave him a hug, and both kissed him on his cheeks.

The man who was pouring himself another glass of wine then spoke.

"There, there, they are warming to you already Bruce. Please stay a while and enjoy the company of these two beautiful ladies. They would dearly like that, would you not."

Jade turned to face Bruce and replied.

"We are here for you Bruce, please come to our room and stay with us for as long as you like. Am I not beautiful and you desire me. I know you do; I can tell."

Tanya, then swoped places with Jade. She put her hands on either side of Bruce's face, and she kissed him on the lips.

"Please Bruce, we need a man with us now. We are so lonely here. Us three could share an intimacy that others only dream of, please Bruce come with us."

Bruce's face had turned to a nice shade of bright crimson. He was sweating profusely, and was definitely aroused.

However, Bruce pushed both woman to an arm's length, and almost sputtered out.

"No, no thanks. OH, what I mean is, maybe some other time. If you are ever in London. Then possibly we could meet up?"

Hearing this Insidious, clapped his hands.

"Please ladies you may now leave us."

Tanya and Jade walked over to the double doors, and they closed the doors behind them.

"What a pity Bruce, they were so looking forward to getting to know you better."

"I must go now," said Bruce nervously.

"I really do need to find my parents. Are you able to help me?"

"No, sorry they are beyond my influence. But, as I have already said, you are very welcome to stay here and enjoy yourself."

"No Sir, I must leave now, please."

Bruce was now feeling hot and sweaty again, and thinking I just want to get out of this weird place.

"Go on then, I shall not stop you Bruce, if you want to go, then go. You know the way out."

Insidious looked over at Bruce and gestured with his hand that Bruce should leave. Then he went to pour himself another drink.

Bruce walked over to the stairway. The stone stairway seemed much darker than it was when they had walked down previously. Bruce grappled around for a handrail or a light switch but there was neither. Bruce glanced over his shoulder to see Insidious leisurely drinking a glass of wine.

Bruce was now panic stricken, and he decided he must leave now!!!

He begun to walk up the staircase as quickly as he could in the dark. He stumbled a couple of times. However, after walking up about 5 large stone steps. The next steps Bruce had noticed that there was something under his feet, something crunching. He looked down towards his boots and there was just darkness. Bruce stopped walking giving his eyesight time to adjust to the darkness. The step surface seemed to move underneath his boots. He was staring down and there was every type of small creeping or crawling creature you could imagine. Every step he took now he could hear the crunching of the creatures bodies. His boots were also now covered in hundreds of cockroaches and all manner of creepy Crawley's.

The uneasy feeling of squashing insects made Bruce stamp on them all the more frantically. He began to panic, and he bolted up the next 5 or 6 steps, almost leaping up two steps at a time. Then as the stairs turned a corner the crunching stopped. Now Bruce could hear a young child crying. She was on a stone ledge above his head. The girl looked about 5 years old, and she had a small dog with her. The little girl stopped crying, and her voice was very soft and sorrowful.

"Can you help me mister. I want to come down."

Bruce looked up to see the young girl.

"Sure thing, grab my hands and I will help you to come down."

Then as Bruce offered up his hands to the girl, the small dog bit his fingers on his right hand.

"Ow, shit, that bloody dog has bitten me."

The little girl began to cry; as she hugged the little dog.

"I hate you mister, go away. You are rude and evil"

Then girl started sobbing loudly. Closely holding the little dog she walked away from the edge of the ledge.

"No, please come back. I am deeply sorry, let me try again please."

The little girl now hidden in the darkness of the recess replied.

"No, way not never, you are a horrid man. Go away and leave me alone, I hate you."

Bruce watched and listened as the little girl and the small dog, quietly faded away into the dark shadows at the rear of the ledge. He also noticed that there was only 4 or 5 steps remaining. Bruce took a deep breath in, and driven by pure adrenaline; he ran up the remaining stairs.

However, at the top of the stairs Bruce pushed a large, wooden door open. But instead of him being outside in the farmyard as before. He was still inside but now in a great wooden barn. Bruce ran over to the double doors. They were closed, and pad locked on the outside. Bruce could see through the slats in the walls. Then he noticed a long timber ladder lying on the floor at the back of the barn. The ladder was very heavy, but he raised it up to the midpoint of the barn doors. He climbed the ladder to the top, and there above him he noticed a small door. It was only a bit higher than where he was. Bruce moved up the ladder very slowly. Carefully he climbed up, holding onto the slats in the wall of wood with his fingertips, and getting a foot grip by using the side of his boots to stand on the very last run of the ladder. Bruce reached the small doors and with a clenched fist he pushed it open. Bruce was very relieved to see the outside world again. However, after balancing himself through that small doorway, he still had the best part of four metres to climb down to the ground. When Bruce, finally stepped onto good old solid ground. He looked around him hoping to see someone, but like before the farmyard was deserted and silent.

Bruce then ran as fast as he could to get away from the farm and towards the distant farm gate. He threw himself over it and landed on his feet with a thump! He mumbled to himself.

"Dead of Winter Farm, if I never see you again, it will be too soon."

Bruce was shocked and confused about what had just happened to him. He needed to get back to reality fast. So, he ran back to the church in Monyash. He was exhausted when he arrived, but filled with hope of seeing someone who might have some answers, to his growing list of questions.

Chapter 4

Arriving at the church open day, Bruce noticed that there were several people tidying up tabletops and clearing away, books, leaflets, and other stuff. Bruce guested that the open day was coming to an end. However, he needed to speak to someone, anyone, who might know where his parents might be. Bruce walked up to one of the tables and he spoke.

"Hello, my name is Bruce Knight, does anybody here know where my parents might be, please."

The four people at the table all looked at Bruce. Then Chris Hughes, who came to the door of Snipe cottage earlier that morning, replied.

"We have spoken to each other, and we do not know where your parents can be, and really in our opinion you should talk to the vicar as he might know more than us."

"Where is the vicar, inquired Bruce?"

"The Reverend Chandler, should be in the vestry."

Bruce walked into the church, and he noticed a door there that had on it, church office. Bruce knocked on the door. The door opened, and Michael spoke.

"Oh hello, good afternoon, Brian."

"It's Bruce, vicar."

"Sorry, Bruce what can I do for you."

"Have you seen or heard from my parents lately?"

"No, not at all, are they still missing, how very strange?"

"Yes, indeed they are," replied Bruce, "and talking about strange things. I just went to the farm called, Dead of Winter. Where I met a real creepy guy named, Insidious Blake."

"Are you sure about that Bruce. Because that farm has been abandoned for about 6 or 7 years, ever since the owner went missing."

"Oh, this guy was real, alright, and he had two lady friends, that were banging, if you know what I mean."

"Yes, I think I do understand, please take a seat, Bruce."

Michael closed the office door, and he went over to his desk and sat down. Michael then said.

"Right, this is what I know. The Dead of Winter farm had been deserted for years. Ever since the farmer who lived there went missing, and was later presumed to be dead. However, some do say, that after his wife passed away. The farmer just gave up the farm, sold all the livestock and probably moved away, possibly to Devon. But this is just village gossip you understand."

"Well, this Insidious Blake guy was real enough. He was a very smartly dressed man, who would not look out of place in the better off parts of London."

There was a moment of silence whilst Bruce thought for a moment.

"Hang on there, did you just say that the farmer had gone to live in Devon."

"Yes, he might have gone there, but this is only speculation you understand. No more than village gossip."

"This absent farmer, was he named Clive Leach; by any chance?"

"Yes, he was, did you know of him?"

"No, I don't know him personally, but the last time I came up here. I ordered a taxicab, to take me to Bakewell. The taxi driver gave me his card, that had on it his name, Clive Leach, and on the back of the card it was written.

"Your parents are in No Place."

"How very strange, remarked Michael. Have you told this information to the police?"

"Yes, I have, but all they said was that the taxi driver was just a stranger using Clive Leach's taxi cards."

"Well, that is possible, people do tend to do their own thing up in these parts, and they have little or no regard for authority."

Michael then stood up and walked towards the door, then opening the door he said to Bruce.

"I am so sorry about your parents, but I cannot spare you anymore time, I have other matters to see too. But please do call in here or at the vicarage, if you get any news of your parents."

Bruce stood up and he replied.

"Thanks, I will."

Bruce walked into the church, as the vicar closed his office door.

Then Chris Hughes came into the church, carrying a cardboard box, filled with books and leaflets.

"Hello, Bruce did you find the vicar?"

"Yes, he is in his office."

Bruce was looking around the church.

When Chris noticed Bruce's interest.

117

"It is a lovely old church is St. Leonards. It dates right back to the 17th Century, originally built about 1640. It has some original carvings and artwork on the walls, over there."

Chris pointed to a part of the church wall.

"Have a look over there Bruce, that section of drawings was discovered when the church was being repainted about 20 years ago."

Bruce looked at the early paintings, that were now mostly worn away. However, there seemed to be letters, o plac.

"Chris, look at this. Did those letters once read, No Place?"

"Well, they might have. I can see the reason for your speculation, but what does it mean?"

"Maybe we should ask the vicar, he might know."

Bruce knocked on the vestry door. The vicar opened the door and spoke.

"Oh, it is you again."

"Please Michael come and look at this writing that is with some paintings on the church wall."

Bruce and Michael walked over to where Chris was looking closely at the vague drawing and the few letters that were discernible.

"Look over here vicar. This young man thinks he has found the words No Place, written on this wall. Do you know what it means?"

Michael looked at the wall where Chris was standing.

"When this artwork and other drawings were discovered back in the 1980's, during the church renovation. It was recorded by a researcher, that the words might signify, No Place and the paintings. That are now extremely hard to define, were that of a wishing well."

Bruce eagerly went to have another look and replied.

"When I went to No Place previously, there was a wishing well there, and it had written on the well, "POUTIA.""

Michael nodded and replied.

"But you now say that you cannot find this, No Place."

"No, I cannot. I have tried several times. But the entrance via a dirt track, it is not there anymore."

After a moments silent consideration, Chris spoke.

"The local wells around here are dressed, with beautiful flowers every May Day, as a blessing for the water in the well. I have lived here abouts for more than 75 years, and I have never heard of a No Place."

"That is true enough." agreed Michael.

119

"I have never heard of a No Place either."

Bruce just shrugged his shoulders, then asked.

"Chris did you know Clive Leach."

"Why yes, he came to this church regularly. He is said by some to be dead, but I think he ran off to Devon."

Michael then intervened.

"Chris, Bruce mentioned that he booked a taxi recently, and the driver card indicated he was Clive Leach."

"Not possible, Clive Leach disappeared over 6 years ago, and even his daughter has never seen or heard from him since. Anyway, vicar, changing the subject. We have packed everything away from the open day. Sadly, there were only a few people who came out to see us today. Maybe, one or two might come back on Sunday, God willing."

"Yes indeed, thank you Chris, and you too Bruce. However, we must close-up now, we once could leave the church open. But, sadly, not anymore."

Bruce walked out of the church and when he arrived back at his parent's cottage. He sat down on the sofa to contemplate what had happened to him today, and very soon he had fallen asleep.

At just after 9pm Bruce woke up. Blimey, this sofa and sleep are habit forming, in this ever so quiet and peaceful place. Bruce switched on the TV, and he called Josh on his mobile.

"Hi Bruce, what are you doing?"

"I'm watching TV, whilst sitting on a comfy on the sofa."

"You know how to play hard and loose, my friend."

"Anyway, where are you? Now let me think its Saturday night nearly 9.30. You are in the Marquis having a pint or two."

"Yes, I am, and you should be here too mate. Not galivanting about the moors, like Sherlock Holmes looking for clues."

"OK, point taken. I will be back on Monday and maybe we could have a drink later that evening," suggested Bruce.

Josh remarked, "alright Bruce, you drive a hard bargain. See you soon."

Bruce was happy after speaking to Josh. He went into the kitchen to look for something to eat. The fridge was empty, and the freezer had just a Cherry pie, and two Chinese Chicken and rice, microwave ready meals.

"Right" said Bruce. "Dinner and desert are fixed."

He turned on the electric oven and after emptying the packaging. He placed the Cherry pie in the oven, and put the two ready meals in the microwave.

Bruce then watched some TV program about women who lived in Essex, and he soon became convinced that he recognised several Tanya and Jade, look-alikes.

After eating his meal Bruce decided to have an early night and he went off to bed at about 11pm.

On Sunday morning Bruce was woken by the sound of church bells. He sat up and thought. I should go to church, maybe someone there might know something about mum and dad. After a wash and shave, Bruce got dressed and ready to walk to the church. He had never been to church before, well when we say never. What that means is that he had only been to a church before. Once to attend a wedding. Once, to a christening. Then twice, to funeral's. But never, a Sunday church service as such. Therefore, when Bruce arrived at the Sunday morning church service, just after 10.30. He held back, momentarily in the church yard for a minute or two, hoping to follow others inside. However, after waiting there, for what seemed more like 5 minutes. Nobody else came past him, so he thought maybe they are already inside.

Inside the church Bruce noticed the vicar, and Chris, and another man. Plus, two women that he saw packing away books at the church open day. One of these women had noticed Bruce standing at the back of the church. She gestured him to come forward.

"Hello dear, my name is Elsie Warrilow, you are most welcome, to sit here next to me at the front."

Bruce sat down on the pew, and rather nervously he spoke.

"Thank you very much."

The others who had been standing now sat down, also on the front pew. Michael, the vicar was standing next to the font. Looking at his watch, he mumbled.

"Where Lord, is that woman?"

Then a female voice from the back of the church.

"I am here darling, ready when you are."

Michael, began the service with a prayer, asking.

"Oh, Lord deliver us from difficult people. Open the doors to our hearts desires. Free us from our chains of sin, and deliver us from evil. Amen."

"We shall now sing from the Hymn book. Hymn number 127: Be still in the presence of the Lord. Lynette, when you're ready."

Lynette was now sitting at the piano, and began to play. Bruce was now standing next to Elsie. She gestured to him to pick up a hymn book and to hymn number 127.

When the singing finished everyone sat down, but not Bruce. Then Elsie pulled at his shirt sleeve, and Bruce sat down.

"We shall have a time of open prayer," announced Micheal.

Bruce heard several of the people there mention Robert and Debbie in their prayers. Then Michael went up to the pulpit to give a short sermon. Entitled, gods grace and favour. Micheal ended his sermon with a short prayer. Hoping that Bruce's parents would be found soon.Then Lynette at the piano began playing, The Lord of Sea and Sky. Everyone stood up including Bruce, this time without any prompting. Elsie whispered hymn number 120. The small congregation lead by the vicar began to sing. Chris came along the people on the front pew, holding a red velvet bag. Elsie whispered to Bruce as a guest you don't have to put anything in, if you don't want to. Bruce took out his wallet, and he put a 10-pound note into the bag. When the song finished. Elsie said to Bruce.

"Please stay behind, and join us for a cup of tea or coffee and a biscuit."

At the back of the church. Chris was waiting for the kettle to boil, and Elsie had opened a box of mixed biscuits. Lynette walked up to Bruce.

"Hello again, my dear, sorry to hear your parents are still missing."

Bruce smiled and replied.

"I am sure someone here must know something?"

"Dorothy, my dear," said Lynette. "Do you know where Robert and Deborah Knight might have gone?"

"No, I don't. I spoke to them on the Sunday morning they were last here at church. Debbie said they were going for a lovely walk that day."

Bruce remarked.

"Did they say where they might be walking too?"

"No, sorry my dear, they just seemed happy and were looking forward to a nice day out, walking in God's creation."

Chris, who was waiting by the kettle.

"Would you like a drink of tea or coffee Bruce."

"No thanks. I might go for a walk myself, seeing it's such a nice morning."

Bruce left the church, and he again walked across the open fields to the point where the path splits. Turning right he soon came to the wooden style. After climbing over, he walked up the lane to the house with the large oak tree in the garden. Bruce opened the small metal swing gate, and he walked up to and knocked on the front door. An elderly man opened the door.

"Hello, how can I help you sonny?" he said.

"Hello, I was wondering if you know the way to No Place?"

"You had better come in, young man."

Bruce stepped into the lounge, where the old man said.

"Please, do take a seat."

The old man was pointing to one of two armchairs. He then sat down, what is your name sonny/"

"I am Bruce Knight, and I am looking for my mum and dad. Debbie and Robert."

"Well, they are not here; are they missing?"

"Yes, they are, do you know anything about a village called No Place," enquired Bruce.

The old man replied, looking deep into Bruce's eyes.

"It is believed to be a village that can only be found, if you are in the right frame of mind?"

"What do you mean a right frame of mind?" Replied Bruce in a loud tune of voice.

"Look at you. You are getting angry and aggressive already," said the old man.

No Place will ever be reached by an angered and aggressive mind. I can tell you that for sure, my friend."

"I am very sorry for raising my voice. Please forgive me. But I don't understand you. What have feelings, and a good frame of mind got to do with finding No Place?"

"A great deal my friend, and that is Gods honest truth. I am telling you. Please you must go now as my dear wife will be returning home very soon."

The old man got up and walked over to the front door, and on opening it. Bruce stood up and as he was making his way slowly out of the house. In to the garden came an elderly woman. She stopped to close the gate and then proceeded to the front door.

"Hello, Elsie," said Bruce.

"Hello Bruce," said Elsie. Fancy seeing you here, it is an exceedingly small world."

Then Elsie went passed Bruce into the house. As Bruce walked towards the gate. He turned around to close the garden gate. When he observed Elsie through the lounge window, she slapped the old man across his face.

Bruce thought this whole place is too crazy for words. No Place is not a place, but rather a frame of mind. What short of stuff is that old man smoking, and as for the little old lady. She goes to church to pray for people's wellbeing, then comes home to physically abuse her husband.

Finally, Bruce got back to his parent's cottage, just as the phone inside was ringing. He ran into the lounge and picked up the phone.

"Hello."

"Hi, Bruce its Trevor, do you still fancy coming out with Brenda and me for a meal and a pint later."

"Oh, yes please, that would be great."

"Good we shall be around to pick you up at 6 o'clock."

"Fine, thank you."

Bruce went upstairs and had a shower and put on a change of clothes.

Trevor and Brenda arrived at 6pm. Trevor beeped the horn of the car. Bruce came outside, and got into the back seat of their car.

Trevor spoke, "we have a real treat for you tonight, Bruce. We are going to, The Bulls head, at Foolow."

After a short drive they arrived at the pub.

Brenda said, "you will like it here Bruce, it is a beautiful old inn. A quintessential English village pub, and the food is the best around here."

Bruce was sitting in the lounge bar with Brenda, both looking at the extensive menu. Whilst Trevor brought over the drinks.

"Here you go Bruce, a pint of Fosters, as they had no draught cider."

Trevor sat down, and commented.

"The 8oz sirloin, or the12oz rump steaks, here are great, but personally speaking. The mixed grill is fantastic. It comes with a with 6oz rump steak, 6oz gammon steak, and a ring of Cumberland sausage. A fried egg, fried mushrooms and tomatoes, and a pineapple ring, and chips."

Brenda also commented.

"Very nice indeed, but I am having the Salmon steak with chips. Are you having a mixed grill Trevor?"

"Yes, I am," replied Trevor.

"What about you Bruce, choose what you like! It's our treat to you."

"Thank you very much, and yes, a mixed grill, would be lovely. Plus, can I have an extra portion of onion rings, and garlic bread, please."

"Are you hungry, dear," said Brenda?

"Yes, I am. Mum, and dads kitchen is now empty. No food left in the fridge or the freezer. I went to the church today and I met some old people there, who said they had no idea where mum and dad had gone. Then later, I went for a walk where I met an old man. Who said that the village known as No Place, was only accessed by your frame of mind. Whatever that means, really, I have no idea?"

Bruce took a great gulp of his pint.

"Honestly, I think I am going mad; nothing makes sense around here."

"What makes you feel like that," said Trevor?

"Well, yesterday, when I was out walking. I went to a farm, Dead of Winter Farm. A farm that has a great big chain and

130

padlock on the gate. However, I met there, a really, posh bloke. Who, must have a tailor in Savile-Row? He introduced me to two gorgeous young women, who asked me to stay with them for a while, and make cosy.

"I have heard of that farm," exclaimed Trevor.

"Let, him finish," replied Brenda.

Bruce smiled and continued.

"Then whilst leaving that crazy place. I upset a little girl, needed my help. But her little Jack Russel dog bit my hand. Then the girl said that she hated me, and I was to go away. Then I had to climb up high in a barn, to get out. All that happened, and still, I cannot find No Place, or my mum and dad!"

Trevor replied. "Well, you did have an adventure, that; s for sure?"

Bruce took another great gulp of his pint.

"Then I went to have a word with the vicar. Where he thinks I am on the hard stuff, Marijuana or even worse. Apparently, because nothing I have just told you, can really make any sense; to any rational minded person."

Brenda looked at Bruce and spoke.

131

"Now, look dear you need to go back home to London. Then have a real holiday, get away from this place, maybe you should visit your sister in Spain. Really Bruce, you need to relax, and stop worrying. Go and see your sister, you know the old saying. Two heads are better than one."

Then Trevor spoke.

"It must be hard for you to believe, that your parents could have just taken off on a grand tour of Patagonia, or somewhere like that. However, Brenda is right, only time will eventually show us what has really happened to your parents. For the record Bruce. My money, is on, that they have gone away, possibly on a world cruise."

"Absolutely true," replied Brenda. "Maybe, they won the lottery, possibly winning millions. The shock, the excitement. Suddenly, they just took off, living life to the full, on an ocean liner, and who can blame them at their age."

"But I found their passports in a bedroom draw, and their clothes and suitcases are there also," said Bruce.

Trevor siled and confidently commented.

"Did you check to see if they are their old passports, from when they lived in London?"

Bruce quickly replied.

"You know, I never thought of that, and the passports are back in London in my flat."

Brenda smiled and patted Bruce on the back of his hand.

"There you go, Bruce, they have new passports, since moving to Derbyshire. So, they are more than likely, on a once in a lifetime romantic cruise holiday."

Bruce was now feeling much more positive.

"Thank you both, so much. For your kindness, encouragement and your generosity."

"It is a pleasure to help you," said Brenda. "Debbie and Robert are nice honest people. They are more than likely having a splendid time on a world cruise."

"Lucky beggars," retorted Trevor.

Bruce was now feeling reassured regarding the wellbeing of his parents. He was happy again, knowing that they were probably having a great adventure. Bruce smiled and spoke.

"I was going to tell you a story about my broken pencil. But I cannot now see the point."

Trevor replied.

"Do you like telling jokes? Here is one I heard the other day. My therapist says I have a preoccupation with vengeance. We will see about that! I snapped in reply."

Brenda then gave her opinion on cooking programs.

"I will never understand why they cook meals on TV. Because, we can't smell it. We can't eat it, or taste it, you might not like it. However, the cook says, this is a delicious meal for you and your family."

"You have a point there Brenda, which is more than can be said of my pencil."

After the delicious meal. Trevor and Brenda returned Bruce back to Snipe Cottage. Where they wished him well, and they again reiterated, that Bruce's mum and dad would be back home soon. Bruce thanked them for a very enjoyable evening, and agreed that his mum and dad were highly likely to be enjoying themselves in some far-off tropical paradise, with not a care in the world.

Chapter 5

In Snipe cottage, Bruce woke up on Monday morning feeling very nauseous.

"God, I feel sick, it must have been those bloody onion rings?"

Bruce ran to the bathroom, and he was sick in the toilet. Bruce had a shower and got dressed, and made his way downstairs. He went into the lounge, and amazingly there in front of him on the lounge floor was a skeleton head. The skeleton face was looking up at him, with red bloodshot eyes. The skeleton head spoke.

"You are a trespasser, and I despise trespassers. I want to make you suffer before I kill you."

Bruce was shocked, he had never seen anything like this!

"What the heck is this about," said Bruce. "I must be hallucinating."

"Bollocks, I'm not an object in your filthy and corrupt mind. I am physically here to warn you to stay away from No Place. Go back to London and rot their you scumbag."

In a deep voice coming from the skeletons head.

Bruce was standing and holding onto the back of an armchair, momentarily trying to gather his thoughts.

"I am not going mad, I am not going mad," shouted Bruce.

Then suddenly in a temper rage, he ran towards the face, and tried to kick it. However, his foot just passed through the skeleton face as though it was made of smoke. Then the head completely disappeared. Bruce nervously ran upstairs. He collected his shoulder bag. He chucked in his clothes, and shaving things from the bathroom. He hurried back downstairs, used his mobile to call a taxi to take him to Bakewell. He quickly went out the back door, locked it and hid the key.

Bruce did not feel at all comfortable being inside the cottage. So, he waited outside on the roadside for the taxi to arrive. Upon getting into the taxi, the driver commented that Bruce was not looking to good. Rather pale, so the driver offered him a sick bag, just in case.

Much later, at roughly 5:30 pm. Bruce put the key into his flat door. Bruce still felt terribly ill. Nervously shaken by his strange ordeal. But he was not convinced that he had seen a skeleton face on the floor. He thought it was more than likely a hallucination brought on by what he had eaten the previous evening. Therefore, nothing more than a case of severe food poisoning at the least; in his estimation.

On Tuesday morning Bruce returned to work and his manager, Andrew asked if everything was now all right.

"No, they are still missing. But friends of theirs, think they might have won the lottery, and gone off on a world cruise or something like that."

"Well lucky for them I say, and as for you, Bruce. Its back to reality today. There is quite a bit of catching up to do here. We have a stock take on Thursday, and I'm leaving it to you; as part of your ongoing management training."

After work, Bruce texted Josh to see if he fancied a pint or two later. "OK," Josh texted back. "Red Lion at 9."

When the two friends met up. Bruce gave the continuing bad news regarding the whereabouts of his parents. Plus, that he had tried to find the village No Place, but he was unsuccessful.

Josh shook this head in acknowledgement of the bad news.

"Look Bruce you have done your very best to find them. You mentioned what Trevor and Brenda have said. That they think that your parents have gone on a world cruise. Possibly after winning millions on the lottery. I have heard that those world cruises take over 6 months, and sometimes even longer. Especially, if a passenger gets off halfway round, for a bit of a mooch about. Visiting such places as

China and the great wall. Australia and the outback. Whale watching off Vancouver. Do you get my drift mate, they could be gone for months, even a year."

"Yes alright, I get it." replied Bruce.

"How long have they been missing now Bruce?"

"About 3 months or thereabouts."

"There you go then, mate. They are only about 3 months into a 6-month cruise. Let it go, do your own thing for the next 3 months, and for heaven's sake stop worrying. I am sure they will be back home soon enough."

"Your right, Josh. Why should I be worrying, when they are most likely living it up in sunny Australia or New Zealand."

"Spoken like a true gent," said Josh. "By the way, that consultation will cost you another round."

"I thought it might. Same again, please."

Bruce offered two empty glasses to the bar person.

Josh then spoke to Bruce.

"To change the subject somewhat. I heard that Stan, a regular in here. Who often brought his little Yorkshire Terrier with him when he came here for a pint. Then there was also Bert, yet another regular here. Who sometimes came in with his big Rottweiler. Anyway, the other afternoon, when the two men had both been in here with their respective dogs. Well, Stan's little Yorkshire Terrier killed Bert's big Rottweiler."

Bruce was taken aback. "What that little dog killed Bert's big dog. How did that happen?"

"Apparently, the little dog got stuck in the big dog's throat." laughed Josh.

As the days went by Bruce and his four good friends. Continued their weekly social gatherings, having fun, in their favourite pubs and clubs. A special occasion was the 5th of November. A spectacular night out, watching the firework display, enjoyed by all. Followed by a great deal of drinking, and finishing with a curry feast in an Indian restaurant. In fact, Bruce was feeling happy and much more positive about life in general.

However, later in November Bruce was brought back down to earth, by a comment from Andrew at work.

"Bruce, are you going to your parents for Christmas?"

On hearing this question, Bruce finally touched base with his emotions. Was he going to Snipe cottage at Christmas? Would his parents be home for Christmas? Would he be getting exotic and expensive presents from around the world?

Andrew continued to say.

"I was just wondering what your holiday plans are, seeing that the university canteen would be closed during Christmas and the new year for two weeks."

Bruce thought about the previous years. when he had always spent Christmas with his parents, and why would this year be any different.

"Yes, Andrew surely, they will be back for Christmas. It is such a special time of the year, family time."

"Very good to hear," replied Andrw.

Bruce then thought about the new year celebrations with his best friends. Bruce was feeling so positive that he booked the coach ticket there and then, on his mobile phone. He would travel up to Derbyshire on the 22nd of December and return on the 28th to London. Just in time for the New Year celebrations.

On the morning of the 22nd of December. Bruce had packed his trolley case, he walked to the tube station, swiped his debit card, and then he travelled to Victoria coach station. He had a half hour wait, before he boarded the usual coach. So he had a coffee, and he phoned his sister in Madrid.

"Hi sis how is you."

"Fine thanks, are you going to mum and dads."

"Yes, I am at Victoria now."

"I have sent them a card but give them a hug from me too, and tell them I shall see them soon, hopefully at Easter."

"OK, will do, what are you doing for Christmas."

"I am going to Barcelona with a group of friends; it should be a nice break away from work. Anyway, do not forget give my love to those two scallywags and ask if they have brought me something nice from their overseas holiday. Bye Bruce, hope to see you too at Easter."

"Bye sis."

Bruce walked over to his boarding point, where he waited for about twenty minutes. When finally, a coach for Manchester, stopping at Bakewell and Buxton arrived.

In Bakewell, Bruce again looked along the line of waiting taxis hoping to see Clive Leach. But he was not there, so in the end Bruce got into the first cab and asked to be taken to Monyash. The cab pulled up in front of Snipe cottage, and Bruce was half hoping to see a light on or a glimpse of his parents. But all was in darkness inside and so when Bruce opened the back door, he walked through the downstairs of the cottage. Switching on most of the lights. At the front door Bruce noticed that there must have been 3 dozen letters, and about 3 months' supply of free weekly newspapers, together with a pile of assorted leaflets and coupons.

Bruce had at first been very hopeful of seeing his parents at their home. However, seeing this assorted pile of papers and leaflets, scattered over the welcome mat. Brought this whole sad episode to the forefront of his mind. Nothing had changed here. He felt alone, depressed, and saddened by his loss.

Bruce picked up all the mail; and the rest of the junk that was by the front door. He carried it to the kitchen table and then dropped it there. Bruce decided to phone his sister again.

"Hello sis, I am up here, and they are nowhere to be seen. The bloody front door was almost blocked by 4 months of post and other rubbish. I need your help."

"Calm down Bruce, you will have a heart attack."

"I want you to come here Denise and help me to find them."

"Stop panicking Bruce, and remember that I live in Spain. What can I do, that you have not already done?"

"Please Denise, I cannot do this on my own anymore."

"Look I will call the police for you, and I will try the local hospitals. But that is all I can do to help you at this moment. Please understand I have other commitments over here."

"Have you got a boyfriend over there, is that it? You cannot be bothered to help me to find our mum and dad, because you would rather shag some Spanish bloke at Christmas."

"Grow up Bruce. I shall call you back if I hear anything from the police or the hospitals, bye."

Bruce felt betrayed by his sister. She had proved that only he cared for his mum and dad. His sister was a self-centred cow and a waste of space, living just for her own selfish needs. He now hated her; she is no sister of mine he thought. Bruce searched through the mail, where he noticed amongst the bills and the advertising offers. An envelope, which was posted in Madrid. Then without a second thought he put all the rest of the post into the kitchen bin. Then he opened the envelope from Madrid, which contained a Christmas card. To the best Mum and Dad. Happy Christmas, from your loving Daughter Denise. Bruce put the card back in its envelope, and then put it in a cutlery draw. Then he phoned Josh.

"Hi Josh, I am up here at Snipe cottage, and they are not here."

"What did I tell you! I told you Bruce to give it 6 months or more. Maybe, even up to a year. A world cruise takes that amount of time, mate. How long have they been missing?"

"About four months, getting on for five."

"Right there, that is my point exactly. They are still coming up through the Panama Canal, with at least another 6 or 7 weeks to go. Sailing up the east coast of America and the Caribbean, before turning east in New York and crossing the Atlantic. However now you are up there, mate. Tidy the place up, put on the central heating to warm it up and hoover up. So, when they finally get home the place is warm, clean, and cosy. That will show them that you really do care about them."

"Thanks Josh, you are a real mate."

"Think nothing of it, until it is your turn to buy a round at the new year eve bash, and then make mine, a large scotch."

"Yeh, alright will do, thanks again, bye."

Josh is a good egg thought Bruce, and he knows how to cheer a bloke up. Now where is the gas boiler and the hoover?

Two hours later, the cottage was warming up. Then whilst Bruce was hoovering the downstairs area. The doorbell rang. Bruce rushed to the front door. He opened it, hoping to find his parents loaned down with bags of presents. However, there stood two police officers.

"Hello," said the female officer.

"Are you Mr Robert Knight."

"No! that is my dad."

"Is your father at home?"

"No! he and mum have been missing for about 4 months".

The male officer, then spoke.

"Hello, are you, Bruce Knight"

"Yes I am."

"I have spoken to you previously, Mr Knight. I am Pc Degg, and this is WPc Dasgupta."

"Oh right, please come inside. I have only just arrived from London. I'm warming the place up and hoovering, please do come and join me in the kitchen."

The police officers followed Bruce along the hallway.

"Please do take a seat."

WPc Dasgupta replied.

"Thank you, but we prefer to stand. We have had a phone call from your sister Denise Knight, in Madrid, Spain. She said you were terribly upset about your parents still being away."

"Well yes, I am a bit upset, after all they could phone me to say that they are alright."

"Have you had an argument with your parents, Mr Knight?"

Enquired Pc Degg, as he took out his notebook.

"No! whatever makes you think that?"

Pc Degg replied whilst reading from his notes.

"You have made several calls to the police regarding the disappearance of your parents."

Turning a page in his notebook, the Pc continued.

"You made a call to Bakewell police station, in August. Stating that your parents had apparently gone missing. Then, you made another enquiry in September at a police station in Tottenham, London. Followed by another phone call, more recently in October. To me here at Bakewell police station. It does seem to be slightly suspicious, that you keep coming up here to Monyash. Then you call the police to ask where your parents might be, because you say they are missing. Now even your sister, who lives in Madrid, Spain. She is also calling the police in Bakewell, regarding your missing parents.

A thought has crossed my mind, that there is something untoward happening here Mr Knight. That might need further investigation by our detectives."

Bruce responded to this accusation that anything was untoward!

"What do you mean exactly? There is nothing untoward here, except the whereabouts of my parents. My mother and Father are missing and have not been seen here, by anybody hereabouts for at least 4 months; nearly 5 months, actually. Why can't you find them, that is what I want to know."

WPc Dasgupta then spoke.

"Please stay calm Mr Knight, there is no need to shout. How do you know that your parents have not been here. On the odd day or two, because as you have said; you live in London."

"I know they have definitely not been here, because of all the post and junk mail that was behind the front door."

Pc Degg was writing this information in his notebook.

"Where is the post now Mr Knight."

"I put it in the bin, over there."

"Do you normally put your parents mail into the waste bin?" Enquired Pc Degg, whilst he was still writing.

Bruce was now busy taking the post back out of the kitchen bin. Feeling frustrated he finally tipped the bin's contents onto the kitchen table.

"Did you know it is an offence Sir. To steal, destroy, or to in anyway obstruct the Royal Mail?"

Explained WPc Dasgupta.

"Look I am sorry. I was angry at my sister, and that my parents are still not here."

"Do, you often get angry Sir," asked WPc Dasgupta.

"No, please don't get me wrong. I am sorry. The post, is here now back on the table."

"Thank you, Sir. We shall make a report that your parents are apparently missing, even though they are still receiving their post at this address."

The two police officers were walking towards the front door. When Pc Degg acknowledged that they would be reporting this situation to the CID.

"We shall give our report on the apparent disappearance of your parents. to a senior officer. Where he or she might ask you for further information regarding your parents, personal details. Such as their Bank accounts, or their Passports. This is normal procedure when investigating into mysterious disappearance."

"Good evening, Mr Knight." said WPc Dasgupta.

Bruce stood at the front door, collecting his thoughts as the two police officers drove off in their patrol car.

Bruce was thinking: What on earth are those two on? My word what a couple of fruitcakes, they were more interested in the post being in the bin, than helping me to find mum and dad.

Bruce decided to walk along to the vicarage and pay a visit to Michael and Lynette Chandler. Bruce knocked on the vicarage door and as the door opened, Michael put his head around.

"Hello oh! it is you again. Do we have an appointment?"

"No! I need to speak to you urgently about my mum and dad."

"Please come in, we have just had dinner, and I was clearing the table. Come on through Bruce, to the lounge."

In the lounge sat Lynette, reading from a fashion magazine.

"Oh hello, were you expected?"

"No, dear, Bruce wants a chat about his parents. You can stay if you like, can't she Bruce?"

"Yes, no problem."

"Please do take a seat." Lynette gestured to Bruce by patting the place next to her on the settee.

Bruce sat down next to Lynette and spoke.

"I cannot get my head around what is happening to me, when I come here to Monyash? I have tried again to find the village No Place. But it has gone, it is nowhere to be found. Believe me it is a mystery; it was there once. But now nothing, not a trace. My parents went to find No Place, because I asked them to and now, they have gone mysteriously missing. Then I went to, Dead of Winter farm, to seek help, and I met there a very smartly dressed man named Insidious Blake. He told me that No Place was beyond his influence. Therefore, he had never been there himself. He then introduced me to, two of the most beautiful women I have seen in my life. They wanted me to stay for a while and make cosy, if you get my drift. There was also a little girl who needed my help but her pet dog bit me and she told me to go away. Then later when I returned to the church, I met Chris Hughes, and he said that farm was abandoned years ago by Clive Leach. What does all this mean, can you fathom any of it out vicar."

Lynette smiled at Bruce and spoke.

"You are asking the wrong man here, darling! Michael finds it hard to follow an Agatha Christie novel. Even when the murderer is disclosed to you in the first scene."

Michael sat up straight in his chair after that cutting remark. "Don't listen to her Bruce, she married me for my brain power, as well as my worldly charm."

"Yes, my dear, there was little else you could have offered me. Please excuse me, Bruce. I have dishes to wash, seeing that my husband's salary here does not go to affording a dishwasher."

"Sorry, about that. Honestly, I can see your frustration, but I cannot see how I can help you any further myself. However, there are prayer requests slips available in the church vestry."

Bruce was now taking some heed to what Lynette had just commented on!

"Really vicar, I was hoping that you could put some answers to a few of my questions. Especially the weird stuff that is happening to me, it does seem strangely demonic, don't you think?"

"Such as what, can you elaborate more?"

"Such as the Morris dances at the Notting Hill festival. One was a tall black, bat winged creature. Who was called the Ancient one. Do you know who that might be?"

"Ancient one, you say. I really don't know who, or even what that might be, sorry."

"How about, Insidious Blake. The man at the Dead of Winter Farm? He was such a posh looking bloke, who would not look out of place in Savile Row."

"No never heard of him before, sorry."

"How about the disappearance of Clive Leach?"

"Yes, I have heard of him before, but sadly he disappeared several years before we arrived. So sorry again but I don't know much more about him. Except that he lived at that farm you mentioned, and that his wife had sadly passed away. Then he disappeared not long afterwards. Supposedly, it is reckoned that he had moved to a location somewhere in Devon."

Bruce was nodding his head in general agreement.

"Have you ever seen or heard of someone. That had seen a skeleton face with bright red eyes. That came up out of the floor."

"Could it speak" asked Michael?

"Yes, it did," quickly remarked Bruce.

"No, never, sorry Bruce, that I could not have been more helpful. In answering your questions. But I shall pray for you and your parents later at bedtime."

Bruce quickly stood up, and was just about to say. You have been no bloody use whatsoever. Call yourself a vicar, a Shepard a leader of your flock. You know nothing, you are an ignoramus. But Bruce thought, no, just let it go.

Michael led Bruce to the front door.

"Sorry, again Bruce, but I am sure your parents will turn up sooner or later, God bless."

Then as Bruce walked away and Michael was closing the door and then bolting it. Lynette walked into the hallway from the kitchen and spoke.

"Why, did you lie to him about Clive Leach. His wife is not dead; she also mysteriously disappeared."

"Leave, it my dear, why should we complicate matters?"

On 23rd December, Bruce slept almost all day. He watched a bit of TV in between snoozing on the comfy sofa. Then he suddenly, woke up thinking, hang on did some mention that Clive Leach had a daughter? I need a drink and something to eat, to get my brain cells working again. It is time I went to the local to sort my thoughts out. Arriving after a very short walk to, The Bulls head, Monyash.

Bruce entered the public bar.

"Hello! can I have a pint of Strong Bow, please. Do you have food as well," he asked the barmaid.

"Yes, we do, the menus are on the tables."

"Thank you." Bruce ordered his favourite mixed grill, and he washed it down with a pint of dry cider.

Bruce noticed a man who attended the church open day. This man had been one of the helpers, selling old books. The man was elderly roughly in his late seventies or early eighties, with a deeply wrinkled face and a large broad and knobbly nose. Bruce's dad had once commented that such a nose belongs to a hardened drinker. Bruce walked over to the man, who was sitting next to the bar. He was reading from a daily newspaper.

"Excuse me. Hello, my name is."

The man quickly interrupted.

"I know who you are sonny. Your Bob and Debbie's lad from London."

"Yes, I am, can I have a word with you, please?"

"I suppose so, if you must. Anyway, what kind of young man are you, when it has taken you more than 4 months of visiting here, to finally find this local pub."

"Yes, I would have been in here sooner, but I have had other things on my mind."

"So, what do you want to know, my friend?"

"Have you ever heard of a village called No Place?"

"We do a pub quiz here once a month, on the last Thursday of the month. That village called No Place. It has come up as a question before. I am sure, It is in Cumbria or was it Northumberland. Yes, Northumberland somewhere up north."

"No what I mean to say, is there a No Place around here?"

"Nope, never heard of it in or around these parts."

"OK, let me try another question. Do you know what happened to Clive Leach."

"Blimey, all this talking is thirst work, you know?"

"Oh, yes, it surely can be, what is your name again?"

"Noel Lightfoot."

Bruce asked the man behind the bar.

"Could you give Noel another pint of whatever, please."

"Hey, Noel you are not sponging off my new customer, are you?"

"No, Jack this young man is asking me about Clive Leach."

Jack the Landlord of The Bulls Head, replied.

"That whole episode was a strange thing, without any doubt. Clive was such a popular man too."

"You are not wrong there, Jack. Clive Leach was a good man. A godly man. A hard worker, and totally devoted to his wife and their daughter."

"Yes, I remember that someone recently mentioned to me, that Clive Leach had a daughter."

"Yes, indeed Bruce, her name is Betty. She lives in Bakewell I think!"

"I really need to speak to her urgently; do you have her phone number?"

"No, Bruce I do not, and you be careful. Don't go upsetting that young woman. She has had enough heartache for one lifetime. She lost her mother and her father, the poor woman."

Bruce then offered to buy Noel another pint, and he paid his own bar bill.

"Are you going?" Enquired Noel.

"Yes, I need to find Betty's address. Do you know if she is still Betty Leach?"

"No, she is not. She is married, with children."

Bruce thanked Jack, and Noel, as he left the bar, heading straight to Snipe Cottage. Finally, he thought, I have a real lead.

Bruce was looking through the local telephone directory, but there was not an entry for B. Leach listed. So, on the off chance, he looked in his mum and dads' telephone number and address book. Sure, enough there was a Betty, listed under church home groups. Bruce rang the number.

"Hello, is that Betty my name is Bruce Knight. I would like to speak to you about my mum and dad, Robert, and Debbie Knight."

"Oh, yes. I remember them from the Fire shed group of Christians friends at St Leonards."

"Yes, that is them, my mother and father."

"What do you want to speak to me about?"

"My parents have gone missing, and I wondered."

Suddenly the phone went dead. Bruce quickly re-dialled the number again, but it went straight on to the answer phone. Bruce, thought why has she turned her phone off? Bruce sat

157

down on the sofa and thought about what he should do now. His thoughts were to leave Betty an answer phone message. Bruce pressed redial on the phone. The recording announced.

"Hello, this is Betty Turner, I am not available at this moment. Please leave your message after the tone, and I will get back to you later."

"Hello, Betty this is Bruce Knight. I really need to speak to you about my mum and dad and possibly the similarity with your mum and dad. What do you know about the village called No Place. Please call me on this number and we can talk; I am presently staying at my parent's house in Monyash. Thank you."

On 24th of December Bruce, waited for a call, but none came. It was Christmas eve, and Bruce was feeling downhearted. Bruce decided he would go back to the pub arriving there at about 1pm. The place was heaving with people getting into the Christmas spirit, no doubt. Bruce stood in a packed bar for about an hour, when a table and a chair became empty. Bruce sat down with his pint of cider. When two men also standing in the bar came over to him. "Can we share this table with you?"

"Yes, please do, but you will need a couple of chairs."

"You talk very posh for these parts don't thee, pal."

"I'm from London, my name is Bruce."

"That is more like an Australian name isn't it, mate."

The other man then spoke.

"Why are you here then, in our part of the country, are you just visiting for Christmas?"

"My parents live here at Snipe cottage, just over the road."

"Are they just, they are bloody foreigners, taking our houses. That are meant for local people."

"They retired here, and they are not foreigners, they are English, just like you and me."

"I'd be careful what you say my friend, you might have insulted us. We are Derbyshire folk first, not bloody English."

"That is what I meant, but we are all English, and live in England."

"We don't need your type around here. Buying up our houses and making out you are the bloody same as us. You want to watch what you are saying, you could hurt someone's feeling, my friend and things might get nasty."

Chris Hughes suddenly stepped forward up to the table where Bruce was sitting.

"Are you alright Bruce."

"He is fine." Replied one of the two men.

"We were just educating this outsider on our country ways."
The two men drank their beer and placed down their empty
glasses on the table, then they walked out of the bar.

"Can I sit with you Bruce, if I get another chair."

"Oh yes, please do, Chris."

Chris found a spare chair and joined Bruce at the table.

"Did those two threaten you, Bruce?"

"No, but I am glad they have gone. I think they wanted an
argument, about outsiders buying local properties."

"Well, no harm done. Can I get you a drink, Bruce?"

"No, Chris, let me, what would you like."

"A pint of Guinness, please."

When Bruce returned with the drinks, Bruce asked.

"I hope you can answer a few of my questions?"

"Better to hang on for a while, as they all should be in here
later, even the vicar and his wife."

Bruce thought this could be an ideal opportunity to ask
questions about Insidious Blake, Clive Leach and Betty

Turner. After a few more drinks with Chris. Bruce new everything he needed to know about Chatsworth House. This is where Chris was employed before his retirement. However, he is still a very keen regular visitor.

Michael and Lynette arrived just after 3 o'clock. Lynette came straight over to sit with Bruce and Chris. Whilst the vicar met with the locals and asked the inevitable question. I hope to see you in Church tomorrow morning, for the traditional Christmas Day service. Bruce, asked if Lynette would like a drink?

"Oh yes please, a G and T with ice."

Chris spoke. "It is my round, same again Bruce."

"Yes, please, thank you." replied Bruce.

"Lynette, have you ever met Clive Leach's daughter, Betty Turner?"

"Yes, I have at the church."

"Do you know where she lives, not off the top of my head dear. But, maybe in the church office, we could find the address there. If you come to church in the morning. I could let you have it."

"Have what," quipped Chris, as he came back with the drinks on a tray.

"Oh, Bruce just wanted me to give him a quick tour of the church in the morning; before the service."

"That will be nice of you, it has many beautiful features.

"So, I shall see you there at 9 o'clock sharp." replied Lynette.

"Can I propose a toast." remarked Chris.

"Let us raise our glasses. To a Merry Christmas, with good will to all men."

"What about us women, don't we deserve good will also" Michael had now come up to the table.

"What about you women." asked Michael.

"Darling, it is said that behind every good man, there is a better woman driving him onward."

"Oh dear, I do hope you are not going on about moving again. The Bishop said, he would consider me for a city position in a few years."

"Not any city, Michael. I want Oxford, or Cambridge, or Ely, or Bath. I do adore Bath, don't you Bruce."

Bruce smiled and replied.

"I am more of a shower person; actually."

Lynette was laughing, and Michael remarked.

"I must remember that one for the next time, I meet with the Bishop."

Bruce finally left the pub at 6 o'clock. Heading for a warm cottage and a comfy sofa. Together, with 4 bags of crisps, 2 packets of cashew nuts, and a bag of pork scratchings.

On Christmas day, Bruce woke up suddenly, at 8:35am. Oh heck, he thought. I said I'd meet Lynette at 9 o'clock. After a very quick shower, and brushing his teeth. Leaving no time for a shave. Bruce was quickly getting dressed. He was out and running down towards the church. There waiting at the church, was Lynette.

"Hello Bruce. You are very punctual. Please do come on in. There is no one else about."

Lynette opened the office door. "Do come in, quickly now, let's keep the warm air inside."

Closing the door behind her, she immediately asked Bruce.

"Do you have a girlfriend?"

"No, not at the moment. I did once, but she now lives in Australia."

"Her loss, is our gain, do you not agree."

Bruce felt a bit unnerved, especially as Lynette was now standing face to face with him. Lynette quickly kissed him on the lips. Aren't you going to kiss me back, after all it is Christmas and there is some mistletoe hanging from a tree in the church yard."

Bruce went to give her a peck on the lips. When Lynette grabbed hold of Bruce's arms, pulling him towards her. They had a full lingering kiss.

"Now that is more like it," suggested Lynette.

Bruce stepped backwards his back now against the door.

"You were going to tell me something about Betty Turner?"

"Oh, yes, so I was." Stepping forward so she was face to face again with Bruce.

"She lives at 24 Station Street, Bakewell. Is that information worth another kiss."

Bruce and Lynette kissed again, which was more of a long snog really.

"I really must go now, my dear. Merry Christmas. I have things to do before the service."

Walking to the door handle. Lynette turned to Bruce and spoke.

"There could be more of this, if you want it."

Then she opened the door, and Chris Hughes was standing in the church doorway.

"Morning, Lynette, morning Bruce. Happy Christmas to you both."

Lynette did not answer, rather she walked straight out of the church, into the church yard and was quickly heading towards the vicarage.

"Did you get what you wanted, from the vicar's wife."

"Yes, she gave me, what I needed."

"Well, the church service is at 10:30, so you have time to go home and have a shave, and get yourself tidied up. The service on Christmas day is always the busiest of the year. Mark my words, it will be packed in here later."

Bruce smiled and walked home. Where he had another shower and a shave. Then got dressed, in his best top, trousers, and trainers.

Then at 10.25 on the dot. He took a brisk walk back to the church. Chris was right, he thought, as he approached the church. There was a line of cars parked on both sides of the road. In the church yard, there stood about 80 people. Bruce took a place at the back of a queue. Where he could see the vicar at the front of the queue shacking the hand of everyone attending the church. Finally, after what seemed like ten minutes waiting. "Morning, Bruce, Merry Christmas," said the vicar, as he shook his hand.

Inside the church it was full, every pew was taken. However, at the back of the church sat Chris and Dorothy.

"Please come and join us sinners here at the back remarked Chris, pointing to an empty chair. We are the Deacons here and we help anyone, if needed."

The service was taken by Micheal and Lynette played the piano when necessary. Micheal spoke about love and hope for all humanity through Christ. After the service ended, there was mince pies and warm mulled wine free to the congregation. Chris asked Bruce if he would help him and Dorathy to hand out the mince pies and mulled wine at the back of the church. Michael and Lynette both stood at the church door, and again they shook hands and thanked those who had attended. When Bruce was leaving the church Lynette grabbed Bruce by the hand.

"So glad to see you Bruce, please do not be a stranger."

Michael, then added.

"Yes Bruce, please, do come and see us again, anytime."

Bruce smiled in acknowledgement.

"Thank you, Micheal I have enjoyed the service."

Then as Bruce walked down the church pathway towards the road. He was unravelling the screwed-up piece of paper that Lynette had put there, when she shook his hand.

Dear Bruce, I would very much like to see you again. Busy on Boxing Day, but can see you at the church on 27th at 1 o'clock.

Bruce, put the piece of paper into his trouser pocket.

Chapter 6

At lunch time Bruce arrived at The Bulls Head.

"Hello, again." Welcomed the Landlord.

"You are becoming a regular here. However, we will be closing after lunch today. Then it's our evening off."

"No, that is fine, but can I still get some lunch."

"I am sure my Chef can rustle you up something."

"Thank you anything will do, and a pint of cider, please."

Bruce picked up his drink, and he noticed Chris, Dorothy and Noel sitting at a table. Bruce walked over to them.

"Hello, may I join you."

"Yes, please do," replied Chris, as he shuffled his chair around a bit to make some room.

Grab yourself another chair."

"Did you enjoy the service. We always have a lovely service at Christmas. The congregation numbered 89, not including the vicar, Lynette, or us wardens".

Noel then spoke, and gave an insight to the church history.

"We used to get over 250 people years ago, men, woman, and children. But times have changed. Nowadays, we are lucky to get 89."

"Where is Else?"

"She couldn't come out this year, due to her husband not being too well," replied Noel.

"I met him the other day. I knocked on his door and he invited me in."

"Are you sure it was him, Bruce." remarked Chris. "Because yesterday, Else mentioned that Bert was at deaths door, with a heavy cold; and been confined to his bed."

"He never comes out of that house these days."

Remarked Dorothy, and she Continued.

"It is not right he needs the exercise. He like to meet others and enjoys a chat. Not to be locked up all the while."

Noel quickly replied.

"Now, now, who said Bert was locked up, you will be giving this young man the wrong idea about us country folk."

Chris then commented.

"It is true, Bert is not as fit as he once was. We do miss him at the church. Bert is an elder with great local knowledge."

"Were Bert and Elsie wardens like you three?"

"Why yes, of course, we are the church wardens all five of us. In fact, Bert is the Head Warden as well. Also, with an ancient title. Guardian of the gate, and Keeper of the Keys."

"What do those titles mean?"

"In the old days, centuries ago cities, towns, and some villages had walls and gates that could be closed at night. On other occasions the gates were closed to keep invaders and the like out. The person who had the authority to open and close the gates, was the Keeper of the Keys."

Dorathy then exclaimed.

"Bert still does, open and close, the gates."

"Speaking, metaphorically, she is," replied Noel.

A waitress came up to the table.

"Your lunch is ready Sir."

Chris stood up and spoke.

"We shall leave you to enjoy your meal, in pease."

"No, please do not go on my account."

"No, we must be off."

Noel, Chris, and Dorathy, walked away from the table and exited the bar. The waitress returned with a roast turkey dinner; with all the trimmings.

"Here you are Sir, a meal fit for a King."

"Well, yes indeed. However, in my case not a King but a Knight; thank you very much."

Bruce did enjoy his Christmas dinner and several pints of cider. But he thought it was strange to eat alone on this otherwise family occasion. He settled his bill, and the Landlord bid him.

"Merry Christmas, see you again soon young man."

Back in Snipe Cottage, Bruce assumed his regular position on the comfy sofa, and he was soon fast asleep. Bruce was woken by the house phone ringing. He quickly picked up the phone and in a very tired voice, he almost yawned.

"Hello."

"Well, a Merry Christmas to you to little brother. Are mum and dad there yet."

"No, just me, as usual."

"Well, personally I'm so glad to be in Barcelona, enjoying myself, at a party with friends. You sound if you just woken up."

171

"I was you woke me up."

"Are you going to wish me a Merry Christmas?"

"Merry Christmas, sis." The phone went quiet.

"Hello, are you still there, sis. Bloody, hell she has hung up on me. What a Christmas this is turning out to be."

Bruce ran upstairs and got into his own bed.

On the morning of the 26th, Bruce was finding it difficult to book a taxi to Bakewell. Phone call one: "Sorry my friend, we are fully booked. Try another taxi company." Phone call two: "Hello can I book a cab." Not today, Sir, we are fully booked, sorry" Phone call three: "Hello, can I get a cab to Bakewell."

"When today, you will be lucky. Where from?"

"Monyash to Bakewell."

"Well, it is your lucky day, my friend," replied the taxi operator. "I have a mini cab going to drop off at The Bulls Head, Monyash at around 12.30. You can come back here with that cab if you like Sir."

"Yes, brilliant, thank you very much."

Bruce was waiting by the pub when a minibus arrived. The side door slides open, and seven men got out of the minibus.

Then they went quickly into the bar entrance. The driver looked at Bruce.

"Are you Mr Knight?"

"Yes, I am."

"Could you slide that door closed, please? You can then sit in the front, if you like?"

Bruce closed the side door and got into the front passenger seat.

"Hi, please can you take me to 24 Station Street, Bakewell".

"Yes, no problem. In fact, you were incredibly lucky that those dancing fools were coming for a Boxing Day drink at The Bulls Head. Normally, you cannot get a cab this time of the year for love nor money."

"What are dancing fools?"

"Oh, they are Morris Dancers, sometimes known as dancing fools."

"I didn't know you had Morris Dancers locally."

"Yes, we do, just like many English shires, and especially where there are ancient wells. It is a tradition you know to play music, sing, and dance on special occasions."

"Yes, I met some Morris Dancers once at the Notting Hill Festival, in London. But they were not very friendly dancers, I can tell you."

"Do you mean they hit sticks together. Banged a drums, and they had little bells on their legs. However, you felt that they were not being very friendly!"

"Well yes, point taken but one did have a sword."

"They do sometimes have a sword and a handkerchief. You don't find silk tissues unfriendly too, do you?"

Pulling up outside 24 Station Street, Bakewell.

"There you go Sir. Would you like a cab back later, as I am going back to The Bulls Head to pick up the dancing fools, at 9 o'clock. So, if you are ready and waiting here at about 8ish. You can get a lift back, and all for a special boxing day price of £40 cash. Is that all right?"

"Yes, that is fine, thank you."

Bruce got out of the cab, and knocked on the door of number 24. A middle-aged woman, with a pale complexion, green eyes, and brown uncombed hair opened the door.

"Hello, are you Betty Turner."

"Yes, who might you be."

"I am Bruce Knight."

"I have nothing to say to you Mr Knight, goodbye."

Betty then quickly closed the door. Bruce was standing outside on the pavement wondering what to do next. When the door opened again, this time there was a teenage girl standing in the doorway. The girl aged about 14 years old, with a thin face, pale complexion, brown eyes, and shoulder length blonde hair.

"Why do you want to talk with my mum?"

"I want to ask her about her mum, and her dad, and why he disappeared suddenly?"

The girl then closed the door. Bruce was again waiting outside, and he was just about to turn around and knock again at the door. When it suddenly opened, and the same teenage girl spoke to Bruce.

"Mum said, you can come in."

Bruce walked through the small living room, of this terraced house, and into the kitchen/diner.

"Thank you for seeing me, Betty."

"You should thank her there. I have been talked into this, against my better judgement, by my daughter Rachael."

"Thank you, Rachael, Merry Christmas."

"Please sit down, Mr Knight." replied Betty.

"Please, call me Bruce."

"What do you want to know about my grandad?"

"Let him, ask the questions Rachael."

"Right, where to start. I have visited recently, The Dead of Winter Farm, and there was a man there named, Insidious Blake."

"Where at our farm, did he know he was trespassing? That is my parents farm, and we are waiting for them to come back one day."

"OK, so, you are waiting for them to come back to the farm. I was told your mother had died."

"What grandma is dead. Who told you that?"

"The vicar told me."

Betty quickly snapped back!

"Well, he is a liar, my mother went missing about 7 years ago. People in Monyash, said she had run off with another man. But that kind of sentiment was totally rubbish. I know my mum, she was devoted to my dad. I know that for sure."

"Do you know where your parents are, could they be in Devon?"

"No Bruce, we only say that to avoid difficult questions from the locals."

"Do we mum, so they are not in Devon?"

"No, love we do not know where they are."

"The funny thing right, is that my parents are now missing too. Some people just say they must be relaxing on a world cruise, or in Las Vegas, living it up, or perhaps peacefully walking in Peru. Undoubtedly wherever they are, having a great time, after coming into a shed full of money!"

"Sounds very nice." Remarked Betty.

"Even the local police, are now saying that my parents are more than likely on a world tour. Which is just an excuse because they cannot find them."

"So, your mum and dad have disappeared too, this is very strange."

"Yes, that is why I am here, to see what you know about people disappearing, around Monyash."

"I don't know, my mother lived with my father on our farm. I lived there also, until I got married to Rachael's dad, and then we moved here to Bakewell."

Rachael then commented.

"My mum has divorced my dad. He now lives in Stoke-on-Trent. Do you know where Stoke is, Bruce?"

"Not too sure, where Stoke is exactly. But I support Arsenal, and we have played against Stoke City, many times before when they were in the premiership."

"My dad wants me to go and live with him, one day."

"Be quiet, Rachael, I have told you before you are not going to live with your dad."

Rachael suddenly got up from her chair and spoke.

"I can do as I want, when I am sixteen."

"Did your father tell you to say that?"

Betty, responded in a raised voice. Rachael ran across the room and went running up the stairs.

"Sorry, about that, teenage girls, and their absent fathers!"

"You were telling me about your mother disappearing, and not being dead."

"Yes, she just vanished without a word. Dad was inconsolable, and I was frantic with worry for both of them. I desperately wanted her to come back to the farm. The talk in Monyash or should I say the gossip in the Bulls Head, was that mum had run off with another man, maybe a farm hand or an agricultural salesperson. But she was a good woman, she went to church on Sundays, and she really cared for dad and me, and they worked hard running that farm."

"So, then what happened to your dad?

"That was even stranger than what happened to my mum. After mum had been gone for about a year. My Dad unexpectedly sold off all the livestock, he closed the farm gate and put a dirty great chain and lock on the gate. Just as if he were, shutting up shop. Like he was mothballing the farm for a later date."

"Maybe he was, Betty."

"I don't follow you, Bruce."

"Maybe your dad knew where your mother had gone, and he decided to follow her there."

"Follow her, where too?" asked Betty.

"That is my next question I need you to answer. Have you ever heard of a village called No Place?"

"No, should I have?"

"It was once on a finger signpost, almost opposite the Dead of Winter farm gate. I followed the sign, and it led me to a very strange little village. No Place it is called, and there was a wishing well there with a sigh above it, written on it was, POUTIA wishing well. Then afterwards, whenever I try to find that village. I cannot for the life of me find it again. Plus, whoever I talk to either in, or around Monyash. They have never heard of No Place. I have asked the locals in the pub, and those at the church. Nobody has the faintest idea of what I am talking about."

"Sorry I cannot help you either Bruce. I am just as confused as them others. I lived at that farm from birth, right up till I got married at 19 years of age. Which was about 16 years ago. Then when I got married, we moved in here. I walked from that farm and opened that gate. Sometimes I even climbed over the gate, heading for the road, and thereby the big old oak tree. I would wait for the school bus. I did that every school day for years Bruce, and I never once saw a lane leading to No Place."

"That's OK, I am beginning to doubt myself. One minute I think I'm getting somewhere then the next minute I am lost again."

"I really don't know where my mum and dad went too either. The talk of them going to Devon, is just local gossip, plain rubbish and I know it. But I can't prove otherwise."

"Who owns the farm now, Betty?"

"I do, but I don't want to sell it in case they come back one day. However, that scumbag of an ex-husband, has tried to get me to sell the farm. Hoping that in a divorce settlement he would get half."

"Do you think that your ex-husband has had anything to do with your parent's disappearance?"

"No, he has not got the intelligence to be devious. He is just a womaniser, and I am best rid of him."

"Betty, when I last came to my parents' house a few months back. I took a cab to Bakewell, and the driver gave me his card. When I got back to London, I noticed the card had something written on the back of it. It was (your parents are in No Place)."

"Did you get the name of the cab driver?"

Yes, I did, the name on the card was, Clive Leach."

"That is not possible."

"That is exactly, what everyone else says, it cannot be Clive Leach, because he disappeared about 6 years ago".

"What did the taxi driver look like?"

"He was white, he wore glasses, and he was about 60ish, with a baldish head."

"That description seems very similar to my father, but it can't be him. No, it could be anyone. Anyway, enough talking, would you like a tea or a coffee?"

"No, I am getting a lift back at 8 o'clock to the pub."

"Well, it is only just coming up to 3 o'clock. You have plenty of time for a drink. Unless you don't want too."

"No, that's exceedingly kind, I would love a cup of coffee, white with 2 sugars, please. Do you have a photo of your mum and dad?"

"Yes, I have, somewhere?"

Betty opened a draw in the kitchen and brought out several photographs. Then showed them to Bruce.

"This one is my dad, sitting on a tractor. The photo was taken about nine years ago."

"He does look familiar. In fact, he looks a bit like my dad, in many ways."

"This photo is my mum with Rachael. When Rachael first went to primary school here in Bakewell, also taken about nine years ago."

"Your mother is tall, and slim, with long shoulder length brown hair. She is wearing sunglasses. I am sure I have seen her face somewhere before?"

Then just as the kettle began to boil. Rachael came running back down the stairs with her mobile phone in her hand.

"I have told dad; you have a man here, and you are talking about selling the farm. Dad said, he needs to know what you are doing here Bruce, because mum if you are selling the farm, it is my inheritance as well."

"What, is your dad talking about, he has got no business telling you to repeat our conversation. Who, does he think he is. Rachael, put that phone away, now."

"He is my dad, and I can speak to him when I want."

"You, silly fool. He left us for his fancy piece. He doesn't care about you. All he wants is the money, so he can spend it on his bit of skirt."

Bruce stood up as the agreement raged in the kitchen.

"Maybe I should go, Betty."

"Yes, sorry, Bruce. I do need to deal with his situation right away, before it drags on all through the coming week."

Bruce walked towards the front door to leave, he could hear Betty shouting at Rachael.

"Now listen here, young lady. Its time you were told a few home truths."

Bruce opened the front door and after stepping outside, he thankfully closed the door. Bruce decided to walk into Bakewell town centre, and possibly get the taxi later from there. Arriving in Bakewell town centre. Bruce phoned the taxi firm and asked if he could he be picked up by the National Coach stop, at the pre-arranged time. Whilst passing the time away. Bruce had walked along the river Wye, and visited the park and gardens. During this leisurely stroll. Bruce was thinking why had the vicar lied to him about Mrs Leach being dead. Who else was lying in Monyash? Where had Mrs Leach gone to? Was she in Devon? Had Mr Leach abandoned the farm hoping to join his missing wife?

At 7:45 Bruce arrived at the National Coach stop. Where thankfully the Mine-bus was waiting.

"Have you had an enjoyable half a day in Bakewell, Mr Knight?"

"Yes, thank you, not too bad. My good friend Josh, back in London, would have liked it here."

"Why is that, I wonder. Does your friend like historic buildings, and peace solitude."

"No, not at all. He would like it here. Because Bakewell has a brilliant Costa. An amazing Greggs, and a wonderful Wetherspoons."

After a twenty-minute drive, the minibus pulled up outside the Bulls head.

"Here you are my friend back at the pub."

Bruce gave the driver £40.

"Thank you, very much and Happy New Year."

Bruce walked back to Snipe cottage. In the kitchen, Bruce was starving and ready for something to eat.

"Now for a proper single persons evening feast."

Opening the carrier bag, he had brought with him. One of Greggs Steak bake, and one bag of Sea salt and Cider vinegar crisps. One of Costas Emmental and Mushroom toastie, one paper cup containing a flat white, with two sugars. Everything needed reheating in the microwave. Then when the coffee and the food was piping hot. Bruce sat down at the kitchen table.

"What a wonderful meal, set out before a knight. I could just as easily be in my flat in Tottenham."

After eating his meal, Bruce, phoned Josh, for a chat.

"How's things Josh, my old mate."

"Good man, we are heading out tonight big time. Marquis at nine, then we have booked a table at, El Paso's, for ten. Then we are all going clubbing at a venue in Leicester square. All except you and Ben. Ben went to his parents in

Bristol, for Christmas. Have you had any luck finding your mum and dad?"

"Nope, nothing at all. No one knows where they are."

"Bloody hell mate. When are you coming back?"

"On the 28th the day after tomorrow."

"Good, we miss you mate. We care about you too. All the team send their best wishes."

"Ok, thanks and tell them I miss them too."

"AR, now piss off, bye."

Bruce switched on the TV, and settled down on his favourite sofa. There must be something about the quality of television programs, especially on a Boxing Day evening. Because Bruce fell asleep within 10 minutes of getting comfy.

On 27th Bruce woke up early. He walked around the village of Monyash, to get a feel of the place. It was early, about 7:30 am, so all was quiet at that time of the morning. The houses here are mainly made of the local limestone, as is the church which has a spire that can be seen for miles around. Most of the houses are built as the Terrace type. The Bull's head is a nice-looking olde-English public house, with a lounge. That has soft pink cushioned seats, and a bar. The public bar has a much simpler feel to it. With wooden tables and chairs. The pub has also a beer garden for those long summer days. The village looked very calm and peaceful, but at Christmas time very cold. Visually the whole place is attractive to the countryside visitor. However, Bruce thought it was niceish, but boring. Where do you get a coffee and a croissant? Or a Bacon Egg McMuffin and a hash brown. Or a bacon and cheese toasty, with HP Sause. No, he thought Monyash is a nice place to visit on a sunny afternoon in the summer. Otherwise, it is like living in a time warp, back in the 1950s. With no fast food, no scrummy milkshakes, and definitely no gorgeous young females. Bruce got back to Snipe cottage, where he searched every kitchen cupboard and shelf space. Looking for a drink or something to eat. There was no bread or biscuits. In the fridge, no food, just a tub of flora margarine. In the freezer, there was, a bag of garden peas and a bag of ice cubes. In a cupboard on the wall, there was a bottle of tomato ketchup, salt, pepper, and vinegar. A box of tea bags (lemon herbal) and half a bag of demerara sugar. Plus, a variety of herbs and spices, beef stock cubes and a parmesan cheese shaker, and a jar of marmite. Bruce stared intently at the lack of food, no bread, no biscuits, no coffee, no milk, not even long-life milk.

"What time does that bloody pub open," he yelled."

Then lying back on the comfy sofa, Bruce waited and waited. The morning TV programs helped momentarily to dull the pain of thirst and hunger. Then suddenly, it was 10 o'clock. Bruce dashed up the stairs, he showered, had a shave, cleaned his teeth. Got dressed, put on his best trainers and he looked in the long mirror in the hall. Yes, he thought, spick and span, hair brushed. Ready for the off, onward to, The Bulls Head, opening time at 10:30am.

"Morning" Bruce spoke to the barmaid, as she was placing beer mats on the clean and polished tables in the bar.

What can I get you Sir"

"Can I have a coffee, americano and a croissant."

"Certainly, Sir please take a seat at a table, and it will be with you in 5 minutes. Bruce was basically gobbed smacked, by the excellent service here. Maybe I have got this country living all wrong? The waitress brought over the breakfast.

"All fresh Sir, and obtained from the Tagg lane farm shop, first thing this morning at about 7 o'clock".

After a real treat of a breakfast, Bruce thanked the waitress and ordered a pint of cider. He then thought about his upcoming meeting with Lynette. Bruce had another pint before he left the bar at 12.45pm. Then he walked slowly over to the church. Bruce was standing in the church doorway, then after waiting 5 more minutes, Lynette came walking across the church yard.

"Hello, Bruce, we need to talk."

"Ok let's talk, can we go inside the church."

"No, not here. Can we go to your house?"

"Yes, I suppose so."

"Good, you go there now, I will wait here for another 5 minutes. Then I will follow you, is that alright?"

Bruce nodded and walked away quickly, back to Snipe cottage. He was waiting in the lounge and looking though the net curtain for Lynette to arrive at the front door. When there was a knock on the back door. Bruce went into the kitchen, and opened the door for Lynette. She walked in and took off her coat and she unzipped her winter boots.

"Where should I put these"?

"There by the back door."

"Right, Michael is at a meeting after a late lunch in Bakewell. He is due back home at 4.30."

"Ok, what did you want to talk about?"

"I don't want to talk right now. I just need to hold you close to me."

Lynette whispered softly, her eyes sparkling with desire as she leaned in for a long, lingering kiss that sent shivers down Bruce's spine.

With a playful smile, she pulled back slightly and looked into his eyes.

"Where is your bedroom?" she asked, her voice barely above a whisper, filled with anticipation.

The atmosphere around them was electric, charged with the promise of intimacy and connection.

Bruce gently guided Lynette upstairs, their hearts racing in anticipation. As they reached the bedroom, the world outside faded away, leaving only the two of them in a cocoon of warmth and intimacy.

Lynette stood there, adorned only in delicate lace, her discarded clothes, a trail that led to this moment of connection. With a soft, knowing smile, Bruce removed his shirt, revealing the warmth of his skin.

They stepped closer, their bodies just brushing against each other, igniting sparks of desire. Holding each other tenderly, their lips met in a passionate kiss, a perfect blend of tenderness and longing that spoke volumes about the bond they shared. In that private sanctuary, time seemed to stand still as they lost themselves in the sweetness of each other's embrace.

Bruce was ecstatic about being in love again. Lynette was whispering sweetly to him of how much she loved him.

Lynette revelled in the warmth of Bruce's embrace, feeling a love that enveloped her like a soft, radiant glow. It was a love so genuine and profound, one she had longed for but had not tasted in years. Every heartbeat echoed the joy she felt in his arms, and in that moment, time seemed to stand still. She wished to linger there, wrapped in his affection, where the outside world faded away and all that mattered was the connection they shared. Yet, the shadows of her loveless marriage loomed over her, a bittersweet reminder that she would have to leave the sanctuary of his love to return to the vicarage. A place devoid of the passion that Bruce ignited within her. Still, as she gazed into his eyes, she felt a flicker of hope. Perhaps love was still possible, and maybe, just maybe, a new chapter was waiting to be written.

"I don't normally do this, you know." Said Lynette, "what I mean is that I married Michael seven years ago, and you are the first person who has made me feel this way again. You've awakened something in me that I thought was lost forever. It's like a spark ignited in my heart, reminding me of the beauty of love and connection. Being with you feels like coming home—a place I didn't realize I'd missed so deeply."

"Same here. I had the one girlfriend. Sarah-Louise, we made love, whenever we could. Such as after school or at weekends. However, she moved to Australia seven years ago, and I was heartbroken, I have never met anyone like her, till now."

"I knew you were a special person, when you first walked into the garden, and I was hanging out the washing."

"I noticed you too, you are incredibly beautiful, even when hanging out the washing, and in your apron and fluffy slippers. What are we going to do now, talk some more?"

"Well, I have got to get back to the vicarage soon."

"Oh, you are a lovely man, in every sense, my darling."

Bruce lay there, enveloped in a serene silence, as he basked in the afterglow of their shared moment.
Lynette, with a playful glimmer in her eye, decided it was time to rise. She slipped out of bed, her heart light and her spirit soaring, while the soft morning light danced around her.

As she descended the stairs, she gathered her clothes with a gentle grace, relishing the memories of their intimacy while feeling the fabric against her skin.

Bruce, still in his nightgown, followed her, his heart racing at the sight of her. When she reached the bottom step, Lynette turned, a teasing smile gracing her lips. "What's the matter, Bruce? Cat got your tongue?" she said, her tone light yet filled with affection.

They exchanged knowing looks, a silent understanding passing between them, as they both indulged in the lingering sweetness of the moment. It was a beautiful morning, filled with the promise of more adventures together.
"Will, I see you again?"

I leave tomorrow morning on the 11 o'clock coach from Bakewell back to London."

"Can't you stay here in Monyash for a while longer."

"I have to go back to London, can't you come with me?"

"You know I can't," replied Lynette.

"Please, darling, leave it with me. I have things to tie up in London," he said, his voice gentle yet firm.

"Don't worry, because as soon as I've finished up there, I'll be back for you. Just hold on a little longer." His eyes sparkled with promise, and in that moment, she felt the warmth of his love wrapping around her like a cozy blanket, reminding her that distance was just a temporary hurdle in their beautiful journey together.

Lynette put on her boots and her coat. She kissed Bruce on the lips, and departed swiftly out of the back door.

Bruce went for a shower, then got dressed and ready again for something to eat. Bruce walked to the bar in The Bulls Head.

"Afternoon, young man can I have a word."

Bruce went over to the corner of the bar where the Landlord was standing. The landlord whispered.

"I overheard the lads from the Morris dancers yesterday, saying that they are hoping to get legal representation to seek a high court injunction. On all properties, that are brought locally by outsiders. Then properties are left empty or rented out as holiday lets. Just like your parents, who seem to have abandoned their cottage, is that not so?"

"No, my parents are just missing at the moment."

The Morris dancers think that all properties should be compulsory purchased, and then re-sold or rented out to a local person. Your, parents' house, Snipe cottage was mentioned as being abandoned."

"No, they have not abandoned anything."

"No, please do not take offence. I am just trying to warn you about matters, that might be forthcoming."

"OK, sorry, and thank you for the tip off."

"Your welcome Sir, now is it a pint of dry cider, and we have a very tasty homemade steak & kidney pie, if I might be so bold to say."

"That does sound delicious, thank you. Yes please, a pint and I will have a portion of the pie with chips."

After eating his meal, Bruce was at the bar ordering another pint. When Chris Hughes came into the bar.

"Hello Bruce."

"Hi, Chris, would you like a pint?"

"Yes, please, a pint of bitter will be fine."

"OK, Chris I am sitting at that table over there, please join me."

Bruce came over with the drinks; and sat down.

"When do you return to London?"

"Tomorrow, morning. By the way, I went to see Betty Turner yesterday, and she confirmed that both her parents went missing between 6 and 7 years ago. Betty thinks that her mother went first, and later her father went to find her. However, she has no idea where they are. But what bothers me is that when I previously, asked the vicar about Mrs Leach. He told me that she had died."

"Are you sure, maybe he was confused about the question."

"What is she missing, no she is dead? The vicar is hiding something don't you think."

"Well, who can tell, the vicar does have a lot on his mind. We live in such a troubled world. I was reading this article in the Daily Mail, that investigated that over 3,000 people disappear every year in Britain alone, and the worldwide figure of missing persons is around 10 times higher."

"I know I watched something recently on TV about missing children."

"However, the disappearances around here are different, don't you think? Two couples have gone missing. Firstly, Mr & Mrs Leach, and now my mum and dad. Apparently, both these couples had good and happy relationships. There is no evidence of either drugs or alcohol problems. There was no physical or sexual abuse apparent, and both couples owned property and had independent incomes."

"When you put it like that, there disappearance is an enigma."

Chris then quickly drank his pint and stood up.

"I must leave you now. My wife Dorothy is expecting me back about now. Anyway, Bruce good luck to you, and I hope you have a safe journey back to London."

"Thanks, Chris and give my regards to Dorothy."

Bruce remained there in the bar all alone. He was still hoping that someone else would come in that might know something, regarding the whereabouts of his parents. Finally, he drank up and gave up, and walked back to Snipe cottage. Feeling very melancholy. He thought about his mum and dad. Where on earth could they be, and why could he not find the entrance to No Place. Even more strange is why had no one around here heard of it.

On the morning of the 28th. Bruce was up early. He had packed his bag, phoned for a cab to pick him up at 10am. He had decided, not to return here again. Well, not until his parents had returned home from wherever they were. Bruce thought it was for the best, let things develop naturally. Stop striving and hoping for things to happen. Instead, let things run their course, and not to feel so negative about his parents or hurt he felt regarding their disappearance. Bruce needed to get on with his own life back in London. Where he was incredibly happy, very successful, and always thought positively about his personal situation. Bruce turned off the heating, made sure everything was clean and tidy. He locked the back door and left the key in the usual hiding place.

The cab arrived 10 minutes early and Bruce was standing outside ready and waiting.

"Bakewell National coach stop, please."

Bruce sat in the back of the cab in silence. When he arrived, he paid the fare and walked over to Costa coffee, to buy a coffee and a ham and cheese toasty. When the National coach was almost due, he walked over to the National Coach stop. Waiting there already was a young man and a young woman. Bruce walked up behind the young woman. When she suddenly turned around, it was Lynette.

With a generous smile, and a twinkle in her eye, she said, Hello, Bruce, are you surprised to see me?"

"Bruce returned the smile, and with a sweet whisper in her ear responded with, "hello beautiful" What are you doing here?"

"I am coming with you to London. I need to break away from Michael and from this place. Anyway, I need you and you need me. Being alone obviously doesn't suit you Bruce. Are you happy, that I am coming with you?"

"Yes, of course I am very happy."

"Your very cheeky, I don't know if you should say things like that to a vicar's wife."

"I never expected a vicar's wife to be so amazingly beautiful like you."

"Oh, my darling, I shall take that as a complement."

Chapter 7

After, roughly 5 hours of travelling, on the coach and on the tube. They finally reached Bruce's flat.

"Welcome, to my London pad."

Lynette looked around.

"Yes, it seems nice. Lounge/diner, sperate kitchen, bedroom."

"With a separate shower room and toilet. Do you approve?"

"Yes, I approve."

Lynette began to empty her suitcase.

"Can I move some of your things around, to make room for mine?"

"Sure, no problem, do as you like."

Bruce was busy phoning Josh.

"Hi, are you going for a pint tonight mate, my mouth is as dry as a camel's crutch."

"Where shall we meet."

"Red lion 8:30."

"Great see you there."

"Who was that, you were speaking to?"

"It was my mate Josh."

"Why didn't you tell him about me?"

"I will later, anyway you are coming out with me, aren't you?"

"Yes, OK, that will be simply fine, I need a drink or two."

In the bar of the Red Lion. Josh was waiting at the bar when Bruce walked in with Lynette.

"High, Josh. This is Lynette."

"Please just call me Lyn, from now on. I prefer to be called Lyn, is that all right?"

"High Lyn, nice to meet you. My name is Josh and where did you guys meet."

"We met in Monyash." replied Bruce, with smile.

"Great, would you like a drink, Lyn."

"Oh, yes please, a Bacardi and coke with ice."

"The usual for you is it, Bruce."

"Yes, thanks mate."

Toni and Rikki, then came into the bar.

"How are you Bruce, Merry Christmas," said Toni as she gave Bruce a hug.

"Thanks, I have missed you guys too. Oh, this is my girlfriend, Lyn, Lyn this is Toni, and this is Rikki. Lyn has come down with me to see how the other half live," joked Bruce rather nervously.

Rikki smiled at Lyn and asked.

"Hi, are you a student or do you work up north."

"No, I am married to the local vicar in Monyash, or I was until I left him this morning."

Toni gave Bruce that, what the heck look.

"Do you play pool, Lyn?" said Toni. Come on, let us girls, go and chill on our own for a little while."

"Rikki, bring me a lager with a dash of lime, please sweetie."

Josh looked at Bruce, with a fixed stare.

"Bloody hell mate, you have run off with the vicar's wife."

"It is not like that," replied Bruce.

Rikki quickly butted in.

"Well, there is one thing Bruce, you won't be going to heaven."

"Why, is that?" Josh and Rikki replied together.

"Cos you have run off with the vicar's wife."

"Quiet, keep your voices down."

"Well, you are a dark horse, Brucie boy. Have you been trying out the vicar's wife, before purchasing?" said Rikki.

"Sure, have and she is the best since, Sarah-Louise."

"You, numb skull, she is the only bird you have had since Sarah-Louise and that was seven years ago," replied Josh.

"Look pal, seven years without sex, is a long time. Even for a Welsh man, who has an allergy against wool. Anyway, she is beautiful, and she needs me, and I absolutely need her. Is that OK, with you guys?"

"No worries, Bruce. If you like her, then so do we, don't we Rikki."

Absolutely, we do, are you ready for another pint?"

Toni heard the call for another pint and came over to the bar. "Right, who's next to take on Lyn at pool, she has beaten me."

Rikki stood up straight and spoke.

"Stand back, I am the pool master here."

Toni said, "she might be posh bird, but she knows how to play pool alright."

That first night as a new member of the group. Lyn won every game, even beating Bruce. Then when Lyn and Bruce went back to the flat. They made love, in fact, this routine of going out almost every night for at least the last 2 hours of drinking time in the pub. Continued unabated. Then on returning to the flat, they made love. Bruce and Lyn, acted like newly-weds on steroids. Bruce had been such a quiet neighbour, but now he was thrusting away every night. With Lyn, shrieking, yelping, and groaning, like a banshee. That before long, some of the near neighbours had complained to the landlord. However, this uncontrolled passion continued for the next two months. Bruce was incredibly happy; indeed, he almost never mentioned his mum and dad. He told Andrew at work that he had a new girlfriend, who was killing him, with immense sexual activity.

"Lucky you," replied Andrew. "My wife and I have been married for 27 years. We make love, on our birthdays, wedding anniversary, Christmas Eve, and New Year's Day, if we are still awake.

Bruce smiled, "You sex maniacs."

On Saturday nights, Lyn, Bruce, Josh, Toni, Rikki, and now Ben, who had returned from Bristol. All six were regular clubbers. Lyn had gradually become a good friend to all. She fitted in nicely. She liked drinking, she enjoyed watching Arsenal play football. She ate Indian and Mexican food, like a native. She could dance the night away till the early hours.

However, on one evening, about another two weeks later. Bruce arrived at the flat just after 5pm. Lyn was dressed, and she had her suitcase packed ready to go.

"Hello, what is going on Lyn?"

"I have had a phone call from my father. He says that Michael is not doing to good, mental health wise. He is on anti-depressants and has been having heart palpitations. He is not coping at all well, since I left him. I need to talk to him urgently."

"But Lyn we are so happy here."

"I know darling. However, Michael needs me now, please try to understand."

There was a ring on the doorbell.

"That will be my cab, can you carry my suitcase downstairs, please."

The taxi was waiting, the driver opened the boot for Bruce to put the case in.

"Bye, my love, see you very soon," she gave Bruce a kiss on the lips.

"Bye" replied Bruce.

Bruce did not take to this new situation, very well. In fact, he became, depressed, and had heart palpitations himself. Josh, Toni, Rikki, and Ben were all shocked that Lyn had gone back to her husband too. They tried not to mention Lyn in conversation, but it just couldn't make Bruce feel any better. Instead, Bruce became, morbid and full of remorse.

"Lyn never really, loved me, she said she did, but we know better now don't we. Even my parents are just the same, they have buggered off and left me too. Even my big sister moved away to Spain. Prior to all this, Sarah-Louise deserted me. She was my first and only true love. I adored her. Yet even she went halfway round the world to get away from me."

Josh had heard enough of this self-flagellation.

"Have you heard yourself lately, mate. You are becoming a real pain in the butt."

Bruce stared at Josh, "Piss off, wanker."

Then Bruce drank his pint, and walked straight out of the bar, without muttering another word. Toni put down her drink and went to follow Bruce, when Josh spoke.

"Let him go Toni, he is not himself lately."

On the following Saturday Bruce returned to his flat rather intoxicated, and feeling a little worse for wear in the alcohol department. Bruce, saw the skeleton head with bulging red eyes coming up from the floor again. Also, this time there were four large plastic body bags, on the floor next to the skull. The skeleton's head was tilted just slightly upward, its gaze—those hollow, red sockets—were locked on Bruce. Not lifeless. Just staring intensely. There was something in the air that was immensely threatening. The silence thickened, and was broken suddenly as Bruce heard the brittle creak of the ancient jaw bones began to move."

"I warned you before to stay away from No Place. But you have tried to return there. If you continue to defy me, those four body bags, will contain your four best friends. Do you hear me trespasser!"

"Bruce Knight, thought to himself, you are not going mad, and started to tell himself, "I am not seeing this." He began repeatedly speaking out to the entity, with a trembling voice, "You are just a figment of my imagination, now go away and leave me alone."

"A figment of your imagination am I indeed!" responded the apparition.

The skeleton's head shook violently, from side to side, and with the sound of demonic laughter echoing in the room. Repeated mockingly, *"He's not going mad. Ha, ha, ha."*

Suddenly the skeleton's head stopped shaking, then it cursed Bruce to hell and torment, unleashing the Dogs of Hades, to take Bruce Knight."

The skeleton head began again to shake rapidly from side to side. During the agitated shaking it changed from a human skull face to that of a snarling dog skeleton face, with a pointed mouth and sharp teeth. The 4 body bags shook, as though something inside desperately wanted to get out. Then sharp claws ripped them open from within; each body bag contained a snarling wolf. When out of the bag each wolf sprang into action. Bruce had by now had seen enough. He to sprang into action and ran out of the open flat door and was descending the stairs, as quick as he could. The 4 growling wolves were running down the stairs, snarling and snapping at his heels. Bruce opened the outside door, and he had run a good twenty metres or so, up the busy street. Before he suddenly stopped and looked back at his pursuer's, but there was nothing. No snarling wolves, no barking no snarling, nothing.

The street just contained ordinary people walking about, going about their business, and the usual sound of traffic from the surrounding area. Bruce urgently phoned Josh and asked him.

"Josh could come around and check that his flat was empty."

Josh turned up in roughly twenty minutes and went into the flat and ten seconds later came out of the flat, and shouted down the stairs,

"all clear, mate. No skeleton heads, no mad dogs, and no body bags."

Later in the Marquis of Granby, the 4 friends met with Bruce. He told them what he saw and what the head had said to him. Toni was very concerned about Bruce's mental health.

"Bruce, you need a holiday, please leave the details to me. You need a break away from your problems here, or you will become very ill, do you understand what I am saying."

Bruce nodded.

Several days later, Bruce met up with the usual group of friends in the Marquis. Toni gave Bruce what she hoped was good news.

"I have some good news for you buddy. I have contacted Sarah-Louise, and she would like you to visit her very soon.

In fact, as a surprise we have all chipped in, and bought you an open return ticket to Brisbane."

"What, when for."

"Next Monday, how about that," remarked Josh.

"But how can I just go to Australia? I have a job and commitments."

"You need to take a holiday, mate, or you will soon be off work sick. You are not yourself lately, and visiting Sarah-Louise might make you feel heaps better," suggested Toni.

"Here are your outward and return tickets."

"Oh, thanks guys, you are all true friends. I raise my glass to you all, true Friends."

"Cheers, to true friends," said one and all.

On the following Monday morning, Bruce, was heading by tube to Heathrow airport. He had phoned his manager, saying he had a severe tummy bug. He had been sick and had been sitting on the loo all night, and that he would be taking a week's sick leave.

Once on board the Cathay Pacific flight, it took 23 hours, calling into Hongkong to refuel, to reach Brisbane Airport. Bruce had plenty of time to think of what to say to his onetime girlfriend. Then arriving at Brisbane airport, Bruce was met by Sarah- Louise and her father Malcolm. Sarah-Louise notice Bruce as he walked through the arrivals gateway.

"Hi, Bruce, over here. We have such a lot to catch up on."

Her father commented on how things had changed since they emigrated.

"Hi, Bruce, things have been noticeably quiet with Sarah-Louise, since we moved here, let's keep it that way, mate.

Sarah-Louise gave Bruce a hug. Then they walked over to the airport carpark.

"We have a long drive ahead of us Bruce, so sit in the back and make yourself all comfy and have a snooze, if you need to. Come on Sarah-Louise we will sit in the front, get in dear, mums waiting for us back home."

"We live near St. George, a nice little town, just the other side of Goondiwindi. Do you still live in London, Bruce?"

"Yes, Sarah-Louise I do. But mum and dad have moved to Monyash, in Derbyshire."

"Nice, place Derbyshire lots of hills and valleys," replied Malcolm.

"Do, you miss not living with your mum and dad," asked Sarah-Louise.

"Yes, very much, and especially now they have disappeared."

"What do you mean, disappeared. Have they gone walkabout?" enquired Malcolm.

"Dad let him rest, it has been a long flight for goodness's sake."

About 2 hours or so later, they arrived at their home. A modern version of an old Queenslander. Timber framed and timber cladding, and built on stilts about a metre off the ground. With a covered veranda that went around 3 sides of the house, and steps leading to a front porch entrance, and another set of steps that led from the back door to the rear garden. Sarah-Louise's mum, Katie, and Sarah-Louise's younger brother, Callum, were sitting on a swing seat on the veranda when the car arrived.

"Hello, Bruce come on in, welcome to Australia."

Malcolm carried in Bruce's suitcase.

"Now, listen here mate," said Malcolm. "Bruce, you can share a bedroom with young Callum. We have a nice folding bed on which you can sleep."

Callum replied, "hold on dad, why can't Bruce sleep in the spare room."

"Cos, your uncle Paul, and auntie Grace, might turn up, unexpectantly, and they will need that bedroom."

Katie spoke, "I didn't know Paul and Grace were coming!"

"Yes, love, they said they might drop in any day now."

"But they live in Ilford in Essex."

"Let it rest, will yar. Give Bruce a cup of tea and a bun, that's a good wife."

After Bruce had drunk his tea, and polished off a large, iced bun. Sarah-Louise suggested they had a walk, maybe down to the local river. As they took a leisurely walk Sarah-Louise asked.

"Toni phoned me, saying you are not very well, and that you needed a break from the pressures back home."

"I am alright honest, it is the not knowing where my parents are, they disappeared about 8 months ago."

"Are you going out with Toni?"

"No, she is a mate, that's all. We meet with the others down the pub."

"Why, do you have a boyfriend over here?"

"Not anymore, I had someone at college, that I liked. But his parents moved to New Zealand, so it ended, a bit like us really."

"Do you ever think of me Bruce, and what might have been if we had stayed in London!"

"Yes, sometimes I did, especially when my parents moved away to Derbyshire. I have a one-bedroom flat, and you could have moved in with me."

"Oh, you are quite sure of yourself, what makes you think I would move in with you."

Sarah-Louise slapped Bruce on the bum, and she ran on towards the river. Bruce quickly gave chase, and when he caught hold of Sarah-Louise's arm. H pulled her around till they were face to face. They kissed each other as passionately as they did many times before. Sarah-Louise, cuddled up to Bruce.

"I almost forgot how much I liked kissing you."

"I never forgot how much you meant to me, when we were teenagers," remarked Bruce.

"Come on let us walk along the riverbank for a while," suggested Sarah-Louise.

Bruce was holding hands with his sweetheart again.

"This is a really lovely place, Sarah-Louise. Just look at that blue sky, and the sunshine is so hot. Can we swim in the river or are there crocodile's in there?"

"No, mate. The Bull sharks ate, all the crocodiles."

Sarah-Louise laughed at her joke, and smacked Bruce on the bum. Bruce hugged her, and they kissed again.

Then Callum came rushing up on his BMK bike.

"Hey, you two love birds, mum and dad, want you home now."

Back at the house, Katie and Malcolm were waiting on the veranda.

"Did you enjoy your walk? We have invited some friends around this evening for a barb, and a few drinks."

"It will give us a chance to get to know you again Bruce," remarked Katie. "Sarah-Louise can you help me to prepare a salad and possibly bake a chocolate cake."

"Yes, mum no problem. What about Bruce, what can he do."

"He can help me with the fire, and the cooking of the meat. Come on Bruce follow me, into the back yard. Now, Bruce, gather up some of that bush wood from over there, and bring it over here to this old tin drum. Then we shall light an open fire in that old barrel, and get it baking hot."

Bruce was gathering the firewood, from around the garden. Mostly, dead branches, tree bark and twigs. Picking the firewood up with his bare hands, straight from the ground. Callum came out of the house, via the back door. He noticed what Bruce was doing, so Callum ran over to Bruce and spoke.

"What are you doing, mate."

"I am collecting firewood for the barbeque."

"Well, yes, I can see that. But out here you always use a stick or a branch or a garden rake to first move the sticks to where you want to pick them up. There are Snakes Bruce, in this place and some are very poisonous, didn't dad warn you about the dangers."

"No, he didn't."

Malcolm came out of the house with a tray full of fresh meat.

"Hey, you two fellers, go in the kitchen and get the tin's, about 100 will do to get us started. OH, and a bottle of sweet sherry for the ladies."

Callum looked at Bruce with a broad smile on his face.

"Come on Bruce, he thinks he is a bloody comedian."

Bruce was amazed at the 4 tall and wide fridges in the kitchen.

Callum said, "these 2 fridges on the right are full of booze. There are 24 cans in a tray, so we need at least 4 trays. I will carry these, and don't forget the bottle of Harvey's Bristol Cream, or the ladies will get upset."

Bruce smiled as he got the joke, and picked up the sherry bottle. In about an hour or so, the guests began to arrive. Sarah-Louise had got changed into a beautiful orange coloured chiffon, long cool dress, exactly right for a warm Queensland evening. Malcolm introduced Bruce as a friend of the family, who had recently lost his parents. Bruce, then spent most of the evening explaining, time and again that his parents had not died, but they had disappeared unexpectantly. By the time Bruce had literally, spoken to everyone at the party. The party was almost over. Sarah-Louise simply asked.

"Where have you been Bruce? Have you been avoiding me?"

"No, it was your dads fault, after him saying that my parents had gone away, or I had lost them."

"Don't you dare blame my dad; he put on this party just for you. So, you could get to know us and our friends."

"Well, I certainly, got to know your friends, alright."

During the next few days Bruce seemed to be taken here and taken there. In the car, and usually by Malcolm. He would initially say, something like.

"Come on Bruce, mate. I am going into town, come with me, and meet some of us real Australians."

They would inevitably go to a bar in the town and have a few cold ones.

"Just a quick one or two, to keep our peckers up."

Then when I asked if I could go home now, to see and spend some quality time with Sarah-Louise. Malcolm would reply.

"Strooth, mate, this is bloke's time, not for Sheila's. I genuinely thought a man like you would appreciate that. I know where this old opal mine is around here. I might take you there tomorrow, as a treat."

By the time Bruce and Malcolm got back home. Bruce was absolutely knackered, hot and bothered, and half asleep. He could just about manage to sit himself down on the veranda swing chair. Then he feel asleep within minutes. Malcolm looked at Sarah-Louise and commented.

"He asked to go with me, sweetheart. It is not my fault; he can't keep up; he's a bit of a wimp don't you think!"

Bruce was woken up, by an anxious Sarah-Louise.

"Come on sleepy head, you are going to be late for dinner. We are going over to the Evens house for a real culinary treat, so mum says."

"Core blimey, mate. Come on Bruce, shake a leg. You can't stay awake for more than an hour. Not much of a party goer, are you?"

Remarked Malcolm as he stood over Bruce, who was still looking worse for wear on the veranda.

After a short drive they arrived at a very modern looking property.

"Look at this place. It was inspired by a house on Australia Grand design, TV program. I do think it is a beautiful building; I would love a house like that."

"Me too mum. I want a house like this one day."

"Well, you'd better find yourself a financier to marry, that's all I can say," quipped Malcolm. Sarah-Louise, nudged Bruce with her elbow. He was still half asleep in the back of the car.

"Do you want to live in a house like this one, Bruce?"

"He would be lucky; this will set you back over $1,9m. That is real earnings love, not in his league, I'm afraid to say."

Susan and Edward Evens, welcomed in their guests.

"Please make yourselves comfortable," said Susan.

"Your house, it is so beautiful," replied Katie.

"Thank you, we love it don't we Edward. I shall show you some of the amazing features, later if you like."

"Can I offer you a drink before dinner," asked Edward?

"The usual for me, please Ed. This is Bruce, he is here from London. He also likes a cool beer."

Susan looked at Bruce and asked.

"Where in London do you live."

"I have a flat in Tottenham, just off the Tottenham Court Road."

"Cor blimey, it is a bit rough around there isn't it, don't you have to carry a knife," smiled Malcolm.

"No, it is genuinely a really nice area."

"Don't take any notice of him Bruce, he is just pulling your leg," replied Katie.

"Come outside with me Bruce, let us sit on the patio."

Sarah-Louise grabbed him by the hand and led him outside.

"It is lovely here isn't it, Bruce."

"Yes, genuinely very nice, but don't you miss the city life, and all that is going on there."

"Yes, I do sometimes. I remember when we used to go to the park, and we would lay down on the grass and you would kiss me, and tell me that you loved me."

"Taking about laying down together and kissing. When can we be alone?"

"Blimey, are you two coming inside or what. Susan has cooked a blooming goose and roast spuds for dinner."

"Coming now daddy, come on Bruce. Let us go and eat."

"Great, tucker this, Susan."

"Thank you, Malcolm. Please help yourself to more."

"When is your boy coming back home, Ed?"

"He is due back tomorrow. I will drive to the airport to bring him home."

"Did you hear that, Sarah-Louise. Dillon is coming home tomorrow!"

Edward was sitting next to Bruce, and he spoke to him about their son.

"Dillon has been over to the States to see if there are any openings for his, talents. In such places like Berkeley."

"It will be Australia's loss, mate. If the likes of Dillon can't get to study nearer home," remarked Malcolm.

After the meal Sarah-Louise proposed, that maybe Bruce and she could walk home, as it was such a lovely evening.

"Ok, dear, that will be nice," replied Katie.

Later when Malcolm, Callum, and Katie, said their goodbyes to Susan and Edward. They left for home, a twenty-minute drive away. Malcolm was not. However, very happy.

"Why did you let those two, walk home. For Christ sake!"

"They wanted to be alone for a little while, that's all. It's not a big deal, is it?"

"Well, I am not happy about it, love. She would be much better off with a bloke like Dillon; she should forget about Bruce."

"Now, listen to me, our daughter is a good girl. She deserves to be happy, and if she prefers Bruce, well that is good enough for me."

Callum was sitting quietly in the back of the car.

"Yeh, dad, Bruce is a really nice guy."

"Ok point taken, now keep your eyes peeled for them two walking, that's a good lad."

Sarah-Louise and Bruce had called into a local diner, for a milkshake.

"Hi, one Banana, and one Strawberry, please," ordered Bruce. "I am getting strong vibes, that your dad is not too keen on me being here."

"He is all right; he just wants this move to Australia to be a success, for all of us. We gave up such a lot to come here. I am sure he likes you really!"

When Sarah-Louise and Bruce arrived home. Malcolm was waiting on the veranda, patiently sitting in a rocking chair.

"Blimey, I could have run a half marathon in the time it has taken you two scallywags to walk home."

"We stopped at Mike's diner for a milkshake," replied Sarah-Louise.

"Isn't that good news, about Dillon coming back tomorrow."

"Yes, dad, it is. He can meet Bruce."

"That should be nice for him, he can tell Bruce all about Quantum Physics. I am sure Bruce will be savvy about that subject. Anyway, I am off to bed, and I suggest you two call it a day too."

In the morning, Bruce was having an early shower, before breakfast. When there was a knock on the bathroom door. "Hello, it's me," whispered, Sarah-Louise, "can I come in?"

Bruce wrapped only in a towel opened the door.

"Hi, Bruce, I thought I might join you."

Sarah-Louise was wearing a short cotton night dress. Bruce beckoned her to come in, then closing and locking the door behind him. Sarah-Louise then pulled up the night dress, up over her head, they both stood naked under the warm shower. After rubbing the sponge into a fragrant soap, they washed each other's back. Bruce had become sexually aroused. Bruce gave Sarah-Louise a big hug and he kissed her passionately, she responded, and they began a frenzy of passionate love making beneath the cascade of the warm shower.

Covered in soapy suds, both were happy again. It was as if they were making up for the last 7 years. Then Sarah-Louise stood with her back leaning on the tiled wall. She had a firm grip on Bruce's buttocks, as they both pulled and pushed to a steady rhythm. Then as they came together, they kissed passionately.

"Thank you darling, that was wonderful," whispered Bruce. Then wrapped in bathroom towels, they kissed each other passionately once more. Then headed for their respective bedrooms. During breakfast, the couple were back as they had been many years before. Always close together, always holding hands, or hugging and kissing each other, at every opportunity.

"Aw, isn't that sweet," remarked Katie. As she watched the two holding hands, while they walked around the garden, on a beautiful bright sunny morning. Malcolm however, glancing over the top of his morning newspaper, replied.

"Mark my words love, this will all end in tears, especially when he wants to go back to London."

In the late afternoon, Edward phoned to say that Dillon was back. Malcolm could not contain his happiness at that news.

"Sweetheart, he shouted, as he walked onto the veranda. Where Sarah-Louise and Bruce were resting. Sarah-Louise, good news darling, Dillon is back. You could call him, to see what he is doing later."

Bruce quietly whispered into her ear.

"Is there something between you and this Dillon?"

"Only in my dad's head," she softly replied.

Katie now joined them on the veranda.

"Why don't you two go over to see Dillon. He might like the company."

"Ok, mum, that's a good idea. Come on Bruce, lets walk over there and see if he wants to party later!"

As the young couple walked away from the house. Malcolm commented again on his deeply held concerns.

"I hope you remember dearest. That two is company, and three is a crowd."

Half an hour later. Bruce rang the doorbell.

"Hello, again you two. I suppose you have come to see Dillon."

Bruce was at first shocked to see the dark skinned, dark haired. Very tall, and slim, young man that came into the lounge.

"Hi, Dillon, how was America?" Asked Sarah-Louise, as she walked up to him and kissed him on the cheek.

"Good to see you again Sarah-Louise. America was brilliant, I might go there to study either Physics or Law. Hello, who is this?"

"Oh, yes, this is my old boyfriend. Bruce he's from London."

"Pleased to meet you Bruce, and you already have a good Australian name."

"Yeh, I'm really liking it here, the weather is so nice."

"Do you think you will stay here, by the way the weather can get very different in October and November!"

"I would like to stay for another week. But then I need to get back home. My parents disappeared about 8 months ago, and I'm still hoping to see them back at their home; anytime soon."

"Aren't you going to stay here forever, Bruce with me." said Sarah-Louise.

"No, not yet, anyway. I need to see my mum and dad first."

Sarah-Louise had tears in her eyes, then she burst into openly crying.

"Please excuse me, I need to fix my makeup."

She ran then to the bathroom. Susan who was standing nearby. Heard the commotion and headed to see if she could help.

"You fellas, have no sense of a woman's feelings. She just gets used to being happy again, and you blokes bugger off again, at the drop of a hat!"

Susan went into the bathroom to see if Sarah-Louise was all right. Bruce and Dillon looked at each other in total confusion. "What did I say," remarked Bruce?

Dillon asked Bruce if he would like a beer? They went out on to the patio.

"Are you an aborigine?"

"Yes, mate, that is a good deduction."

"I don't mean anything against you, or other Aborigines."

"None taken. I was adopted when I was about 2 years old. Good people are mum and dad, they treat me as their own. Always have, done. Bruce, do you know anything about aboriginal culture?"

"No, mate, not much. We don't get a lot of information in Britain about Aborigines, even at school."

"Well Bruce, you are due for your first lesson. Because, the day after tomorrow. There is a local tribal gathering, and you are now invited."

Just then Sarah-Louise came out onto the patio. Seeing her the men stood up,

"Sorry if I upset you," replied Bruce.

"Can we walk home now Bruce; we need to talk about us."

"See you soon," said Bruce to Dillon. Sarah-Louise gave Dillon a parting kiss on the cheek. Then as the two begun their walk home. Sarah-Louise had a few crucial questions to ask Bruce.

"Bruce, are you planning on going back to London?"

"Yes, I am, but not right now."

"So, when are you actually going back. I thought we were back together, especially after what happened this morning in the shower. I don't give myself to anyone you know. I went out with a lad from college here, and for a whole year. But we never did, what you did to me, this morning."

Bruce stopped walking and on turning to face her. He gave Sarah-Louise a big hug and a loving kiss.

Back at the Queenslander. Callum asked, "did you guys see Dillon?"

"Yes, we did. He has invited us to a tribal meeting, and cultural event, that is happening this weekend."

Malcolm and Katie arrived back from a visit to the shops.

"Hello, we have brought a real treat home for dinner. Fish & Chips. I hope you like salt, Bruce, as the girl put loads on."

The following day, Friday. Sarah-Louise and Bruce went into St. Georges, just to mooch around and to have lunch at a restaurant, by the river. Sarah-Louise was looking in the window of a jewellery store.

"Come and look at this ring here Bruce, it is a solitaire diamond, and it is so beautiful. Don't you think."

"Yes, it is, but the price $65,000, that is a lot of money".

"Well, you are going to be a catering manager soon, aren't you? Then you will be able to afford such a beautiful ring, for the woman you love."

"Wow yeh, I suppose. How about that big opal ring over there, that is a real beauty and its only $18,000."

"Yes, it is genuinely nice, I agree. But a diamond ring comes first, then an opal ring maybe later."

Bruce, did feel that the conversation over lunch, was a bit to clingy, to say the least. Sarah-Louise talked on and on, about the beautiful diamond engagement ring. Then she mentioned how she wants a traditional white wedding, with hundreds of guests. Bruce could invite all his friends from London. She also had a plan for a wonderful honeymoon in Hawaii. Bruce felt extremely uncomfortable about the tone of the conversation. He does honestly love her very much, and it was good to be back together all lovey-dovey. After all, they have been an item since year 8 at the High School. But he was not yet ready for marriage. Romance yes, sex definitely yes. But marriage, not until I am at least 33 years old his best friend Josh would have insisted.

When they got back home Sarah-Louise was quick to tell her mother all about the Diamond ring, she had seen in the jewellers shop.

"It was so beautiful mum, I loved it straight away."

"Did Bruce like it too?"

"Yes, he did. He said it was beautiful."

"How much was it?"

"Only $65,000, then we had lunch, and all we talked about was our wedding plans, and our honeymoon in Hawaii."

"Oh, I am so happy for you, my dear. Is he going to ask your dad for your hand?"

"I think so mum. Oh, I'm so excited."

Bruce was meantime, sitting on the veranda, with a cold beer from the fridge. His thoughts were more on how bloody hot and humid it gets in Queensland. Later that evening when Malcolm got home, from his evening-shift at the water treatment plant. Katie called him into the kitchen to tell him about Sarah-Louise's good news.

"What, you're joking. I am not happy about that love, no way. He might take our girl back to London, is that what you want?"

Malcolm continued to speak his thoughts regarding Bruce...

"No, no way is that bloke good enough for our beautiful girl."

"But what if he asks you for her hand," replied Katie.

"Hand, he will get my bloody fist first, the pomme bastard."

At the breakfast table the next morning. Malcolm was anxiously waiting for Bruce to say something. So, he could slam him down, as an undesirable bloke. As far as marrying his wonderful, beautiful, daughter was concerned. Katie was joyfully happy for Sarah-Louise. Thinking also that Malcolm had slept on what he had said, the previous night. Hoping he might now be in a better frame of mind. Callum was just waiting for someone to say something. Such as, what would you like for breakfast. Sarah-Louise was hoping that Bruce would announce their future intentions, by going down on the knee. Asking her to be his beautiful bride. Plus, Bruce ask her father, for her hand in marriage. Sarah-Louise was not sure which way round; those two vital ceremonies are meant to happen. But, what the heck does it matter when you are so happy. However, whilst others might be contemplating joyful tiding. Bruce was wondering if to have the granola or the shredded wheat. The deathly silence was broken only by the house phone ringing. Katie answered the phone.

"Hello, yes, they are here having breakfast. Its Dillon, asking if you are still going to the Aboriginal tribal event."

"Yes, sure thing we are," said Bruce.

"Ok, I will tell them, to be ready for 11 o'clock, bye."

"Dillon said he will be here at 11 o'clock to pick you up."

Sarah-Louise was sitting next to Bruce, giving him the what the heck look!

"Bruce, are you going to ask dad something?"

She gave Bruce one of those, we are waiting for you, looks. Where Bruce was still enjoying his bowl of crunchy cereal.

"Well, Bruce are you, asking him?" she shouted loudly.

Bruce's mind was undoubtedly elsewhere, when Sarah-Louise poked him in the upper arm with a forefinger.

"Oh, yes sorry, sweetheart. Malcomb would you and Katie, like to come with us today. Oh, and you too Callum."

"Under the kitchen table Sarah-Louise kicked Bruce on the shin.

"Ouch that hurt, what was that for?"

"No, you youngsters can go, we have things to do around here, don't we my dear," smiled Malcolm.

"Can I still come with you, please?" said Callum

"Yes of course you can," replied Bruce. There was total silence now in the kitchen. Noone said anything for ages. Then Callum broke the silence with.

"Dillon's here in his pick-up truck.

"Hello, are you two fellas' OK, sitting in the back, there are only two seats in the cab."

Bruce and Callum made themselves comfy on some empty sacks in the back of the truck.

"Hi, Sarah-Louise are you alright, you look rather sad. Have you been crying again."

"No, I am fine, I just hate people who let you down."

"Not, me, I hope."

"No, not you, you are fine."

The drive was about an hour, to where the Yarandali Tribe, were holding a cultural dance and art meeting for locals and tourists, alike. The display consists of tribal singing, music and dancing. Aboriginal art and mythological story telling.

When the four arrived, the dancing and music was in full swing. There was at least two hundred Yarandali people, and another five hundred spectators. Dillon led the way to a small village building that had a display of Aboriginal art.

"This is my favourite part of the gathering. The opportunity to see new artwork from new Aboriginal artists."

"What are the shapes meant to be?" asked Callum.

"These are drawings and paintings of mystical beings that brought the Aboriginal people to this place from across the ocean, to the land of the Dreams."

The four then left the art building and they walked over to the main arena. Where the visitors were watching a group of six Aboriginal men dancing, and two others, one playing a didgeridoo, and one playing clapsticks.

Dillon explained that the dancers were imitation wild animals and birds.

"These dancers are re-enacting the Dreams of a time that had no beginning and no foreseeable end. The land of Dreamtime."

The dancers stopped, and one dancer announced.

"Please welcome to the arena, our spiritual leader, Yawura." The crowd around the arena gave an applause, as an Aboriginal man walked in and joined the other dancers. Then a new dance started, and the dancers began to act out the indigenous animals of Australia that make Dreamtime a special place. The dancers imitated, Kangaroo's, Emu's, Koala's, Lizards and snakes.

When the dancers had finished their display, they were mingling with the crowd of visitors, and the inevitable selfies were taken.

"Come on follow me," said Dillon.

He led them over to see the spiritual leader, Yawura. Who was standing in front of a hut. Dillon was smiling at the Spiritual Leader, hoping to get his attention. Dillon wanted to talk to him, regarding if it was wise for Dillon to go to live in America. However, unexpectedly, and very suddenly, the spiritual leader stepped forward towards the group of four. Yawura then spoke.

"One of you, is of the spirit world!"

Dillon was just about to say, "Yes, I am an Aborigine too."

"You, man." Yawura was pointed to Bruce.

"You are a visitor to the spirit world."

Thinking it was a joke or part of the act. Bruce replied.

"Well, yes, I am visiting here from Tottenham, London. The great spiritual home of our beloved Arsenal football club."

"No, man listen to me. You four people follow me now."

Yawura turned around and he walked into the side door of a small building. All five were now in the building and standing still. Yawura the spiritual leader, put out his arm and he held his right palm towards Bruce's forehead. No one said anything, for what seemed like two minutes.

"You have visited Dreamtime, are you a messenger my friend."

"No, I don't know what you are taking about. I'm from London in the UK, over here visiting my girlfriend."

Dillon then spoke.

"Please uncle, explain what you mean."

"This man here has been to the spirit world. I know he has. It takes one to know one, as you English people say."

Bruce replied. "No, honest I have never been to Australia before."

"Listen to me, you don't have to be here in Australia. You may have visited Dreamtime, elsewhere. The entrance to these hidden places, can be a tree, or a rock crevice, or even through still water, such as a lake."

So, dreamtime exists in other countries, not just Australia? Remarked Dillon.

"Why yes, as far as we know, these spirit realms are everywhere. Through, these realms, the living can meet the Kingdoms of Heaven here on earth. We go there to gain strength and wisdom."

"Can you explain that again," please said Bruce.

"Through Dreamtime the living can visit the place where the living can be transformed. By spiritual knowledge and healing. We Aborigines believe that our ancestors have disappeared from the sight of mere mortals. But continue to live in a secret place made by the creator. We believe it is our destiny to go to the secret and hidden places. Either dead, or when alive. There we will receive an understanding of the very essence of life, and the reason for us being here on earth."

Dillon asked, "Uncle, has Bruce been to this secret and hidden place."

"Yes, he has, I know he has."

"Hold on a minute, mister," said Bruce. "I went to a small village about a year ago, called No Place. But I have not been able to find it again."

"Was the entrance in a cave, or a rock crevice?"

"No, it was a small dirt track, that descended down a short slope, then turned into a village road."

Yawura again held out his arm and holding the palm of his right hand just millimetres above Bruce's forehead.

He finally spoke. "Was there a tree, a big old tree, near to the dirt track."

"Yes, there was a big old oak tree, in the garden of a house nearby."

"That is, it, my friend. That old tree is the entrance."

Bruce was now thinking fast, this unexpected meeting could solve the disappearances.

"How is it possible, for an old tree, and the mysterious village to be connected?"

"We Aborigines believe that there are special places, that are a way back to the beginning of time. These special places are physical sites, such as Uluru or Aye's rock as you English called it. These places lead you into another realm, where you can speak to your ancestors to learn how to cope and survive in the natural world. Visiting Dreamtime, we call it, people can enter those places and come back again if they choose to do so. However, we must perform certain ceremonies, and sing customary songs regularly. To keep the entrance alive and open. We have kinship with them who live in Dreamtime, if they chose to come back or if they choose to stay, we respect that decision."

With that said by Yawura. A young Aboriginal man entered the small room.

"It is time to go Uncle; there are tribe's folk waiting to see you."

Yawura acknowledged this messenger, and he then held Bruce by the right hand.

"Go spiritual brother, and seek those who have gone before you."

Yawura then walked out of the building. Leaving those remaining totally inspired.

Dillon and Bruce looked at each other. Bruce finally spoke.

"Can you explain that to me one more time please."

Dillon smiled at Bruce's confused expression.

"You have previously found a way into the realm of the past and present. Known here as Dreamtime. There is a big tree that is the entrance to that special place. You must be in a positive frame of mind, full of hope and happiness, to open the entrance. Always remember this, your mind set, your thoughts, they can open doors, as well as close them. That my friend, is the same wherever you go in the world. Also, there must be local people, that know of that entrance. Because, someone needs to sing and dance through certain ceremonies, and do this regularly. Only that will keep the entrance open. Dreamtime is a concept embodying the past, present, and future. You can walk in to visit, then walk out again, or you can stay there amongst the spirits and the living."

"Good grief, thank you Dillon!" exclaimed Bruce. "I know where my parents are!"

"Where are they Bruce?" said Sarah-Louise.

"They are in POUTIA!"

Bruce had a eureka moment. Bruce clicked his fingers, and he smiled. Dillon congratulated Bruce with a pat on the back.

"You know now what you must do my friend."

Bruce nodded in acknowledgement, and put his arm around Dillon's shoulder.

They walked back to the truck, and Dillion drove them back home. Not a word was spoken on the 50-minute journey.

However, on their arrival, Callum jumped out of the back of the truck, he could not wait to tell his parents, about the magical, spiritual man, they had spoken to.

"He was really, cool mum and dad. A real Aboriginal leader. He was called Yawura, and he speaks to the spirit world in Dreamtime."

"It is all a load of mumbo jumbo," replied Malcolm. "There is only one way to heaven, and that is through believing in Jesus Christ."

"But dad, he told Bruce his parents were in Dreamtime."

"Dreamtime, I think its past your bedtime sonny."

Outside Sarah-Louise and Bruce were talking to Dillon. Bruce asked again, what does he need to do?

Dillon reiterated, "You need to go to wherever you were before. Then and only then, will you be able to access that hidden secret place."

"Ok, said Bruce, I understand what I need to do. But I have been there again and again. Believe me there was no entrance to be found!"

"Look Bruce, if Yawura says, that it was there, then you must believe it too. Both in your heart, and in your mind."

"Alright, I will try once more."

"Good on you, buddy, see that you." Replied Dillon.

Dillon got back into his truck and drove off.

Sarah-Louise, who had been unusually quiet for ages.

"Are you really thinking of going back to London."

"Yes, I must go back. I honestly don't believe I have a choice?"

Sarah-Louise burst into a flood of tears, and ran towards the house.

"What is up with you," shouted Bruce.

Sarah-Louise ran quickly into the house and went straight to her bedroom, slamming the door behind her. Malcolm had heard his daughters sobbing, and the slamming of a door. He went to the front door, to find out what was going on. Where he met Bruce very slowly walking in.

"What have you done to my girl, mate? You'd better not have hurt her."

"No way man, she is upset that I am going back to London."

"You are what! Oh, dear never mind, do come in, and sit down over here with me." Malcolm, pointed at the lounge.

"Callum was just telling me you had spoken to a medicine man, and he told you that your parents were dead and gone to heaven."

"No, he did not say that at all. He said, my parents are alive and in a special place very similar to Dreamtime. Yawura said, it is called Dreamtime here. But, in Derbyshire it is probably called, No place or Poutia."

Then Katie came into the lounge.

"I have just spoken to Sarah-Louise. She is terribly upset with you Bruce. You were planning to get engaged soon, weren't you? Now you are leaving her and going back to London."

Malcolm suddenly spoke…

"No, not at all, my dear. Take it easy on the poor fella. Bruce needs go back home. Because he has been told by an Aboriginal medicine man, where he can find his parents."

"Since when, did you start to believe in Aboriginal culture?"

"Now then, Katie my love, we must all respect the indigenous people, and their beliefs, and culture. If Bruce wants to find his mum and dad, so be it, I say!"

"Callum come with me to the study. I want you to look on the internet, for an early flight back to London tomorrow, if that is OK with you Bruce."

Katie, then sat down on the sofa next to Bruce.

"Bruce, our daughter loves you very much. She was heartbroken when we left London to emigrate here. She missed you so much. She would cry uncontrollably at times. Then she met a nice lad at college. Craig was his name. Craig liked to see Sarah-Louise at college and by all accounts he loved her dearly. But Sarah-Louise was extremely nervous to get too deeply and emotionally involved again. Just in case he left her, and strangely enough he did just that. When after about a year of dating each other. His parents suddenly up sticks, and moved to New Zealand. However, this time, she coped and got on with her life and her college work. Then you have come back, and genuinely out of the blue. She thought, she was blessed to have her first true love back in her life. You could literally take up, where you two left off."

Now Sarah-Louise came into the lounge, still looking very upset.

"How, are you feeling, are you alright now, my dear."

"Yes, thanks mum, a little better."

"Well good, I have just had a word with Bruce, and I have told him what you have told me. Especially about how you want him to stay here, and build a loving future together,"

Sarah-Louise smiled at her mother. Suddenly, Callum and Malcolm rushed in.

"Great news Bruce. Callum here the wizard of the internet, has just found you a spare seat on a Cathay Pacific flight back to Heathrow tomorrow night at 9 o'clock".

Sarah-Louise burst into floods of tears. Katie, put her arm around her daughter's shoulders and as they walked slowly out onto the veranda. Katie turned around to face the men. "You blokes, are such unfeeling bastards."

The next day Katie and Sarah-Louise had got up early, got ready and they went shopping, as a therapeutic remedy for bad news. Malcolm was on an early shift that day. So, Cullum, and Bruce, were left alone to have a lie in. When Bruce, woke up he showered and got dressed. He was eating a bowl of cereal when Callum came into the kitchen.

"Bruce, what is it like living in London?"

"It's great, you have everything there. Loads of places to drink and eat out. Theatres, cinemas, night clubs, and brilliant football clubs."

"Who do you support, Bruce?"

"Arsenal, the best team in London, and some say in the Premier Leage."

"I want to come to London, when I go to uni."

"Brilliant which uni. do you want to go to."

"I don't know yet; it depends, I suppose, on who will have me."

"If you go to the University of Central London. Well, you might see me there."

"Aren't you going to come back here, to marry my sister?"

"Yes, maybe later, but I am hoping that she will come and stay with me for a while in London. Especially before we commit to getting married."

"Can I stay with you as well?"

"Maybe you could. However, we might need to get a bigger flat, first. Mine has only one bedroom."

"Alright, that is a brilliant idea. I shall mention it to mum and dad, as a idea for the future."

Bruce had finished his breakfast, so he went to sit outside on the veranda. There he texts Toni and Josh, saying that he would be back in London on Wednesday, t.t.b.a. and he had good news to tell them about his parents.

Malcolm had finished work at 2pm on the early shift. He had gone to pick up his wife and daughter in town. However, they ended up in a local cafe, for a coffee and a chat.

"Why are you helping, Bruce to go home," asked Katie. We want him to stay here with us, and eventually marry Sarah-Louise."

"Aren't you girls jumping ahead a bit. Maybe, Bruce is not the marrying type, or he has other plans for his future. Have you asked him, or do you just take him for granted."

"Look dad, I know you are only trying to protect me from being hurt again. But I really love Bruce. He is my only real boyfriend. I feel happy with him, and he loves me. I know he does, so why can't we get married?"

"Have you heard yourself! He is just some bloke; you met at school in London. When you were only 12 years old, and remember we left there seven years ago. We came here to make a better life for us all, sweetheart. If you carry on with this relationship, believe me he will want you to move to London to be with him."

"Oh no, you wouldn't move away from us would you dear."

"That is my point, exactly," said Malcolm. "Long distance relationships don't work. One or the other ends up moving to make the other one happy, and then bears a grudge that they gave up everything for the other."

When they got back to the house, an excited Callum met them. He ran out to their car, and immediately told them.

"Bruce says we can stay with him in London, you sis, and me."

"Who you, you are staying here my boy." Insisted Malcolm, as he jumped out of the car.

"Bruce, where are you?" Malcolm shouted.

Hearing the shout, Bruce walked out onto the Veranda.

"What is all this rubbish about you, inviting my kids to live with you in London."

"I only mentioned it to Callum, for future reference. That if he goes to uni. in London."

"Look here mate, Callum is not going anywhere, especially London and that is a fact."

Katie quickly ran up to Malcolm and held his hand.

"Calm down dear, or you will have a heart attack. Now Bruce, we need to talk to you in a civilised manner. Everyone, please take a seat at the table in the kitchen."

Then as everyone took a seat at the kitchen table, Katie continued to have her say.

"When we were shopping today, we talked about your plans Bruce to marry Sarah-Louise. Are you planning to come back here, after you have found your parents?"

"Well, that depends," replied Bruce.

"Depends on what, exactly." said Malcolm.

"Well, I have a job there in London, and I have started a six year part-time degree course as a football manager/coach."

Sarah-Louise, who was trying hard not to burst into tears.

"I thought we were an item again Bruce!"

"We are, aren't we. But what is the rush. Why can't we take our time and just enjoy life together."

Katie explained the way they see the future.

"What Sarah-Louise means is, she thought you were staying here in Queensland. Together from now on. Getting engaged, planning to get married, finding a house, etc."

"I do love you Bruce, and I just want us to be together; always."

"I know that you love me, and I feel the same way about you. However, I need to know where my parents are, and that they are safe and well. Please try to understand my feelings towards my parents, I need to go back."

Sarah-Louise could not hold back her emotions any longer. She began to cry again.

"There, my dear don't cry, come with me onto the veranda."

Katie took Sarah-Louise out onto the veranda. Leaving Malcolm to interrupt the conversation.

"Now let us all stop this madness. Bruce is going back to London later today. Whilst there he will go and try to find his parents. When he has done that. Then we can talk again on the phone, and see if he still wants to come back here, and marry our daughter. Does that make sense to everyone?"

Half an hour later Bruce had packed his suitcase, and Malcolm was driving him to the airport, roughly 4 hours before the flight. Sarah-Louise felt far too emotional and upset to go with them. Therefore, Katie and Callum were going to stay at home with her and have a nice meal together. Bruce gave Sarah-Louise a hug and a kiss as he was leaving.

"I will be waiting here for you Bruce, love you, bye."

However, on the journey to Brisbane airport. Malcolm took the opportunity to speak his mind.

"Now listen to me Bruce. I know you have believed this cock a hoop story, that your parents are in another place called Dreamtime, or whatever it's known by in Derbyshire! However, don't lose heart, if they cannot be found. They will show up sooner or later, because as you first mentioned to us. They have more than likely won the lottery, and gone crazy spending millions on a world tour. That scenario is not unrealistic, now, is it? Katie and I would more than likely do the same thing if we had won a truck load of money. However, please think about what we have said to you. We came here for a new beginning, a new life, together with our kids. If you are serious about marrying our beautiful daughter. Then I ask you now to respect our wishes, that we all stay here in Australia. Cos believe me fella; there is no chance of us giving our blessing to Sarah-Louise. If moving back to England, is the option you are offering to her. I say this in good faith mate. You can come back here, to stay with us. Believe me there are plenty of good job over here, for a smart young chap like yourself. Then you and Sarah-Louise can get engaged, and have a grand engagement party. You can invite your folks to come over here, for the party and for us to get to know them better."

"Ok that sounds like a good plan to me Malcolm."

However, when they arrived at the airport and as Bruce shook Malcolm's hand, and said, "goodbye, see you soon."

Bruce had already begun to think about, his friends back in London. Josh, Toni, Rikki, and Ben. The band of five. Bruce and his buddies, the best mates ever, he thought. Furthermore, he considered that a life in Australia, without his friends; would be unthinkable and unbearable. I cannot leave them, they are my past, my present, and my future. It is Sarah-Louise, who was part of his past life, and maybe she should stay there. In fact, if she really loved him, she would readily move back to London to be with him. Admittedly, she is very beautiful on the eye, and her soft firm figure, was to die for. But on the other hand, maybe not as perfect a body, or as charming a personality as Lynette. Then as for living in Australia. Well, that is a non-starter, they don't even have a Premier League, that is as good as the UK, and what is that Aussie rules game; all about, he wondered?

No, thought Bruce. Australia doesn't seem to have any place in my future life, whatsoever. On that enlighten note, Bruce boarded the London bound flight and relaxed. Sitting there in a window seat, with his mind filled with positive thoughts about finding his parents, and undoubtedly watching the next Arsenal home game with his mates.

Chapter 8

It is an awfully long flight back to London, via Singapore. Bruce had slept about half of the time. However, that still left about 12 hours of trying to make some sensible explanation to what he was told about his missing parents by the Aboriginal leader Yawura. On arrival at Heathrow, Bruce had texted Josh about meeting up with him, and the others for a welcome home drink. The return message was, we are pleased you are back in town, and Toni has a surprise waiting for you. Bruce took the tube back to Tottenham. He arrived back at his flat, in the late afternoon about 4 o'clock. He was totally knackered, so he fell asleep in an armchair. Then at just after 6pm the doorbell rang. At the intercom, Bruce answered, "Hello, who is it."

"It is me Toni, and I have something here for you."

"Come on up." replied Bruce. Presses the button that opens the downstairs front door. Bruce opened his upstairs door, where he noticed Toni coming up the stairs. But she was not alone, he had to look twice, to see it was Lynette.

"I have been looking after someone for you, while you were away."

Bruce was shocked to see Lynette.

"What are you doing here?"

Lynette had then reached the top of the stairs. Whilst rubbing her tummy and smiling at Bruce.

"I have something of yours in here."

Toni responded by giving Bruce a kiss on the cheek.

"You are a very lucky man; indeed, you are, Bruce Knight."

Toni began to go down the stairs.

"Hope to see you chaps later, in the Marquis about nine."

Lyn had her suitcase with her.

"Well, are you surprised to see me, darling."

"No, yes, I mean, just come on in, let me take your case for you."

Closing the flats door, they sat down on the sofa.

"So, when did this happen?"

Bruce was looking at Lyn's tummy.

"I think you did it when I was here last, all that alcohol and rampant sex, should do it."

"No, I mean you went back to Michael, didn't you?"

"Yes, I did, but only to put him straight about us, and to tell him to grow up, and to pull himself together. Then whist I was there, we had a visit from the bishop. He asked me if the marriage was over, and I said yes, it is. The bishop then agreed to offer Michael a new position in Truro, in Cornwall. Seeing that we had officially split. So, I phoned my father. To come and collect me and I came back here. I have been staying with Toni, for the last week and a half. She is a good person, and now a new friend."

"How did you find out, what I mean is, how is our baby doing."

"She or he is fine. I am about 12 weeks pregnant; the baby is due on the 29th of November. I told my father that I think I am pregnant, when he came up to Monyash to collect me. He is so sweet. He wants to meet you soon. He is a retired army, Major; he now lives on his own since mum died 5 years ago. Are you happy about the baby?"

"Yes, I am very pleased, and you look amazing Lyn."

"I don't suppose we could go to bed for an hour could we."

"I think we should, for old times' sake."

After making love, Bruce and Lyn were resting in bed.

"When I was in Australia, I went to an Aboriginal gathering called a Corroboree. At that event I was watching the dancers, as you do. When an Aboriginal man, known as Yawura, came right up to my face, no social distancing, and he said that I had been to the spirit world. What he called Dreamtime. I at first, thought he'd gone nuts, or something like that. But he then explained to me, that there are secret hidden places around the world. That we can visit if we have the right frame of mind. In those places we can not only meet our ancestors and ask them questions, about life and how to find happiness, etc. We can choose to stay there or leave. He then said that the entrance key is either a tree, a rock crevice, a cave or sometimes even through still water, such as a pond. I think in Monyash, it is the big old oak tree in the corner of the garden, that is the key to No Place."

"That is fascinating news, Bruce, and I have got a snippet of news myself. When I was talking to Michael about our life in Monyash, and why I thought our marriage had failed. He then made a comment, that I was going crazy, just like some of the local people up there. Because he had once caught the old deacons, singing and dancing, in the church. He had told them to stop as it was very odd behaviour. They told him, not to mess with things he didn't understand. That they needed to sing and dance in the church regularly, to keep the spiritual access point open."

"We are on to something here, my love. Would you like another cuddle, before we meet the others."

"I think we should by the feel of what you have down their sweetheart, is it by chance a didgeridoo?"

257

"Funny you should think that my dear. It is an instrument of sorts; would you like to play it. My word, you have a strong grip. Oh, good grief," remarked Bruce.

Later in the Marquis of Granby, at around 9 o'clock. The usual group of 5 friends, now becoming 6 of the best. Had gradually assembled around the pool table in the bar.

Josh had recently celebrated being 27 years old. Josh had dedicated at least ten of those years, developing a fine acquirement of eating red hot curries, and drinking ice-cold dry cider. A real trooper, you might say, and a very good friend. Sometimes he could be a bit of a cheeky blighter. But ultimately, with a heart of gold, and always positive, and completely dependable.

Then there is Toni, a very pleasant, and likeable 25-year-old, with the confidence of a lioness. She is or was until just recently. The only female in this group of friends. She is no fool either, very intelligent. She has ambitions to climb the civil service promotional ladder. She can sink a pint of lager, quicker than most other men or woman.

Rikki was the quiet one, and the youngest, just 23 years old. He is a very smart looking young man, very savvy. He lives for his football, a real soccer fanatic. However, he also cherishes his single mum, and his younger twin brothers.

Ben, known as the dark destroyer, on the pool table. Never has there been such an easy-going guy. 26-year-old, six-foot, three-inch, monster of a gentle guy. In fact, only Toni had ever beaten him at playing pool. However, did she really win? Ben insists she won because he is a true gentleman, therefore he let the lady win.

Now there is Lynette or Lyn, as she now prefers to be known. The newest member of the group. Lyn is of slim build, with very attractive, we might say. Photo genic facial features. Her hair is light brown, with blonde highlights, fashioned at shoulder length and with a natural curl. Lyn is 34 years old, extremely intelligent. She is also witty, confident, and knows what she wants out of life. Lyn is determined to seek happiness, after enduring a loveless relationship for the past 7 years.

Josh had ordered the drinks, and he proposed a toast.

"To the baby, if it is a girl, may she be as lovely as her mum, Lyn. If a boy, let him be as good a friend, as Bruce."

"Cheers, to the baby," they all raised their glasses.

Bruce was explaining what had happened to him in Australia, especially when he met with Yawura. The group listened carefully, trying to understand the meaning of this complicated message. Josh initially replied.

"So, you think your parents went into this No Place village, and it is just like the Aboriginal Dreamtime. A place that exists but we normally can't see it!"

Ben was not so sure about this No Place.

"Man, you are dealing with the occult, here. My dad has told me about the medicine man, when he lived in Africa. The medicine man was said to curse people, and they would later die. You need to be very careful when dealing with the spirit world"

Toni was also confused and concerned, she butted in.

"Hang on a minute, let us bring some reality back to the table. Who here in their right mind, thinks that heaven actually exists? Oh, sorry Lyn, I forgot you are a Christian."

Bruce quickly responded to quell the fears.

"OK, let everybody here say their peace. What do you think, about this Dreamtime theory, Rikki."

"Bloody, hell I don't know anything about such stuff. But I do know that if you don't try something, then you will never know."

"Words of wisdom from such a young man," remarked Josh. "If this Aboriginal guy says there is a place where heaven and earth meet. Then I think we should know about it and have a look."

Bruce looked at Lyn and held her hand.

"Should we attempt one last trip to Derbyshire?"

"Yes, I believe we should."

Josh looked at Bruce and remarked.

"Mate, don't you go anywhere, before you buy another round of drinks, sonny Jim."

Bruce brought another round of drinks and as he placed the drinks tray onto the table.

"Are we all up for an adventure to find No Place," he asked.

Josh held up his pint. Then looking at the friends gathered around the table, he proposed.

"To No Place, your place, my place, his place, her place, their place, what place, that place, this place, any place you like. We will go anywhere, with a true friend."

"Cheers everyone, please lift up your glasses. Cheers, to a true friend."

Before finally leaving the bar that evening. Josh commented that the May Bank holiday would be a good time to go on their adventure. Seeing that by then, the football season would have ended, and most of the friends would have that weekend off work. Bruce was to hire a self-drive minibus, for the journey, and everyone would contribute an equal share of the rental cost, and the fuel for the round trip.

After this meeting of the friends.

Bruce and Lyn, settled back into their home routine. back at their flat. Their alarm went off at 6.45am and they made love in bed, before Bruce and Lyn went for a shower together. Then they got dressed and they walked to the local Costa coffee for breakfast. After breakfast Bruce went to get the bus to work, and Lyn would return to the flat. In the evening after work, Bruce would return to the flat. Lyn would be waiting for him. Usually, just wearing one of Bruce's shirts, and nothing much else. They would then make love on the sofa or more than likely go to bed. Then they would shower together, and head out for dinner at the local Wetherspoons. Then possibly meet one of their friends at either the red Lion or The Marquis of Granby.

Finally, on the day of the trip to Derbyshire. Bruce was collecting the hire vehicle. The friends met in the carpark of the Red Lion, at about 11am. Josh and Bruce were to do the driving. Josh was going to drive first, and he will drive to the Watford Gap Services. Apparently, he heard that everyone stops there; even the rich and famous. During the drive, up the M1 motorway. Everyone had to sing a song, to entertain the rest, and they could join in if they wanted to.

Bruce began with, a plucky rendition of. You'll never walk alone, which had a roaring chorus from everyone.

Bruce always the joker told this story.

"Did you know that Yul Brynner, the famous American actor. He supported Liverpool FC, and after he had a shaved his face and head. He never put on aftershave. Yes, Yule never wore cologne."

There was a moment of silence in the minibus, with the customary tumble weed passing through.

Lyn's turn. she sung. In the Summertime, when the weather is high. You can reach right up and touch the sky...

Ben was up next. He gave a resounding rendition of. Dreadlock holiday, and again the chorus was amazing, and with tapping and thumping sound effects.

Josh then gave an almost operatic version of. "It must be love," yes, a real touch of Madness.

Toni then surprised everyone in singing, Puff the Magic Dragon, who lived by the sea in a land called Hona Lee.

Rikki had thought that they needed to end with a classic. So, he gave a very cockney style rendition of. Take me home country road, to the (No Place) where I belong, West Virginia, mountain momma take me home country road.

After the singing had finished, it seemed better to turn the radio on and they listened to, Sounds of the Sixties, with Tony Blackburn. "Nice."

On arriving at Watford Gap services. It was time for a necessary caffeine fix, and everyone was also starving. So, they all had a meal. That ranged from a sausage roll and chips, steak pie and chips, chicken tikka and rice, twice, a jacket potato, cheese and baked beans, fish and chips, and a strawberry and chocolate Sundae with waffle pieces, because Lyn was feeling anxious.

On leaving the Watford Gap. Bruce took over the driving and soon they had left the M1, and they were heading for Bakewell and Monyash. Arriving at Snipe Cottage, at about 4pm. Bruce opened the back door, and as previously he nervously hoped to see mum and dad. However, not at all, the cottage was quite empty. He had mentioned that they would need to get some provisions later as the fridge and cupboards were bare. Then as everyone came inside via front door. After Bruce had opened it.

"Josh you can take my old room, up the stairs first on the left. Toni you can have, my sisters' room, first on the right.

Ben and Rikki, do you mind sleeping on the sofa and the armchair, that sofa over there is really comfy."

Rikki quickly jumped on it.

"It sure is, and its mine."

"Thanks, friend," remarked Ben as he looked at the two remaining armchairs.

"Lyn we are upstairs in dad and mum's room. When we have all unpacked there is a pub in the village called The Bulls Head."

After a quick unpack and a queue at the bathroom door. Everyone made their way to the public bar of, The Bulls Head.

"Hello again, glad to see you back and with friends."

"Yes, it has been a long and thirsty journey, and we have, and we have an appetite too."

"I bet you do. Oh hello, Lynette, nice to see you again. What can I get you?"

"Good evening landlord. Joshua Snow, from Tottenham."

The landlord eagerly shook Josh's hand.

"Can I order, 2 pints of your finest dry cider, 2 pints of lager, a pint of Guinness and a Coke with ice, please Landlord, if you would be so kind."

They also ordered, fish and chips, for six. Followed, by more drinks, and playing darts.
The six friends returned to Snipe Cottage extremely late, and they had just settled down for the night. When there was persistent knocking on the front door.

"Who can this be? It's nearly 12:30."

Being downstairs, Rikki had answered the door. He came running up the stairs, then he knocked on Bruce's door.

"Hay, man it is the cops, for you Bruce."

Bruce put his jeans on, and a polo shirt. He came down to the front door. Waiting at the front door were two police detectives.

"Hello, can I help you," said Bruce.

"Are you Bruce Knight," asked a detective.

"Yes, I am. What do you want at this late hour."

"We are DI Danter, and DS Wooddale. We would like you to accompany us to the Police Station. Where we have questions to ask you regarding your missing parents."

"Have you found them?"

"No Sir, not exactly, but we would like you to come with us, so we can continue our investigation."

"When, now?'

"Yes, now if you don't mind, Sir."

"But I was in bed, can't this wait till the morning!"

"No Sir, we have some particularly important questions that we want to put to you immediately, and this is a good time for us."

Lyn had got dressed; she came downstairs to the front door.

"What, is all this about, officer?"

"We want to take this young man in for questioning."

"Can't this wait till in the morning."

"No, not really madam. Now sir, we would like you to come with us in a voluntary capacity."

"Are you arresting me?"

"No, not if you come with us voluntarily. But if you refuse, we may be back in an hour or so with a warrant for your arrest."

"I will go with them love; it cannot be that important."

"Can I also come with you?"

"No, sorry madam, you may not."

"Do you know who I am?"

"I know who you think you are mam, but that will not affect my judgement."

"Are you coming with us, Sir?"

"Yes, I will come with you."

"Please get me my shoes, love."

Lyn came back with his trainers and a jacket.

"Here, put these on."

"Where are you taking him?"

"Bakewell Police Station."

"We shall follow you there Bruce."

"OK thanks love."

In the police car Bruce had been asked to sit in the back. The detectives got into the front. Nothing was said, during the half hour drive to the police station. Then at the police station, Bruce was led inside, and taken to a room on the first floor.

"Please take a seat in here Mr Knight."

The door was opened, and the light switched on, then closing the door the two police detectives went into the opposite office. The older and more senior officer, Detective Inspector Danter came again into the room where Bruce was now sitting with his head resting on the desk.

"Are you tired, Sir?"

"Yes, I am, we have driven up from London today."

"That is interesting. Why are you up here, Sir? Is it business or pleasure."

"Neither we are here to find my parents."

"Are you indeed. We have our suspicions that your parent's apparent disappearance might not be that straight forward! In fact, we believe that they might have come to some harm."

"Who told you that." quipped Bruce.

"Oh, it is a theory we have, especially when investigating mysterious disappearances like this case. We consider that something untoward might have happened to your parents."

"Your barmy mate, why can't you just find them, by doing some traditional detective investigations." retorted Bruce.

"Indeed, that would be advantageous. However, one of our uniform officers here has a theory, that your parents are in some way involved in an insurance fraud."

"Insurance fraud, what are you talking about, my parents went missing and we intend to find them, very soon."

"Where do you think they are, Mr Knight?"

"Well, they are …. Bruce now hesitated, for a moment. He did not want to say too much about the secret hidden place. They are either on holiday, or they are missing somewhere in the local countryside."

The detective went on to say.

"We have obtained information that your parents were over excessively insured for £200,000 each. Don't you consider that amount of life insurance to be very unusually large. Especially, for pensioners like your parents."

"I really, have no idea maybe they just wanted to look after each other, if one of them passed away."

"Yes, quite so, or if they mysteriously disappeared. Presumed dead. Then you and your sister, would be well off. Plus, their cottage in Monyash; that must be worth roughly £400,000 in today's highly inflated property market."

The detective concluded the conversation at this point and on leaving the room. "Please wait here Sir."

The two detectives had a theory that Mr & Mrs Knight, had been killed by Bruce, whilst they were out walking on the moors. Possibly for their life insurance, a total sum of £400,000. Then their bodies had been buried, or disposed of somehow. This whole cockamamie story, that they had mysteriously disappeared. Was just a subterfuge to throw the police off the truth. There is also an alternative theory that had been proposed by Pc Degg. His conjecture is that this is an insurance fraud. But where Mr & Mrs Knight, had faked their own disappearance and probable death. Involving their son Bruce, and their daughter Denise. Meanwhile the missing parents are now possibly living abroad, maybe in Spain. Waiting for Bruce to convince the police, and others that his parents had mysteriously disappeared, just like Mr & Mrs Leach had done previously.

The two detectives were convinced that something untoward was happening here. Possibly murder for the insurance money, or perhaps that of a family bent on fraud. The two detectives came into the office, where Bruce was still waiting. One detective sat down opposite Bruce, and the more senior detective stood by the door. The detective sergeant spoke first.

"Now then Bruce, we want you to answer a few key questions, regarding the apparent disappearance of your mother and father. Firstly, where do you think your parents are at this moment."

Bruce was thinking what to say, he did not want to mention his thoughts regarding No Place, so he replied.

"I don't really know where they are. Maybe they are on a holiday in America, or they went away, such as a world cruise or something like that."

The detective sergeant replied.

"So, if you think that they are on a world cruise, or something similar. Why do you keep coming to your parents' house, and continue this assumption that they are somehow missing. Are you hiding the truth from us Bruce?"

"I don't know what you mean, I am hiding nothing. I just want to know where they are."

The senior detective who was still standing by the door, then joined the conversation.

"Do you know what I think Bruce. I believe you and your parents are trying to make a false, and fraudulent life insurance claim!"

"What you are mad if you think that."

"Am I indeed. Well, we are not convinced by your pathetic story. You have on record telephoned the police, no less than seven times during the last 6 months. Always claiming that your parents are missing. Yet you continue to visit their home here in Derbyshire. You continue to ask questions locally regarding their apparent whereabouts. We are talking to people about you, and your comings and goings. We are watching you Mr Knight, you are under surveillance."

Then the detective sergeant spoke again.

"There is an alternative theory that our colleague PC Degg has put forward, and he might be on the right track. Regarding you and your so-called missing parents. The constable thinks that when you have made phone calls to him. You are deliberately highlighting the apparent similarity between the missing couple Mr & Mrs Leach. PC Degg continued to give his opinion that you are trying to initiate in our minds a similar copycat scenario, with regards to your parents. Well, are you trying to bamboozle us, into thinking that they too have just miraculously disappeared."

"You two are completely off your rockers!"

The senior detective then spoke.

"I am asking you once more Mr Knight, is there anything that you would like to tell us, about the disappearance of your parents, that you have so far withheld."

"No nothing, absolutely zilch."

The two detectives walked towards the door, and the detective sergeant turned around as they were leaving the room.

"Please wait here Bruce, we shan't keep you much longer."

After another quarter of an hour of just sitting in an office, wanting desperately to leave and get some sleep. The younger of the two police detectives. DS Wooddale opened the office door and spoke.

"We have completed our initial investigation, and you can leave Mr Knight. Thank you for your time, in helping us with our enquiries. We may need to speak to you again at some point, but for now please follow me to the reception area."

Bruce walked into the reception to be greeted by Lyn and Josh.

"Hello, darling, are you alright." Lyn gave him a hug, and a kiss.

"Yes, I am alright now, come on let's get out of here."

Outside of the police station Lyn continued to speak.

"Josh, drove your parent's car here, hope you don't mind."

"No not at all."

"Shall I drive back," asked Josh.

"Yes, if you don't mind. The police think this all an insurance fraud. My parents have faked their death, or even worse. I have killed them and disposed of their bodies, and all for their life insurance, valued at £200,000 each".

"Bloody hell mate are they daft or what. But, on the other hand if you did cash in their insurance, we could all go to the next world cup."

"You are joking, aren't you."

"Maybe I am, but just think about it. £66,000 each split six ways, not a bad amount of money, mate."

"Don't you mean nine of us, if we include Bruce's parents and his sister."

"Yes, sorry, Lyn, so that is £44,000 each."

Bruce was however, not in a happy mood. He snapped back.

"Will you two just stop mucking about. We are going to find my mum and dad tomorrow, and that is a fact. They are not dead and there is no insurance money, OK."

"Ooh, we have got out of bed on the wrong side; haven't we." Remarked Josh.

"I wish, I was in bed, so shut up and let's get home and go to bed."

"Me too Honey bun." relied Lyn.

"Is that all you two think about, sex, sex, and more sex. It is a good job I am here as a steadying influence."

"One more wise crack like that mate, and you will be walking back to Snipe cottage." said Bruce with a smile.

When the group of friends finally woke up the next morning. It was already almost lunchtime. Then it was passed lunchtime, when everyone was finally, washed and dressed.

"What is the plan of action." asked Josh.

Bruce had a plan to walk to No Place.

"Alright everyone, we are going to walk to No Place, it will take just over half an hour."

"What now, what about lunch?" asked Rikki.

Ben eagerly agreed with that sentiment.

"Yeh man, lunch before walking!"

"OK, let's go to the local pub, but only for a quick bite to eat. Not a drinking session."

"Now you are talking, we need sustenance." suggested Toni.

There followed a very eager walk to The Bulls Head. Then after drinking two pints of their normal choice each. Then each consuming the chefs special. Lamb Rogan Josh, with rice, and nan bread. Everyone was ready for a brisk walk in the countryside. Bruce led the way down the road, followed by Lyn, Toni. Josh, Rikki, and with Ben at the rear moaning, are we there yet.

Crossing the fields by following the public footpaths. They arrived at the old house with an even older oak tree in the corner of the garden. Bruce looked back at the dishevelled looking group, and he shouted.

"Come on you lot, last one to No Place, buys the drinks later."

With a great deal of pushing and shoving, and the tendency to grab the person in front, and hold them back. Our intrepid group of 6 friends reached the bend in the dirt track. There was a high hedge, on the lefthand side. With no gaps in the hedge, no finger post, no slope downward, nothing. On the opposite side of the track. There was a sturdy wooden gate. Chained and padlocked, The Dead of Winter Farm.

"Bloody hell. It should be here, right bloody here, opposite that gate!"

"Where is it then?" asked Josh.

Lyn, put her arm around Bruce's shoulder.

"Never mind love, we will find it around here somewhere."

Josh spoke. "Who lives up there in that farm?"

"It is empty, the farmer and his wife are both missing. Hang on though, when I went to the farm before. There was a man there, Insidious Blake and he had two gorgeous women companions."

Josh replied. "What are we waiting for! Why, don't we give this guy a visit, and ask him what he knows about No Place."

Ben eagerly agreed. "Good idea man, come on let's get started." Ben began climbing over the gate.

"Will you be alright getting over there in your condition?" Remarked Toni. "We could wait here."

"Yes, I think I can get over the gate, if you help me too."

Ten minutes later the friends arrived at the farmhouse. But just as before it was quiet, no animals, no people. Bruce rang the doorbell. However, after standing and waiting for what seemed like 5 minutes. Rikki ran at the door, and he kicked it open.

"Come on, let us find this mysterious guy, and get some answers."

Rikki, Bruce, and Josh went inside. Leaving Lyn, Toni, and Ben, to search the outbuildings. Inside the farmhouse there was nothing untoward. The furniture was as before, but there was a thick layer of dust on everything.

"Hello anyone at home." shouted Bruce. But there was no reply.

"We should split up. Rikki, you go that way. Bruce, you go that way, and I will see if there is anyone upstairs."

In less than 5 minutes, everyone was back outside. Nobody had found anything that might suggest that someone lived here.

Lyn spoke to the others as they gathered in the farmyard.

"This farm is empty. There is nothing here and I would say no one has been here in years."

"But love, I was here only six months ago. and there was someone here, and the place was much tidier. Except for the beetle's and other creepy Crawlies all over the stairs."

"What, where, are these bugs and beetles." asked Toni.

"Come on let's head back, there is nothing here." Replied Ben.

Half an hour later arriving back at Snipe cottage, all six were silent; presumably deep in thought about the mornings escapade.

Rikki was the first to utter, his thoughts.

"What actually are we doing here? There is No Place, in this place. We saw with our own eyes. Bruce, you must be mistaken about the entrance to that village."

Ben then piped up.

"Yes, you are crazy man. If you think that there was a lane leading to No Place, opposite that old farm gate. It isn't there, is it? Lanes leading to villages don't just disappear, and reappear; do they? I remember you said once that you and your parents went to a village called, Lathkill dale on a walk. This happened the day before you supposedly went to No Place. Well, I did a bit of research on the internet, and Lathkill dale was a mining area for Galena. Galena is the mineral that contains lead."

"Yes alright, so what are you implying here Ben. That I am in some way, now insane with lead poisoning?"

"No that is not what I meant. But it could explain why you see something that is not really there."

"What, do you really think I'm making this up. Possibly my parents are just wandering aimlessly in the Derbyshire dales in a lead induced trance. Can't you see I just want to know where they are, is that asking too much?"

Josh could see this situation was pointless.

"Ok, you guys calm down. We are all with you Bruce. But there is something peculiar going on here, and it is not easy for any of us to understand. Now I suggest we go to the pub, and relax over a few drinks and a bite to eat."

The friends soon calmed down and enjoyed a usual night out. Ben and Rikki played pool. Josh and Toni played darts. Bruce and Lyn sat it out in the lounge on a comfy sofa. They outwardly tried to put a brave face on a head full of doubts.

"Lyn, do you think that Ben was right."

"No, you are not mad, and neither are your parents. We are all confused about what we have found here, or should I say not found here. However, we will find your parents, darling. I'm very sure of that. Anyway, Bruce we need to find your mum and dad, to tell them that they are going to be grandparents."

Bruce gave Lyn a high five and suggested that they go back to Snipe cottage.

"See you guys later, we are going back to the cottage. Walking back Lyn remarked.

"I hope you are not going to take advantage of me tonight."

"Well, if I do it is purely in the interests of science."

"What do you mean?"

"Well, Ben thinks that the Lead deposits hereabouts, might have affected my brain. Possibly giving me hallucinations. Where, I am now wondering if the Lead, might instead be in my pencil, making it even harder than before. Shall we see if my hypothesis is right."

"I suppose so, if we must."

The two got undressed, and into bed.

"Oh, good grief Bruce, that is harder than a lead pipe. Oh, dear, the things I do for science."

Chapter 9

The next morning all the sleepy heads upstairs in Snipe cottage, rose at around 9 o'clock. Downstairs, both Ben and Rikki. Were dressed and had already packed their bags as the others came down the stairs.

"We are going back to London, today," announced Rikki.

"Why, what is up, can't you stay a few day more?" replied Josh.

Rikki continued to elaborate his and Ben's misgivings.

"Frankly, we feel this search for No Place is pointless. Bruce's parents are more than likely in some far-off place, just enjoying themselves in the sun."

Ben wanted to add his own particular take on this matter.

"Look at the facts, please. We also came here for the Bank Holiday weekend, today is Monday. Rightly we should be heading home. This weekend might not be the outcome Bruce was hoping for! However, we cannot help feeling it's all a wild goose chase, and we don't want any part of it. No hard feelings, mate." Ben looked at Bruce. "But we honestly feel that we must get back to London."

Rikki asked if he could use the house phone, to call a taxi. Within 10 minutes, they were all outside waiting for the cab to arrive. When Bruce asked Josh, Toni, and Lyn.

"Do you three want to leave also?"

Toni gave Bruce a hug and replied.

"No way mate, we are sticking with you."

"Yes, we are, determined to get to the truth." Spoke Josh.

Lyn held Bruce's hand, and gave him a kiss.

"Darling, we do believe you. There is no turning back now, until we find this baby's grandparents."

The taxi arrived; Rikki and Ben gave everyone a hug; before getting into the taxi.

"Bye Ben, bye Rikki." As the cab drove off the 4 remaining friends waved goodbye.

Bruce was now more determined than ever before.

"OK, we need a plan, something we can focus on, don't you agree?"

"Right on, are there any clues to be found here in this cottage, such as a written note or a message on the phone!"

"Good thinking Toni," replied Josh. "The phone, have you checked the answer machine, Bruce?"

"No, come to think of it; I have not!"

Back in the lounge Bruce picked up the house phone, and sure enough there were five messages. Bruce put on the loudspeaker mode.

The first message, was from the doctors, asking if Debbie wanted to visit the surgery nurse for a general check-up.

The second message was from Michael, the vicar. Enquiring if they were alright, because they were very much missed at the Sunday mornings services.

The third message was from Trevor asking if Bob and Debs fancied a drink on any Saturday or Sunday evening. If so, please ring either Trevor or Brenda.

The fourth Message was from a double-glazing firm. Now offering tripe-glazing.

The fifth and last message. "Hello Bruce. This is mum and dad. We have just walked down the dirt track. We are now looking at the sign to No Place. Dad is so happy, and I am in tears. We have reached the little lane that goes down the little hill. You were right. Oh, love we have found it! At this point, the message ended, just as though the mobile signal had somehow failed. Bruce was shocked, he had tears running down his face. Lyn gave him a cuddle, and they sat down in the sofa..

"They bloody found it; did you hear that message. Finally, it confirms where they are."

Lyn took the phone from Bruce, and she played that last message again.

"This message proves that the lane was there, all the time. Even though we had been there only yesterday, and it was not."

"My guess is that there is another dirt track. An identical lane, but further on up the road." Suggested Josh.

Bruce replied shaking his head.

"No, I have already looked further up the road, and there was nothing there; I can assure you."

Toni then spoke.

"Surly Josh is right; we should at least look again. If only to eliminate any possibility of another identical lane. Please Bruce, just to be sure."

Lyn agreed with this logical idea of an alternative explanation, just to keep the peace.

"Come on darling, that idea does seem logical, after all we do need to search out all possibilities."

"Ok, let's see if there is another secret hidden lane. However, I am sure there isn't, but what the heck. I see you all need to check my parents word."

"Don't be so pompous, mate. We are with you all the way here." replied Josh.

After getting their all-weather gear on, for the walk. Boots, thick socks, denim jeans, jumpers, waxed jackets. Typical clothing for a Spring Bank Holiday in late May! The group of friends began the usual trek across the fields. But when they reached the road, and walked up to the house with the big oak tree.

Bruce said, "Hang on a mo., please wait here and I will be right back."

Bruce ran down the dirt track, half hoping to find the way to No Place, just like before. But, alas no lane, no finger post, no way in. Bruce arrived back to greet the others with a

"Sorry, it is not there."

"Come here my love," Lyn gave him a reassuring hug.

"Right, onward. No worries, we shall continue to walk up this road, and maybe there is another lane to explore further on." Explained Josh.

"Yes, come on, let's get a wiggle on," smiled Toni.

The friends walked on for at least another mile and a half, maybe more. But there was no other lane. Josh finally stopped,

"Hold it there, maybe this is the wrong direction. Have you thought of that Bruce!"

"What do you mean, the road in the other direction goes to Lathkill dale." Remarked Bruce.

"Let us go and see, OK. We will go back to the big old oak tree, but then continue to walk down the road in the opposite direction,"

"Believe me it will not be down there. I have walked down that way before, after a half mile you get to the footpath that goes to Lathkill dale."

"How do you know it is not a little further on," speculated Toni.

"I just do. I know it's not further on up this way, and equally it's not further down that way."

Bruce was adamant about this.

However, Lyn interrupted, she was feeling the need to visit a toilet, sooner rather than later.

"Please Bruce, let us go and see if it is there, what have we to lose?"

"Ok, alright, come on, let's waste more time walking the bloody other way. If it makes you all happy."

"You can be a right pain, you know sometimes," said Josh.

Bruce led the way back down the road, and after passing the big old oak tree. Bruce noticed that the finger sign was missing at the beginning of the lane.

"Wait a minute, hang on. There was a wooden sign up there next to the hedge, it read, Public Footpath. Is that a clue!"

"Maybe the signpost has fallen down," remarked Lyn.

"Are you sure it was there, Bruce?" asked Toni.

"Yes, it was here, I remember seeing it on my first visit."

Bruce walked over to where he thought the signpost was before. There was no wooden post, not even a square post hole, where it might have stood.

Josh was getting bored of all this idle speculating; he wanted to find firm evidence of the entrance to No Place.

"Come on let's get back to what we were doing, remember we are going down this road to find another hidden lane in a mile or two."

They continued on their way in this opposite direction. But after a half mile they came to a signpost that read, Lathkill dale.

"I have been here before. I came here on a walk with my parents one day. That style and footpath over there will take us back across the fields to Monyash."

"Ok, we have not found another hidden lane. Therefore, I suggest we go back now via that footpath you just mentioned to Monyash, and a toilet," eagerly recommended Lyn.

"Are you that desperate to go, you could go behind that bush;" suggested Toni.

"No, I'm not desperate enough for that at the moment, but I am getting there."

About twenty minutes later the friends arrived at The Bulls Head. Bruce and Josh went to the bar. Lyn and Toni went to the ladies to spend a penny. When all four friends were sitting around a table in the bar. Bruce spoke first.

"I really thought the entrance to NO Place, was triggered to open, by something in or about, that old house with the big oak tree. But it can't be right, can it?"

"I don't know Bruce, we need help. Surely, someone local knows something about that mysterious village," replied Lyn.

Toni was also feeling down beat and disillusioned.

"I am not sure we are even thinking straight anymore. Why can't we logically except, that your parents have gone on an exceedingly long holiday, after winning a shed full of money."

"Have you lot heard yourselves," pleaded Josh. "The answer is here somewhere, I know it is. We need to speak to someone who is a local."

"Who do you have in mind," inquired Bruce.

"The locals that attend that old church, is my best guess. They are very likely to be part of this whole mystery."

Miraculously, just as if a prayer had been answered. In walked, Noel Lightfoot. Bruce stood up and called to Noel.

"Hello, Noel, could you come and sit with us, please."

Josh got up and offered Noel his chair, and asked, "Can I get you a drink my friend."

"Thank you, a pint, of bitter please."

Finally, with everyone sitting around the table, Bruce spoke.

"We went for a walk today across the moors to the lane next to Bert and Elsie's house. We had hoped that the old oak tree was in some way the guardian of the secret hidden lane. The lane that leads to No Place. But we were wrong, and we just walked about aimlessly up and down the road, and we found nothing."

Noel lifted his pint and took a good sip, then placed the glass back down on a beer mat.

"I can see you know more than you realise. There is a way to gain access to No Place near to where you were today. However, I cannot say more than that in here."

"Can you help us, please?" asked Lyn.

Noel drank the rest of his pint, he stood up and before leaving.

"Please come to the church at 6:30 tonight, but tell no one that you are going there."

Noel thanked Josh for the drink, then walked out of the bar.

"Well, he is a peculiar old chap, if there ever was," said Toni.

"They are all like that up here deary," replied Lyn.

"Meow, Meow." murmured Josh.

"Well, I don't know about you guys, but all this thinking, talking, and walking makes me hungry," announced Bruce. "I'll get the menu off the bar,"

At around 6:15pm, after they all had a short nap over at Snipe cottage. The four intrepid friends began their walk to the church. Waiting in the vestry was Noel, Chris, and Dorothy. Lyn entered the church first, followed by the three others. As Lyn walked forward, she looked at the alter table and said, "father forgive me."

"Hello," said Chris. "Please do come in, we need to close the door behind us."

Dorothy began the conversation.

"We are aware of your quest, what do you want from us."

Bruce replied.

"We know that my parents are in No Place. What we need to know is why we can't find the entrance."

"The pathway is blocked by your negative thoughts." Replied Noel.

"What do you mean, blocked by our negative thoughts?"

"Please, listen carefully to what we have to say to you, before questioning us," replied Chris.

"We three, plus two others are the guardians of the well. The well in No Place was once like many other wells in villages around here, sacred to the local people. It was back in ancient times their only source of fresh clean drinking water.

However, it was rumoured, that an evil spirit got into all the wells locally, and poisoned them. That is how they thought in those ancient times. Actually, the wells became polluted, by people who had the plague. They contaminated the water and the people then abandoned the villages. That was many hundreds of years ago, during the Black Death. It was not uncommon that a whole village would have died out, every man, woman, and child.

 Some locals hereabouts, prayed for forgiveness and salvation. They were offered by the Guardian of the Gate. To go to a secret village where the well was clean and safe to drink from. Can you guess where that secret hidden village might be? The descendants of those people now guarded the entrance to the ancient village. The village was spared from destruction, and it was forever hidden from thereafter. Only those who lived in that village, knew it was there. The name POUTIA was changed to No Place. Presumably, so that if a villager was visiting elsewhere, in Derbyshire. Then someone simply asked where are you from? The reply simply being No Place, could not be more accurate without giving the location away."

There was silence for a moment, then Josh spoke.

"Are you suggesting that the village of No Place, has a mind of its own, and it lets some people in but not others."

"No, not a mind as such, but it detects a spirit of joy and happiness, within a person." replied Chris.

"So, if we go again to look for No Place, are you saying that we must have a clear mind set on happiness. Then and only then, will we find it," asked Lyn.

"Yes, Lyn, you will discover it fully, and experience the peace and tranquillity of that special place." Happily, remarked Dorothy.

Bruce was still confused on how a place, a tree, a house, or anything else can read your mind.

"You mentioned that you three, are guardians and two others. Are you referring to Bert and Elsie Warrilow."

"Yes, I was indeed," answered Chris. "The Warrilow family have been guardians of the entrance since the 16th century, to my knowledge. But that legacy might be coming to an end."

"Why, what has happened," asked Lyn.

"Bert and Elsie have not had a son and their one and only daughter Barbara. Well, the locals here in Monyash think that she is missing and probably absconded with a lover."

"Barbara, no one ever mentioned Barbara to me before. Who was she," asked Bruce.

"She is Mrs Leach, Clive Leach's wife."

"Good grief is she indeed. Now things are beginning to make more sense," said Bruce.

"Blimey, if they are, can you explain it to me." said Toni.

Bruce smiled in response and spoke.

"I sure can. Barbara Leach is the daughter of Bert and Elsie Warrilow. Therefore, she was very aware of the entrance to No Place. Barbara went into No Place, just as I did many months ago. Only she decided one day, not to come back out. Then later, maybe 6 months or more. Her husband Clive. Gave up, or more likely gave in, to the inevitable. So, he sold off the livestock, mothballed the farmhouse, and put a chain and pad lock on the farm gate. Then he followed his wife into No Place, never to return."

"Well done, young man, a particularly good deduction if I might say so." acknowledged Noel.

"So, your mum and dad are in No Place, too."

"Yes, I believe that they absolutely are, Josh. When I took the cab once to Bakewell. It was Clive Leach in the flesh. Who was trying to tell me that very fact, by giving me his business card. With your parents are in No Place, written on the back."

"Michael, once told me, that he had caught you all dancing and singing in the church, late one night."

"Yes, Lyn, we do have such love in our hearts for creation, that it makes us want to dance and sing for joy. Plus, the way to No Place is kept open by us singing and dancing."

"Well, on that subject. I recently went to Australia. Whilst there, I saw that the aborigines also dance and sing. Their spiritual leader, Yawura, explained to me that there is a spirit world beyond our world. They know it as Dreamtime. Yawura, also and respectfully, known as Uncle. Explained to me that the entrances to Dreamtime, are to be found through such things as a crevice in a rock, a cave, or even a tree."

Chris nodded in recognition and answered.

"I am not aware of the aborigine Dreamtime. But there are places where we can visit, that separates us from the here and now. Secret hidden places, that lift our spirit, and give us joy and happiness."

"Can we go there now." inquired Lyn.

"In theory yes, but sadly not at the moment." said Dorothy.

"Why is there a problem." asked Josh.

"You might as well tell them." said Noel.

"Alright," replied Chris. "Something has happened to Bert and Elsie. They are not at their house, and no one in Monyash, has seen them lately."

"Could they have gone into No Place, just like the others!"

"We are not sure, about that Bruce. But it is a possibility. They are the guardians of the gate. Therefore, they should not enter without returning." declared Chris.

"Ok, we will leave you now, and we shall attempt to enter No Place, first thing tomorrow morning." said Bruce.

"We shall pray for you." said Dorothy. "Proverbs: 4.23. Above all else guard your heart for everything you do flows from it."

Noel was opening the church door, so that they could all depart.

"To enter paradise on earth, you must have a pure and joyful heart, together with a clear conscience."

"Thank you, very much. You have all been immensely helpful. Good night and God bless, to you for helping us to understand." Said Lyn.

Returning to The Bulls Head. Then ordering another round of drinks. Bruce, Lyn, Toni, and Josh sat for a while in silence. Again, they had a lot to consider. Bruce was staring down at his feet, when he lifted his head and spoke.

"How the heck, are we going to get into No Place, if we must be pure of heart, joyful, and have a clear conscience?"

"Well darling, you might have a problem there, but I have a beautiful baby to look forward to, I am so happy.

Josh had his own idea regarding happiness and contentment.

"Arsenal will be Premier league champions soon."

Toni thought for a while, before giving her considered opinion on the pathway to joy and happiness.

"Just give me a chocolate cream egg, Mac flurry, and I will have more than a pure and joyful heart."

"Last orders," called the Landlord. "Are you requiring another round before closing?"

"No thank you," replied Lyn. "We need to get a good night's sleep."

"Will you be staying here for the weekend activities!" Enquired the landlord.

"Yes, we are staying for a few more days."

"Marvellous news." replied the Landlord.

"It is our, Grand Village Fate, this coming weekend. There will be the local Morris dancers. Known as, Dancing Fools. They will be performing here live in the car park. On both Saturday and Sunday. Plus, we have a BBQ in the beer garden on both days, weather permitting."

"The village fate sounds very nice. We shall look forward to it." Remarked Bruce.

Arriving back at Snipe cottage. Lyn noticed something different about the white PVC double-glazed front door.

"The door is dirty, look, someone has tried to paint it."

Bruce walked up to the door, then looking closer.

"Let me have a look, bloody hell, its blood. Someone has thrown a bucket of blood at the door and window."

Josh had a close look too, and he remarked.

"This place gives me the creeps, come on let's get inside. We can clean this mess in the morning."

Settling down for the night in their bedroom.

Lyn snuggled up to Bruce all nice and cosy.

"You feel stiff again Bruce."

"Yes, sorry, it's known locally as thrombosis of the middle wicket. It's quite common in these, cold, damp, dark, parts of northern England."

"But it's June, and almost summer. The temperature is quite warm!"

"It might seem warm to you, my love. But feel this sweetheart, is that not frozen solid or what."

"Oh, dear yes, it is rather. Oh, good grief…

After a well-deserved sleep in, our four friends began to get ready for a day of opportunity. Bruce and Lyn came downstairs to find, Josh and Toni standing outside on the front porch. They had washed the front door and window.

"Morning, you randy beggars, we could hear you last night. You need to get a grip on why we are here," said Josh.

Lyn smiled at Josh and confessed.

"I think getting a grip, was the start of our noisiness!"

"Anyway, to change the subject. The blood on the front door and window." Toni was explaining. "There was written in blood, GET OUT. Then as we thought, a bucket of blood was thrown over that."

Bruce replied.

"Yes, as you stated Josh. This place doe's give you the creeps. However, now that we are all up and about. Maybe we should phone our workplaces, to inform them that we need a week's annual leave. To cover this week. I think it is now obvious that we shall remain here until at least Sunday."

"Yes, I suppose we should mate, and you can call the mini-bus hire. To extend the rental for this week also." Suggested Josh.

Their plans were now somewhat altered. They would be staying for the village fate. Hoping, that those who might attend could know something. It was definitely worth a try thought, Bruce. The mere idea of walking back and froe to find No Place, during the next couple of days was not an enviable choice. For Lyn, especially as her feet were aching. So, she suggested they did something else. During the next two days Bruce thought that a trip to Bakewell in the minibus. After all, hey say a change is as good as a rest. Bakewell has shops, where they could buy, coffee, milk, sugar, bread, butter, etc. This would make their stay at Snipe cottage a little more homely and relaxing. After a trip to Bakewell, and an excellent lunchtime session in Wetherspoons. The following day was spent cleaning the cottage from top to bottom. Hoovering, moping, and dusting. Outside windows cleaned, back and front. The bedding was washed and the kitchen and bathroom shined like a new pin. However, every evening was spent at the Bulls Head, eating and drinking, and just having fun.

At 10 o'clock on that Saturday morning, the Bulls Head. Suddenly, burst into live music, with an 8-piece brass band playing in the beer garden. Inside the bar there was a group of Morris men in different stages of dress. Bruce noticed that Noel was in the lounge sitting on a bar stool and reading a newspaper.

"Morning Noel can I get you a pint." asked Bruce.

"No thank you, I already have a tonic water and ice. Today is our big day in Monyash. We sometimes get several hundred visitors today, and even more up to 500 on Sunday."

Toni, Lyn, and Josh, came in from the beer garden. Where they had been listening to the music from the Brass band.

Toni spoke first.

"There are Morris men here with black faces, and roughly the same type of costume that we once saw at the Notting Hill carnival."

"The Dancing fools are a local Morris tradition." replied Noel. "They have blacked faces. Originally, using soot to hide their identity, this tradition goes way back to the 16th century. It was done this way to hide the individuals face from the local priesthood. Who might take offence to a pagan ceremony taking place amongst his congregation. The pub was therefore the Morris dancers natural home base, rather than the local church. Also, the dancers were always paid with ale."

Josh replied. "Did you hear that Bruce, just imagine mate, being paid in ale."

Bruce then reminded the other why they were there.

"Now let's not get carried away with the party atmosphere. We need to go and see Bert and Elsie Warrilow."

"Ok, are we fit to go, let's go then," replied Lyn.

The four friends arrived at the old house with the big oak tree in the corner of the garden. Then after knocking on the front door, and not getting an answer. Josh and Toni went around to the back of the house. Several minutes later they returned.

"Nothing there the place is deserted." said Josh.

"Do you think they could be in Monyash, after all there is a party atmosphere and plenty of things to see and do."

"OK, all right, but we could have a quick look down the dirt track. Just on the off chance that we can get into No Place. But, if not maybe we should mingle in the village, and try to talk to local people there."

As they walked out of the garden gate. Lyn smiled and asked.

"Have you got a happy heart darling. We must be happy, or we will not get in."

Bruce linked arms with Lyn and Toni, and together with a spring in their step, they sang.

"Where off to see the wizard the wonderful wizard of oz." They were all happy, singing and being jolly as they went down the dirt track. Even Josh joined in with a rendition of, Happiness, happiness. The greatest gift that I possess.

But, alas, there was no entrance to No Place on that day.

The walk back was steady, and slow, as Lyn is now experiencing the development of the baby.

"He or she can't get comfortable after I've been walking for more than 30 minutes." Explained Lyn to Toni.

"How far are you now?"

"Roughly 12 or 13 weeks, or just over 3 months."

"Have you always wanted a baby?"

"Yes, I suppose I had, but with Michael it would have been a real difficulty."

"Why was he against having children?"

"No, he was against having sex. We got married and he diligently consummated the marriage on our honeymoon. However, after that he never touched me again!"

"Wow, now that would have been a real problem, if you wanted children."

"Are you seeing anyone, Toni?"

"No not my style, sweetheart. Men are a pain in the butt, sometimes; don't you agree. Anyway, I enjoy my freedom to much. My mum and dad, fought like a cat and dog. But they stayed together for us kids, me and my sister. But that is not a life for me. I leave the fighting to the likes of Tyson Fury. I want peace, prosperity, and pleasure, and generally in that order."

Arriving back in Monyash the four friends went to the church. Firstly, hoping to see Bert and Elsie there. However, the church was empty, except for Chris. He was in the vestry just tidying up. He saw the four coming into the church, through the open door.

"Now that Michael has gone to Truro, in Cornwall. We do not have a vicar anymore. There will be no Sunday service or prayer meetings anymore."

"I am so sorry, Chris, I know you love the Lord and this holy place."

"It is not your fault, Lyn. I am sure we will have another vicar assigned to us in a week or two."

Bruce then spoke.

"We went to see if Bert and Elsie were at home, but they are not. Do you know if they will be at The Bulls Head later?"

"The best solution is to go and see, my friend."

So, there followed a brisk walk along to The Bulls Head. The four friends went directly into the beer garden, found a table and chairs. However, suddenly, Bruce noticed a familiar face within the growing crowd. Bruce walked towards the person, and as the person turned around. Bruce smiled and spoke.

"Hello Betty, would you like to join us for a drink."

"Oh, hello, well I don't want to intrude."

"You're not, so please come and join us."

Bruce led the way over to where Lyn, Toni and Josh, were sitting. This lady is Betty Leach daughter of Clive and Barbara."

"Hello, well I am really Betty Turner, but I am divorced, so I could call myself Betty Leach, I suppose."

"Where is Rachael, is she not with you." asked Bruce.

"She is having half term week with her dad in Stoke."

"Betty, we went to your grandparent's house earlier today, and they were out. Have you seen them lately?"

"No, I called around there also, earlier this morning. Seeing that they were out. I came here, hoping to see them."

Lyn then spoke. "Bruce, look over there to your right, the black faced Morris dancer standing by the gate. He has watched us for the last few minutes; look he is staring at us now."

"Who, Oh him over there, I am sure it is nothing."

Betty suddenly stood up. "Oh, is it that time, I must go and mingle around a bit more, and try to find my grandparents."

"That is, alright Betty," replied Bruce. "We can see you later, if you like."

However, before Betty had given a reply, she had gone. She walked very quickly to, and through the beer garden gate, that led to the carpark. The Morris dancer standing there, by the gate seemed to follow her. Bruce, Lyn, Toni, and Josh had finished their drinks, and they attempted to follow Betty out of the gate. But when they walked through to the carpark, she had gone.

"Where can she have gone too," said Bruce.

However, there was about 150 people milling about outside the pub. Those in the carpark had been waiting for The Dancing Fools. The Morris dancers were almost ready to begin their traditional display. The road outside the pub had several market stall. Where visitors to the fate, could purchase things. Such as, homemade fudge, scented candles, trinkets and other novelties. People arriving in cars, etc. We're being directed to a nearby field to park their vehicle.

"We need to go back to the church, and have another word with Chris, maybe he will know what's going on," explained Bruce.

"Now hold on a moment please Bruce. Can Toni and me, hang on around here whilst you and Josh, go to see Chris. If we see Betty again, we will get her to stay with us, until you two come back."

"Yes, all right, good idea. Come on Josh, let's go and see Chris again, and maybe Betty will be there."

At the church Chris was sweeping the stone floor.

"Hello, you two, what can I do for you now."

"We just had a word with Betty Turner in the beer garden. However, she suddenly got up and was gone, before I could ask if she had ever been to No Place. Also, there was a Morris dancer there in the beer garden. He seemed to be staring at us, and maybe that freaked out Betty and she went elsewhere."

"There is unexpected danger lurking ahead."

"What do you mean by that, can you further explain," asked Josh.

"It is hard for me, in case I say too much, as a Deacon of this church. We are sworn to keep the faith, and to protect the way ahead. Sorry I cannot elaborate more; in fact, I have said too much already. Please go now, and re-join your friends."

"Look Chris, you are not making any sense, whatsoever. Where are Bert and Elsie Warrilow, please tell us, we need to know."

"They have gone away, now please go."

"What do you mean, gone away, gone away where?"

"They have probably gone into No Place, to be safe."

"Safe from what or who, please Chris, come on tell us, what you know."

"Alright, I shall tell you what I know, Bruce. When you entered No Place, several months ago, it was purely by chance, a mistake. I can say that for sure. Bert and Elsie are old people, in their early nineties. They get easily worried about things. They became aware that there was strange happening at their old farm, The Dead of Winter. There had been sightings of strangers up at that farm. The way ahead to

No Place could be compromised and therefore lost, possibly forever."

"I know I met someone there myself, he said his name was Insidious Blake. He was very strange; he gave me the creeps. I was glad to get out of there."

"Well, that might be his modern name, all I know is that he is not like us!"

"Who is not like us, can you be more precise. Chris my friend, you are not making any sense." Replied Josh.

"The entrance to No Place has been compromised, by that stranger, up at the farm."

"OK, I get it Chris. But what did you mean, when you said that I got into No Place by mistake."

"Well, you did, on that occasion a mutual friend. Should have met you and turned you back."

"I think I know what you mean, the stranger, the man in the garden of the first house."

"Yes indeed, that would be my old friend, Clive Leach."

"What on earth are you two talking about." asked Josh.

"I am saying that you are getting closer to understanding the truth behind No Place," remarked Chris.

"What exactly is the truth please explain it to me, my mind is now on overload. I am completely lost to where this conversation is going, and who is the stranger you are talking about. What is all this about the entrance to No Place being compromised." Frantically replied Josh.

"Josh, hold those thoughts you have for a moment longer." Bruce exclaimed. "All will become clear, very soon!"

"Yeh, Clear as mud." said Josh.

Chris reiterated his thoughts.

"The truth is whatever is your heart's desire. Those thoughts that make you happy and joyful. However, your thoughts must be pure and not sinful."

Josh was looking rather dazed; he had never needed to question his thoughts before. He considered his judgements as either black or white. Right or wrong, and definitely no grey areas are allowed in his opinion.

"So, to enter No Place. One, I need to be thinking of my heart's desire. Two, I need a pure and sin free attitude of mind. Three, I need to be genuinely happy and joyful. Well, I wonder if like the lyrics of a very famous song, Two out of three, aren't bad."

"Ok Josh very funny, should we re-join the others now at, The Bulls Head."

Chris asked if he could come along, as his cleaning duties were now done. Therefore, the three gentlemen joined the two ladies in the beer garden. However, also sitting around a table in the beer garden was, Lyn, Toni, Noel and Dorothy.

"Hello everyone, did you find Betty?"

"No Bruce, we have no idea where she is."

Dorothy continued to speak about the difficulties ahead.

"Please be aware that the entrance to No Place, now has no gate keeper, or keeper of the keys. This situation must be rectified immediately, or the entrance could be lost forever."

Chris then intervened.

"Yes, my dear, we are aware of the dire situation. May I propose that you; Dorathy my dearest. Being a cousin of Clive Leach. That you should hence forth become Keeper of the Keys, and Guardian of the Gate. All those in favour say aye."

"Aye" replied Dorathy and Noel. Bruce then asked so where are we going from here?

Dorothy replied with a new confidence.

"When you just asked, where do we think Betty is. Well, I now consider that she has also gone into No Place."

"Yes, she will have gone to her grandparent's house, to see if they were alright." said Chris.

"Do you know why she left in such a hurry, and why there was a Morris dancer watching her and us," Lyn asked Chris.

"We can only speculate on why she left and why the Morris dancer might have followed her. However, I know that there needs to be some changes around here. We were once extraordinarily strong in our purpose. To keep the secret of the hidden place. We feared nothing, but our God in heaven. However, recently we have become weak, and afraid. That there are evil doings all around us."

Bruce was having none of this doom and gloom talk.

"Personally, I thought we are winners, not losers, and what is all this talk of the evil one."

Toni also spoke in a positive tone.

"The evil one, who, Jose Mourinho. Remember, we are Arsenal fans the invincible Football Club. The Gunners."

Josh then appeared from the bar with a tray of drinks for everyone. "Cheers ladies and gentlemen, it's drinkie time, at the village fate."

"Thank you, Josh, what a good man you are," proclaimed Noel. "Cheers, to Josh, a good man." Everyone. Cheered.

The party spirit continued in the beer garden. for the remainder of the afternoon and into the evening. The atmosphere was one of merriment, and good humour. The brass band playing joyful tunes, that many a person joined in with the singing of traditional and popular old songs. There was also a barbeque with a roast hog, and jacket potatoes. Baked in an open wood burning oven. Then in the adjoining car park the Morris dancers' musicians played their harmonious tune on the Penny whistle, Tambourine and Accordion. The eight Morris dancers held wooden sticks. As they danced, there little bells, which are attached to their leggings jingled. The Morris men danced forward and then backward skipping as they go, and at the point where each Morris dancer meets the opposite dancer, they hit their wooden sticks together.

Another ancient activity was a large wooden barrel filled with cold water, that had been placed in the centre of the beer garden. Then roughly 20 apples had been put into the water. This is the ancient game of "The bobbing Apple." Where a person puts their hands behind their back and then they try to grab an apple with their teeth. This game is very popular, or should I say, it was very popular. When fun was just a laugh, a bit of a giggle. Where you inevitably, get very wet, and by the way it is not easy to bite a wet and moving apple. But nevertheless, great fun, was had by all present.

Chapter 10

Early Sunday morning in Monyash, was a very subdued affair, even with The Bulls Head, not opening its doors until midday. That late hour sets the tone for everyone else, even on the village fate weekend spectacular.

Still in bed at 10:45am Lyn asked.

"What shall we call our baby if it is a boy?"

"Lucas is a great name, or Aaron would be just as good!"

"Are they names, from your family?"

"Well, yes, my football family at Arsenal."

"Don't be silly we cannot name our son after a footballer."

"Why the heck not. Alex is also a good name, and so is Danny."

"No way, we are not naming our child after a footballer; not even Stanley as in Matthews."

"Who? Alright, so what name do you have in mind my dear."

"I would like to name him after my father, Sebastian.

"Yes, Seb or Sebby would be cool."

However, if we have a girl then my late mother, had a lovely name, Marigold."

Bruce stared at Lyn in total disbelief.

"What, you are kidding me, we will be hoping for a boy then. Because there is no way, that we want to name our baby daughter after a pair of yellow kitchen gloves," winked Bruce as Lyn hit him with a pillow. Toni knocked on the bedroom door.

"Are you two decent yet, we are going to the pub for something to eat and a drink it's nearly lunch time."

"Ok, see you here," replied Lyn. Lyn then darted from the bedroom into the bathroom. Where she showered and she was cleaning her teeth. When she heard a tapping sound on the bathroom door.

"Is that you, knocking Bruce?"

The reply from behind the door.

"It is not why I'm knocking my dear, but what am I knocking with?"

Lyn opened the bathroom door.

"Oh, I see, does it want something!"

"Why don't you go down there and see what it wants."
"Hello, Mr, stiffy, do you want me to help you!"

"Oh, I do love you, my darling" whispered Bruce.

In the bar of The Bulls Head, Josh and Toni had just enjoyed an all-day brunch. When Bruce and Lyn finally arrived.

"We have already eaten," remarked Josh.

"So, has Lyn," smiled Bruce, just as Lyn slapped him hard on the back.

"What is the plan for today." asked Josh. "Are we going for our usual walk to nowhere."

"You mean No Place, don't you?"

"I know what I mean." replied Josh.

"Ooh, we are touchy today, aren't we, touchy, touchy."

"Well mate after all that talk last night from those three old timers, about the good, the bad, and the ugly. Plus, all that other stuff, it is just a load of bollocks isn't it" exclaimed Josh.

"Please guys, let us keep an open mind, to what is happening around here. As for Chris, Dorathy, and Noel, they can't help being old."

"Yes, let's not think negatively. I suggest we should go along to the old house with the big oak tree, and see if Bert, Elsie, and Betty are there," remarked Bruce.

"Can you manage the walk down there again Lyn," asked Toni.

"Yes, if we take it slow and steady. I'll be fine."

Bruce began to make a comment. "Yes you do like it slow."

"Don't you dare say, one more word Bruce, or I shall alter your Knight, into a Castle without a draw bridge, got it."

"Absolutely, my dear."

Arriving at the old house with the big oak tree in the garden. Bruce knocked on the door. A voice from inside spoke.

"Who is it, what do you want?"

"Hello, is that you Betty, it's me Bruce, and I'm with, Lyn, Josh, and Toni. Can we come in and talk with you, please."

The door was unbolted from within, and Dorothy opened the door.

"Come on in, and take a chair." she uttered.

Sitting down in the living room was Chris and Noel.

"Where is Bert, Elsie, and Betty, why are they not here?"

"No, they are not here Bruce, we came here late last night, and again first thing this morning, but they are not here."

"Do you know or have an idea, where they are."

"No not for certain," exclaimed Dorothy.

Chris stood up, and he walked over to a window.

"Where do we suppose, they have gone. Might you ask! Then to answer your question, we think you should seek the answer at the Dead of Winter farm."

"Why would they go there," inquired Bruce.

"I don't think they had much choice in the matter. They needed to know, who or what is happening at their old farm. Betty knows the truth now about her mother and father, and she will want answers, just like you do."

Noel then spoke. "The truth is that Clive and Barbara, abandoned their farm more than 6 years ago. From there they went to live in No Place. We know this because, Clive has returned here several times over the past years. Probably through curiosity and possibly to check on Betty, Bert and Elsie. Deep down Clive and Barbara knew that it was not their turn to go to No Place. It is Bert and Elsie, who should have entered there to live; if anyone should have."

"What do we need to do now." asked Bruce.

"You do not need to do anything." replied Noel. "However, if you want to help us, you need to go to the Dead of Winter Farm. There you need to confront who or what, is there."

"Why don't we call the police," asked Toni

"This is not an earthly problem, my friends. The police would find nothing there, but an empty and abandoned farm."

Dorathy then continued to speak about the farm.

"We need to know who or what, we are up against. Is someone trying to get into No Place or are they trying to stop us from going there; ever again. We can also tell you this house, or to be more precise the old tree in the garden. Is the key to the entrance gate, to a secret hidden place. The Keeper of the Keys, and the Guardian of the Gate; must live in this old house. Only the keeper of the keys and guardian of the gate, should enter and return from the way ahead. The sole purpose of this ancient position is to be resident in this house and to protect and conserve that old tree."

Noel then spoke about the problem up at the farm.

"There are dark forces that want to close this gateway permanently, thereby closing that way ahead forever."

Josh remarked with some sense of ore.

"Are you saying that there are loads of these gateways all around the world?"

"Well, yes, of course, they are everywhere around the world. In far off Australia, as Bruce has explained about Dreamtime. Then there is Shangri-La, rumoured to be in Tibet. Xanadu possibly in China. Asgard in Norway. Panchaia, a magic island in the Arabian Gulf. These are just to mention a few. Secret hidden places."

 Lyn then thought about, what they needed to do.

"Who is up at the farm, do you know?"

"He is not a person as such, but he looks and acts like a man. When he wants to, he can be charming, polite and has unquestionable logic. He does nothing notably wrong, but he is extremely devious. He will try to befriend you, and encourage you to stay with him. He is highly intelligent, and he understands everything here on earth. So, beware he is very treacherous."

"He sounds just like Insidious Blake to me," remarked Bruce.

"He is known by many names. The ancient people of Derbyshire knew him as MOROG the deceiver. But do not underestimate him. He might seem genuinely nice to you. But basically, he is pure evil; a demon." insisted Chris.

Bruce walked over to the front door, then turning around he spoke.

"I must go now to the farm, will you my friends come with me?"

Lyn got up from her chair and replied.

"I am with you my darling, forever."

Josh smiled at Bruce and earnestly spoke.

"A mate in need, is a true mate indeed."

"You can count me in too. I am up for it, yes to right I am." Remarked Toni.

"Be careful, please don't underestimate the danger you might face at the farm, do take care." said Dorothy.

Josh gently pushed aside, Toni, Lyn, and then Bruce. Until Josh was stranding by the door and then opening the door.

"Right come on, let's go. I can't stay in this place any longer. I am getting severe Gregg's withdrawal symptoms. I need a steak bake, urgently. If this Insidious Blake bloke, is all that's standing between me and that slice of steak bake. Then he's done for, he has met his match; got it!"

The four friends soon arrived at the Dead of Winter farm gate. Climbing over was a bit of a problem for Lyn. But, with Toni pulling and Bruce pushing all was well in the end. At the farmhouse, Bruce rang the doorbell. Josh kicked the door, as Rikki had done. The door swung open.

"Come on," rallied Josh. "Let's get this over and done with."

All four descended the stairs into the large living room. Where now everything had gone, there was no furniture, just lots of dust.

"This room was where I was with Insidious Blake, about 7 months ago."

"Well mate, no one has been here for a while, I would say. Anyway, now we are here let's look around the place."

However, all the rooms were empty, both downstairs and upstairs. There was no visible indication of anyone being there for quite a while.

"Come on, this is hopeless we need to get out of here. We must not lose track of why we are here."

Bruce then ran up the stairs expecting to reach the front door. However, there was no front door. Just a large wooden barn door. Bruce pushed the barn door open. But just as before he was instead a wooden barn, and not outside in the farmyard.

Bruce was amazed at this coincidence.

"This happened to me before; it is so strange. I had to climb up there. To escape through a small opening. Right up there."

Bruce pointed to roughly where the small door was situated, roughly about 4 metres up.

"I cannot get up there in my condition."

"Don't worry yourself. Josh will get us out of here." Replied Toni.

"However, there came a sound from outside of the barn. The jingle of little bells. Then a harmonious little tune, played on a penny whistle, and a rhythm tapped on a kettle drum.

A song then followed.

"Morris men, Morris men, bade you al well today. Morris men, Morris men, be this day sweetly divine. Morris men, Morris men, make our water taste of the vine."

Running up to the timber barn door, our four friends peeked through the wooden slats. They could now see Morris dancers, about 10 of them all dressed up in black and white outfits. All with painted black faces. The Morris dancers continued to sing, dance, and play their merry little tune.

"Oh, what shall we do with an unruly knave. Why not put him in the grave. How should we kill this mischievous fellow. Maybe with a trusty bow and arrow. Oh, why waste a precious arrow. Let us cut his throat and gloat. Hurray, Hurray, Hurray. He is dead and we are jolly. We shall dance and sing to that. Raise your glasses cause life is merry with a glass of cider perry."

Then from behind the Morris dancers there appeared a small ball of dark grey smoke. The ball of swirling smoke, not more than the size of a tennis ball. Then the ball of smoke grew bigger until it was the size of a football. The Morris dances stopped to watch the increasing ball of smoke. Gradually the ball of smoke grew to a very large smoky spinning ball. Roughly about 2 metres wide and high. Then as the smoke began to drift away. The clear human shape of a tall black creature, with bat like wings. Stood upright and motionless.

Suddenly, all the Morris dancers cheered, aloud.

"Ancient one, ancient one., ancient one!"

The creature opened its eyes and spoke loudly.

"Suspicious of the truth, are you Bruce Knight. You seek a tree to give you entrance, to a place where you cannot die. But your quest has already failed; you shall not enter there. Good Morris men of the hills and dales. Go forth now, quickly mind you, and destroy the sacred old tree.

I command your loyalty to do as I bid."

The Morris dancers were bowing, in adoration to this sinister dark demon creature Morog.

"Go now, do not dally, go" …

The Morris dancers ran eagerly towards the distant farm gate. The tall dark creature walked forward right up to the barn door. The grey smoke began to swirl around the creature. The thicker and darker the smoke got, the creature within disappeared. The smoke then began to enter through the slits and cracks of the barn door, just in front of the four friends who coughed and choked on think smoke. With hands covering their mouth they moved back towards the centre of the barn.

The ball of smoke began to form again. This time on the floor of the barn. As the ball of smoke became bigger, the black bat winged creature again stood silently. When the smoke cleared away, the creature opened its eyes.

"You have a baby boy I see, congratulations."

"What, how can you see inside someone?" said Bruce.

"I can see through to the baby, and it is a fine, healthy boy."

"Why are you here, and what do you want from us?"

"I am not your enemy, Bruce Knight. I am trying to protect you from something terrible happening to you."

"What, that's a laugh. You're trying to protect us. We know who you are, you are a demon tormentor, from hell."

327

"If you do know who I am, Lynette Chandler. You know that I could kill you all if I wanted to. However, I am your friend, and I want to help you, and save you from making a terrible mistake!"

"Bullshit, what have you done with Bert, Elsie, and Betty."

Demanded Bruce.

"They wanted to go to that other place. I begged them not too. I got down on my knees, and begged them not to go. But they would not listen to reason. They are foolish people, and they have gone away possibly forever, but I swear I didn't harm them."

"You are a liar," spoke Lyn. "A deceiver, you are evil and not to be trusted. You only speak what is false. You have murdered them, haven't you.

"Be careful in what you say. If you judge me, then I could ask to judge you."

Lyn stepped forward towards the enemy.

"We shall not be outwitted by you, demon. We have already conquered you, by the blood of the lamb. Lead us not into temptation, and deliver us from this evil. Amen."

Lyn then began to walk towards the creature. Holding out the crucifix she wore on a chain around her neck.

"We are not afraid of you; you are already defeated. Go now whilst you still can, or we shall destroy you."

Bruce was impressed by Lyn's boldness in the face of adversity. He began to walk forward, and also, he asked.

"Are you the skeleton face that came up out of the floor, and those hounds, that appeared from nowhere?"

The creatures' eyes turned bright red, as it glared at Bruce.

"You are all going to die, leave here now, while you still can; you fools go back to London!"

"Maybe your right, we are going to die, but not today."

Lyn stood within a metre of the creature's body. Still holding her crucifix. Finally, she pushed it almost to touch the creatures face. Confidently she spoke directly to the demon.

"You shall not put the Lord, our God to the test."

The creature suddenly was gone, without a further remark or a glare from its piercing eyes. Bruce clicked his fingers in joy.

"OK, come on we need to get out of here, and fast."

Josh began to climb up the frame of the wooden barn door.

"Up that way Josh, more over there towards the middle. Hold onto the barn door frame as you climb up. That's it mate, there is a little door just above you now, right there."

Bruce pointed and Josh punched the smaller door, and it flung open. There was a resounding cheer and hand clapping, for Josh as he climbed out, and he was soon on the ground outside.

"There is a pad lock on the door." remarked Josh.

"Go and find something to smash it with, and hurry."

Bruce, Lyn, and Toni, were looking through the wooden slats, wondering where Josh had gone.

"Can you see him yet, Toni?"

"No, he went down that way towards the other outbuildings." replied Toni.

Then after another 2 minutes had gone by, there was a dull sound from outside the barn. Chug, chug, chug, bang, bang, bang. The spluttering sound of an old diesel engine trying to start. Then suddenly, the engine roared into the distinctive sound of a very old tractor engine.

Toni smiled and spoke.

"Oh blimey, he has only got a tractor. Stand back quickly."

Toni shouted, as the tractor sped up the farmyard. Then rammed the barn door open, literally smashing it into many pieces.

"It is an old Massy Ferguson." said Josh smiling from ear to ear. "Not bad Eh, what a motor. I wonder if I can keep it."

"Come on Josh, get off that tractor. We need to go back to the old house, pretty dam quick."

The four friends quickly walked along to the farm gate. Then after another agonising session of pushing and pulling Lyn over the gate. The four eagerly, but cautiously, approached the old house. Where they noticed that the old oak tree was completely cut down. There were pieces of the once mighty oak tree strewn all about the garden, and on the nearby road. Chris, Dorothy, and Noel were standing by the stump of the once mighty oak tree. Bruce walked slowly over the fallen branches, leaves, and twigs.

When Noel remarked.

"What a bloody mess this is. Those crazy Morris dancers came here. Ten of them, with a chain saw, several axes, and bow saws. We watched them through the window. Within half an hour they had completely destroyed a wonderful old oak tree, that must have stood here for at least 250 years, if not longer."

"Vandals." insisted Dorothy. "Whatever possessed them to do such a thing."

Toni then muttered.

"The dark creature, up at the farm, it told them to cut down the sacred tree in the garden."

There was a moment or two of silence.

Then after some consideration Chris spoke.

"The sacred tree, in the garden!"

Bruce was visibly confused.

"Why, yes. The dark creature told them Morris Dancers. To go and cut down, and destroy the sacred tree in the garden."

"Well, no wonder they are called Dancing Fools." said Noel.

"Why, what do you mean!" Enquired Bruce. "Surely, that old oak tree, is the entrance to No Place; isn't it?"

"Poppy cock." replied Dorothy. "This is Yew Tree Cottage, it is the Yew tree over there by the gate, that is the sacred tree."

 There was a general feeling of relief amongst the four friends, as they turned around to look at the somewhat smaller Yew tree.

Dorathy continued to explain.

"That little Yew tree over there is more than a thousand years old you know. Half buried, as it is, in that old hedge line; of other small trees. Size is not everything, apparently."

Bruce was just about to make a derogatory comment regarding something Lyn had mentioned earlier. When Lyn quickly interrupted Bruce's thought pattern.

"Don't you dare mention anything about size being important, Bruce Knight; or you might also get the chop."

"So, it is the Yew tree that is the secret entrance." said Josh.

"Yes, it is, and all is now well here. Thanks to you four intrepid individuals. Not forgetting those foolish Morris Dancers. Who have unintentionally given us enough logs to burn on our fire, for the next 20 years." Cheerfully remarked Chris.

Lyn then spoke softly.

"The dark creature told us that Bert, Elsie, and Betty are dead."

Chris cheerfully smiled and replied.

"More like, dead tired. They went off to Blackpool, for a short break away from all this hullabaloo."

"What, when did this happen?" Enquired Bruce.

"Yesterday afternoon, when Clive Leach returned here. He blackened his face, and put on a Morris Dancers costume. So, no one would recognise him at the village fate. He got those three together, and sent them off by taxi for a well-deserved holiday at the seaside."

"Where is Clive Leach now." asked Bruce.

"He went back to No Place to be with Barbara his wife. He is probably now waiting for you." replied Dorothy.

"You mean the entrance to No Place, is now open!" answered Bruce.

"Yes, it should be, why don't you go back up the lane and have a look." suggested Dorothy.

The four friends walked out of the garden gate, and as they walked slowly down the dirt track towards the Dead of Winter farm gate. They were filled with trepidation. Then there it was, the small dirt track with its metal finger post pointing to No Place. Where just 30 minutes earlier there had been a tall dense hedge. However, now as it was once before, Bruce looked astonished. He smiled as he recognised the small track, that lead down a slight incline. Bruce was so happy to see the open way ahead, he grabbed hold of Lyn's hand, and they ran part way down the track to the little bridge. Then as Josh and Toni, caught up, they all walked over the small bridge that covered a babbling brook.

Bruce was ecstatic and trembling with excitement.

"I am so happy to have found this track again."

He held Lyn's hand tightly, as they walked onward up a little incline, through a small, wooded area.

"Come on Josh, Toni, keep up."

Bruce was so excited, his heart was racing. He was running on pure adrenaline. Then ahead there was the stone wall to the left, together with an old-style gas streetlight.

"We are here, at long last. We are in No Place."

Lyn gave Bruce a kiss and a hug.

"I knew you would find your way here again, after all it is your heart's desire."

"Look, there is the wishing well, over there. With its dusty little sign above, look! POUTIA Wishing Well."

Then a voice came from a garden on the left-hand side of the road.

"Hello, stranger. I am pleased to see you here again."

Bruce instantly recognised the man's voice. Bruce walked over to the man who was now standing behind a small garden gate.

"Well, Clive Leach. I am so pleased to finally meet you and shake your hand."

"Bless you my friend, you have had a real adventure to get back here."

"Yes, I have. Can I introduce you to Lyn, Toni, and Josh."

"Good afternoon to you all, and may I welcome you to our home. The village called No Place."

"Are my parents here?"

"Yes, they are, just continue to walk along this road till you come to the village green. They will meet you there."

"I need to know, was it you that gave me the business card in the taxi?"

"Yes, it was Bruce. I wanted to let you know that your parents were here, and they are safe and well."

The four friends then continued walking along the road. Passing the blacksmith, then the chapel. Pausing, at the little shop, where a lady was standing by the door waving her hand.

"Hello, my name is Barbara Leach, it's so nice to see you again Bruce." Bruce waved back. "Pleased to see you again too, Barbara."

As they walked past the old garage. They noticed that there were two people walking towards them from across the village green. Bruce blurted out in a tearful shout.

"That's my mum and dad,"

With his eyes full of tears that ran down his face, he ran as fast as he could towards his parents. The three were soon hugging each other. Debbie and Robert were crying with the gladness of seeing their son again. After a period of being apart, with no means of other communication for almost ten months.

"Where have you two been for the last 10 months?"

His dad offered him his handkerchief out of his trouser pocket.

"We have been here son waiting for you to return."

Debbie used the handkerchief to wipe the tears off Bruce's face.

"Why don't you answer your phones?"

"They don't work here, darling."

"Then why didn't you go back home to Snipe Cottage?"

"Sorry son, but we were too frightened to leave here, just in case we couldn't find it again. It is such a beautiful place.

After all, how often can you find heaven on earth before judgement day," answered Bob.

The other three had joined Bruce and his parents on the village green.

"Hello, my name is Lyn, do you remember me from the church. I am now Bruce's girlfriend, partner."

"Oh, mum, dad, we are having a baby."

"You are, we are delighted for you, aren't we Robert."

"Yes dear, it is about time you settled down, my lad."

"Hang on a moment. I have a few more important questions to ask you two, before we take about me settling down. Firstly, why have you two stayed here all this time, you must have guessed that I would have been going crazy. Thinking that I had lost you two. I have been worried sick, people have said, you had won the lottery, and gone off on a world cruise. Then the local police have questioned me over your apparent disappearance, and a possible life insurance fraud."

"Now then, dear, never mind. We are here now all together in our idea of paradise, aren't we Bob."

"Yes, we love it here, it is so calm and peaceful. Anyway, that is enough, please come with us to our new house."

"What, you have a house here too."

"We do my dear and its lovely," replied mum.

"Oh mum, dad, these are my friends from London, Josh, and Toni."

"Pleased to meet you, do come along to our home for a nice cosy chat," said Debbie.

Then as Debbie and Robert led the way across the village green, the four friends noticed that the green was surrounded by at least two dozen houses. All in different styles. There were several traditional black and white, Tudor style thatched cottages on the left-hand side of the village green. Then twice as many stone-built houses with slate roofs, and picture postcard size Georgen style windows, on the right-side of the green. These stone-built houses had either a red or white rose climbing up and over the front door. There was even an old English tearoom, with a thatched roof and a glorious wisteria hanging down from the first-floor window level. There was an A board outside the cafe door that had written on it. (Paradise found café. Whilst waiting for a prayer to be answered, why not try a refreshing cup of tea.)

"That is our home, over there, the one with the dark green gate, Laburnum house."

"Mum, why have you got two houses, this one and Snipe Cottage."

"We must be lucky, I suppose!"

Opening the gate and then putting the key in the door. Debbie stopped and politely asked if they would like to come in.

"Please come on into our humble abode and I shall put the kettle on. Let's have a chat over a cup of tea or coffee, and a slice of my home-made chocolate cake."

With everyone seated comfortably in the lounge. Bruce began the conversation with Lyn and his good news.

"We are having a baby boy, apparently and we would like to name him Sebastion Robert."

Debbie replied. "They are lovely names, when is the baby due?"

Lyn replied, "29th of November."

Bruce asked, "Will you visit us after the birth in London."

Debbie was unsure of how to respond, she considered that leaving here was not easy. How do we explain to friends. Who ask where do you live. She began with a few facts.

"Let me explain to you. Your father and I have found paradise on earth. It is real, much more real than anything we have ever known before, and we are happier than we have ever been." "

The truth is Bruce" interrupted Robert. "There is nothing that your mum and I want in life, except to live our life here." Robert continued, "if we lost this new life, then life would not be worth living. That is how we feel. I apologise for being so frank, but we mean every word."

Debbie added. "We will miss you, and Denise, and we understand that you two, must live your life in the way that you want to."

Lyn was inspired by their honesty. "Is it really that special here, that you are willing to forsake everything else. Are you really planning to stay here now and forever?"

Robert replied. "I can honesty testify, there is nothing, in comparison to the feeling of love and happiness we get from being here. The world out there offers us nothing but a ritual of working for material possessions, spending all your hard-earned cash to buy or rent the house, that you will never really own."

Robert continued. "What I mean to say is when you die, you cannot take anything that you worked so hard for with you. The car, the furniture, or any other monetary goods. Don't you see it is all for nothing."

Debbie suggested. "Why don't you and Lyn and the baby, stay here in No Place with us, you can if you want."

Bruce and Lyn almost answered simultaneously "No, not now." Lyn continued. "We have plans and need to see my father and other stuff."

Debbie answered with a smile. "Of course you do, we understand there is no hurry. After all true happiness is being with the one you love, and that deep happiness cannot be bought or sold."

Toni decided to add to the conversation.

"Well, speaking personally, to me happiness is the result of what people do. They earn money to buy things that they need. Some people get happiness from playing a sport, or by watching their favourite team. Some people like music it makes them dance the night away."

"I am not so sure that stuff gives us lasting happiness. Most of the people I knew on the outside were constantly looking for some form of quick fix, to give them a temporary happiness. Such as their lifestyle choices, and their little special treats. Like a holiday in an exotic place for two weeks every year. But really, I wonder how many people do find true happiness, even when they apparently have everything money can buy."

Bruce had listened to his dad's opinions. But there was, he thought something missing.

"I thought you both said previously, that your family was more important to you than anything else. That we would regularly see each other. Spend quality time together. What has happened to those sentiments."

"Yes Bruce, of course, we want to see you, but you are doing your own thing now. Living in London, working there, studying there, and now you have a girlfriend and a baby on the way. Please try to see our point of view. We still love you and your sister. We always will. However, we also love it here, we are happy, and we want to stay here forever."

Toni had an idea. "Excuse me for asking, but is this paradise place just for old people. I don't mean to be rude, but this is not my idea of paradise on earth."

Robert replied. "Point taken, this is only one of a multitude of paradises hidden here on earth. Each one is a heart's desire and will become that person's reality."

"Wonderful," replied Toni. "How do we get to those other paradises from here?"

"You just continue walking through this version of our paradise, my dear, and onto the next, and the next, until you find your heart's desire. Especially, if you don't feel contented here, because this is not your idea of paradise, you will feel more at peace with yourself as you get closer to your own personal place of happiness."

Josh then spoke about his previous thoughts regarding what makes a physical place a paradise.

"I once knew real happiness when I was a boy. My parents went every year to West Mersey, in Essex. We stayed with my auntie Maud; she had a little cottage by the seaside. It was so peaceful and quiet there. Every day of the weeklong holiday was tranquil and calming. Nothing at all like Hatfield where I grew up."

"Mum, dad, will you ever come back to the real world, with us?"

"Who, says this is not real," insisted Debbie. "Please Bruce, be happy for us, we are happy for you, and Lyn, and the baby."

Then Robert had a suggestion.

"Snipe Cottage is yours to live in, if you want to, or to stay in at any time. Especially, when you want to come and visit us, and the same goes for Denise. Otherwise, you could sell Snipe Cottage; and split the proceeds with your sister."

"It is not going to be the same out there without you two."

"You will be fine son, and you now have Lyn to love, and a baby coming soon. I expect you will hardly miss us at all, when you get back to London. We have found real freedom here. We don't ever feel threatened, we have no money worries, in fact we don't need much money at all. You just give what you have, or work for something you need. We have no illness here, and we feel physically fit all the time. We don't worry about anything, and everyone here is so kind and thoughtful. Paradise is here on earth; in fact, you are never more than 3 feet away from your own personal paradise. But sadly, most people out there will never find it, because they are simply looking for happiness in all the wrong places." Robert thought he explained that rather well.

Debbie then asked if anyone would like another cup of tea or coffee and another slice of chocolate cake."

While Debbie went to the kitchen to put the kettle on Robert continued to say.

"Usually, people out there in the world are seeking only material things. They want to own nice things that make them feel happy. But this material gratification is only ever temporary, and the desire to own new and better objects can never be satisfied. Where happiness here is permanent. Out there in the Towns and Cities, there is too much noise, and everyone is far too busy rushing around. Our thoughts are that people never really get a chance to take stock of their lives, once they are on the treadmill, of education and work. Their life becomes an obsession of meeting external demands, and there is little or no time to listen to that quiet inner voice that is saying, surely there is more to life than this? Then they delude themselves by choosing to relax on their days off in a shopping centre, or a leisure centre. Which are full of other people, all far too busy to rest and be still for even a minute. How do they ever hope to find true happiness. I really don't think they ever will!"

"But dad, that is what people do on their day off, they go to places, to have fun and meet friends."

"We know son, but it is all an illusion, a deception, they are all just going around and around in never ending circles of routine drudgery. Where real joy and peace comes only from experiencing a quiet place. Time spent there in those peaceful places, on your own or with the ones you love, is a wonderful experience. The feelings of happiness gained there, will last in you, and them forever."

"I do understand what you are saying, dad. That happiness is only temporary, and maybe just a day or two in a whole year. But I still feel a need to go back to London and to get on with my life."

"That is only natural my dear," replied Debbie as she carried in a tray of drinks and slices of chocolate cake.

"Life is for living, and we have chosen here, and you need to do what is best for you and your new family."

"I never knew you felt that way, mum."

"Neither did we, till we came here. Revelation is something that happens to you personally. At first it is hidden from you, it is only experienced occasionally, or seen obscurely. Possibly as a child, you had an imaginary thought. Maybe of a beautiful garden, or a wonderful holiday location that made you feel very happy and contented. Then maybe one day, many years later as an adult. You came across a secret hidden place. That you previously knew nothing about, and therefore, it did not exist. However, it does exist, and every sense you possess, is telling you that it is real, it is true. It is so infallibly true."

Bruce was not feeling enlightened rather he felt disheartened. "So, what is the point of life, if it is not to make you happy?"

Robert replied. "The point is son; can we ever be materialistically happy in a world which we consider is a counterfeit reality. Real peace and happiness don't cost you anything, just your time. Being contented with what you have. Heaven is here on earth and sometimes it is right next to you and yet you can miss it completely; because life is full of distractions."

The next morning, following a good night's sleep the four friends were having breakfast with Robert and Debbie.

"We must head back today. There are things we need to do back in London. Like return a mini-bus and work will be wondering where I am. Lyn needs to register with a doctor."

"We understand Bruce, you have a life to live back in London. We will see you again soon, definitely when the baby is born."

Toni had an announcement. "Bruce, Lyn, we are staying here to, if that is all right with you guys."

"What, you want to stay here, in No Place!"

"No, not quite here, we want to move on a bit and see if our hearts desire is out there somewhere."

"What are you two an item now." Enquired Lyn.

Josh held Toni's hand and kissed her on the lips.

"Yes, we are. I love her."

Bruce was shocked. "But what about Arsenal, The Marquis, The Red Lion, Costa, and Greggs."

Josh shrugged his shoulders. "We grew up mate. Well, what I mean. Is I have grown up, since we came here with you to Derbyshire. I want to be with Toni; she makes me happy."

Toni gave Josh a hug and a kiss.

"We are going to look just along the road a bit. Where we might come across a beautiful sun kissed, golden sandy tropical beach, surrounded by a warm clear blue sea, that is our idea of paradise."

"We shall miss you." Lyn gave Toni a hug.

"We will be back one day soon, and you can buy us a celebration drink." Josh smiled.

"Goodbye mum, dad, give me a hug. We must be going too."

"Take good care of Lyn and the baby, and most of all be happy together." Replied Debbie as she wiped away her tears.

"Love you too, see you soon, have a safe journey home." Robert smiled and gave Debbie a loving hug.

The two couples, Bruce and Lyn. Josh and Toni were now walking across the village green. At about halfway across. They stopped, hugged each other. Josh spoke first.

"Bye my friend, look after yourselves, until we meet again." Josh then gave Bruce a mighty man hug. Toni then gave Bruce a big hug, then switched to hug Lyn. "I will miss you both, love you, be happy together."

Bruce's eyes were welling up again as he spoke.

"Good luck on your adventure. Don't forget to look us up, when you guys get back. Remember we will have baby Sebastian in roughly 5 months. We would like you two to be his god parents."

"Take it as a certainty, mate," smiled Toni.

"Come on Toni, we have an adventure in paradise waiting ahead of us." Josh and Toni walked away holding hands, their hearts full of love and hope.

Bruce and Lyn also walked arm in arm, onto the road beyond the village green. They walked past the old garage, then past the little shop. Their pace became a little quicker, as they went past the old chapel, and the blacksmiths. Finally, reaching the old POUTIA wishing well.

"I shall miss this place, Lyn. It will always be a very special to me."

"I know it will honey bun. It's where your mum and dad live. Anyway, come on let's go home now sweety pie. We have plans to make for a new life together. You, me, and baby Sebastian."

"Where is home nowadays, Tottenham?"

"Yes, dear, that is our home for now. By the way it is an anagram, did you realise!"

Bruce gave Lyn one of those looks with narrowed eyes.

"What is an anagram?"

Lyn smiled at Bruce, "The name on the wishing well, POUTIA, of course."

"Never, whatever makes you think that, are you sure?"

To which Lyn replied, with a cheeky smile, as she smacked him on his bottom.

"You know. I sometimes wonder about you, Bruce Knight."

The End

Epilogue:

As a young man of 15 years of age. The author of this novel sadly lost his mother to cancer. To add to this tragic loss his father abandoned him. David then found a room to rent, and fortunately he still had his maternal grandparents that lived nearby.

He began work in a warehouse of a local pottery factory, as a labourer. This employment gave him an income and a reason to get up in the morning. He went to his grandparent's house on a Friday evening after work, for a traditional home fried fish and chips dinner.

However, he did miss his mother greatly, and the excuse given to why his father had abandoned him. Seemed rather pathetic, it was inferred, that he just couldn't cope anymore. However, the author had to cope, what other choice did he have.

His life was at this time very subdued, with too many painful thoughts. Such as why his mother had to die. It should have been his useless father. Surely, the world would be a better place without his spinless father.

To escape this unfortunate reality, the author took up cycling. Firstly, as a way of getting to work and back. Second, cycling as a pastime at the weekend. There are many canals in the local vicinity, and the towpaths are remarkably flat, for easy cycling. Such as the towpaths on the Trent & Mersey canal. Going south from Stoke-on-Trent towards Trentham, and onward to Barlaston, and finally to Stone. A total distance of about ten miles. Alternatively, in the northern direction from Stoke-on-Trent, the Trent & Mersey canal towpath went to Etruria, then Longport, and onward to Kidsgrove, and the Harecastle Tunnel. Which leads to the Cheshire plain. However, there is not a towpath through this canal tunnel, therefore the journey north usually ended here.

Back in Stoke-on-Trent, there is another canal, the Cauldon canal. This waterway sneaks its way through the industrial landscape of Stoke-on-Trent. Past all the forgotten hopes and dreams of glory, that once typified this city of pottery excellence and innovation.

The Cauldon canal moving outward into the peaceful, and calm environment of rural North Staffordshire. Firstly, Milton, Baddeley Green, and Stockton Brook. Finally, reaching the Leek branch canal, which veers off near Cheddleton.

Leek is a very nice market town. It has a look and feel of North England. Leek is well worth a visit. However, going back to our journey on the Cauldon canal. Heading on the towpath from Cheddleton the best parts of this canal are not yet done. A remarkable place and a must visit site is the

Churnet Valley. This beautiful site has a river, a Steam Railway, and the canal. How cool is that a real gem of a find. However, there is still a good way to go before the Cauldon Canal reaches its halt at Froghall Wharf.

This little-known area of North Staffordshire, that surrounds the town of Leek. Truly, it is a joy to behold. There are many little hamlets to find and explore. It has been noted many times before, in travel guides, etc. That the Peak District of Derbyshire is a wonderful place to live, or just to visit for a day. Yet those in the know, have previously exclaimed that the best bits of the Peak District are in North Staffordshire. The author knows this fact only too well. He had on many times previously cycled to Leek and beyond. Taking the Ashbourne Road from Leek as far as Onecote. Then continue to Butterton, where the view from the roadside is eternal, you can see across the top of every hill for miles and miles.

Then from the delightful hilltop village of Butterton, take the very steep and narrow road to Wetton Mill. You will be amazed at the breathtaking beauty of the Manifold valley, especially the farm Wetton Mill. Gaze from here down the valley to where in the far-off distance. You will see the majestic entrance to Thors cave. The Manifold valley is a hidden secret place. The author as a young man. He would have on Saturday morning cycled to here from Stoke-on-

Trent, about twenty miles. Then on arrival had pitched his small tent next to the river. Here in the depth of the valley, there is a pleasant tranquillity. Along with the harmony of bird song, from the Dipper, and the Grey Wagtail. Plus, the babbling of the slow-moving water in the little river. This peacefulness encourages the imagination to run wild. Such as, what if you could live in an idyllic place. In peace, with the one's that you love dearly, and they love you equally. Then wouldn't that be everything you would ever want to do? Who could wish for anything more than this, really is this not heaven on earth?

Inspired by those memories of this happy place. The author developed the idea of writing POUTIA secret hidden place.

Other books available for you to enjoy:

The Forgotten Children. by David Wiggins

Discover a Story That Needs to Be Told. Help with the Voices of the Forgotten Be Heard.

The Forgotten Children is a powerful, fictional tale rooted in the dark realities of **child abduction, human trafficking**, and **feral childhood**. Written with deep compassion and a commitment to **child safeguarding**, this gripping novel gives a voice to voiceless children who have been abandoned, exploited, or simply forgotten.

Through the eyes of a feral child, this story invites readers on an emotional journey of survival, resilience, and hope. It's a difficult but essential read — not just a novel, but a call to action.

◆ **100% of the author's royalties are donated to charities** supporting orphaned and feral children, providing them with shelter, care, and education.

◆ Every purchase directly contributes to changing a child's life.

Available now as a **revised edition on Amazon** and as an **e-book on Kindle**.

📖 Learn more and join the mission at:

Halfpennyman.com

The author's autobiography is now available on Amazon as a paperback. Hardback to follow at a later date.

Autobiography by David Wiggins:

Life between an Angel and a Rabbits Foot.

An interesting life to say the least, would be the authors honest comment. However, that is a true understatement of a life from birth to retirement. A happy, witty, nostalgic story in many places, but equally there are frequent heartaches. Disastrous partner choices because of their infidelity. Constantly moving away from trouble, causing financial hardship. Plus, my kneejerk reactions to remedy our problems, and just too much bad luck.

A story of tenacity, determination, mixed with foolishness, obstinance and poor life choices. However, coming from a culture of do or die, mend and make do, nothing ventured, nothing gained. Always looking forward, never regretting, but always doubting. A life full of hope for better times ahead.

CLASSIC COMEDY Laugh Out Loud by David Wiggins.

This is an excellent remedy for the malcontent. You know who I mean. Those that are just too quiet for their own good. The poor souls with no apparent sense of humour. The type that says, it's too boring for me; I'd rather stay in and have a snooze. Well do you want to help such a person? To Wake Up. Get a grip, smile, feel happy and Laugh Out Loud!!!

Then this my friend, is the book you have been waiting for. There are no less than 7, yes seven brilliantly funny comedy stories. Containing, satire, sarcasm, and innuendo. Plus, there are bonus pages of classic jokes. Do you see the potential of this awesome comedy book. You do!!!

Then go for it. The book is available on Amazon or ask your local bookshop to obtain you a copy. Marvelous you won't regret it. You will be too busy Laughing Out Loud.

A note from me to you.

The author had in his previous role as a High School Teacher. Taught thousands of students to aim high to reach their goals. However, he also let them into his life long considered opinion, and he would very much like to also share it with you.

Don't let what you can't do. Stop you from doing, what you can!

THANK YOU & GOD BLESS